THE TARANOCK

XIII

XII

I

XI

II

X

III

IX

IV

VIII

VII

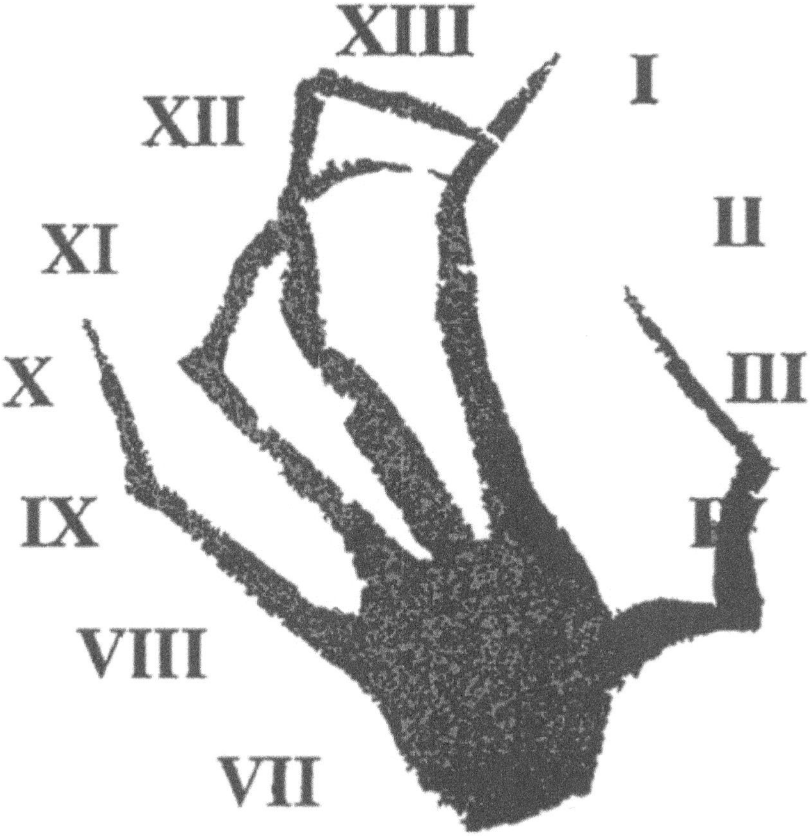

WILLOW HEWETT

Edited by Toni Glitz
glitzedit.co.uk

Veneficia Publications
January 2024

VENEFICIA PUBLICATIONS UK
veneficiapublications.com

TABLE OF CONTENTS

CHAPTER 1
The Offer

The house stood before them, shadowy and imposing. From its position on a large incline, it towered over the house next door. It looked old and was in desperate need of love and renovation.

Arthur wasn't sure he liked the look of its gothic-style structure, but from the expression on Amelia's face, he knew she'd make an offer by the end of this viewing. He'd never had much say in anything they did together, and this was no exception.

To him, it looked like something out of an old black-and-white horror movie, with its murky, eighteenth-century windows and muddy-orange bricks. The other houses around it were typical modern homes, warm and welcoming, in contrast to the drab and shabby-looking house in front of them. It was also situated slap-bang in the middle of a quiet little village called Whitely Bay on the outskirts of Yorkshire, surrounded by bare winter trees, a rocky coastline full of old boats, and an endless view of fields on the other side. He didn't like the fact that it stood at the end of a road which went on for miles—further than the eye could see— eventually leading to another quaint village called Calamar Bay, where everyone knew each other, and they knew no one. It felt like he was about to walk into a snake pit.

He could already sense the neighbours' eyes on them as they left their car parked on the street, just outside the large rusted gates leading up the steps to the house.

Amelia looked up at the house, her baby-faced features curling into a devilish smile as she took in everything it had to offer. She adored old homes, and this one was ideal in every way. Yanking one of her hair bands from her wrist, Amelia twisted her dark curls into a tight bun on top of her head.

From the corner of his eye, Arthur noticed this, and he knew that whenever she did this, she meant business. His heart sank as he realised she had already made up her mind, before he had even had the opportunity to step inside the house, but that was how their relationship worked. He noticed her eyes sparkle with determination, which he used to like about her, but now it just frustrated him.

His mother had warned him about marrying a strong-willed woman, but he had ignored her advice, and now look at him: he was a shell of his former self. His hair had begun to grey, reminding him that he was soon to turn forty, he had more lines on his face than a map of the countryside, and his once brilliant and vibrant brown eyes had faded to a very dull, muddy colour.

He didn't want to admit that his wife and children had sapped his zest for life, but he couldn't help but think that he had enjoyed a life before them. These days, he worked nearly every day for a pittance to provide for them, and she was about to blow all his life savings on a pile of bricks that he didn't even like. He could see this house was going to need some work to bring it up to its full potential, and judging by the way the roof slanted to the side, he knew it was going to eat into his limited funds.

Amelia took Arthur's hand in hers and led him up the steps. They were dangerously steep, with bits crumbling away at the edges; someone could easily slip and break their back. Arthur made a mental note to speak with the estate agent about it, hoping to negotiate a lower asking price. A large, picturesque garden encircled the old building, which was surrounded by a tall, new-looking wooden fence. At the very least, he wouldn't have to pay for another fence, he reasoned, as he observed the garden with its fine stone statues spitting water. The previous owners had planted large rose bushes all around the house, which were now climbing the walls. The floral splashes of red and white around the exterior did make it more appealing. It even made him smile as he picked one of the flowers and inhaled its natural scent.

Amelia looked at him with hope in her eyes, smiling as Arthur admired the rose in his hand. She already knew he'd say yes to anything she asked, so this would be no different. She planned to make an offer this evening, if everything went well. This house was ideal for her, it was large enough for the twins to play in and eventually have their own rooms. It even had an extra one in case they ever tried for another baby but for now, that room would go to her mother.

With her mother's frailty and limited walking, she would be better off living here with her, rather than having to fork out for a carer to turn up every day to see her, with the added bonus of leaving Amelia more inheritance after she sold her mother's house on the other side of the country. It was for the best, and this house would give her the best memories for her and her family.

Amelia looked up at the old Victorian windows and noticed how filthy they looked. That would be one of the first tasks on her to- do list.

A large archway protruded from the front of the house, supported by grey pillars covered in green moss.

Arthur grabbed the iron knocker and slammed it down hard, shocking Amelia. She shook her head in disgust and lightly tapped on the door. Footsteps could be heard hurrying towards them from inside the house. The door creaked open, revealing a well-dressed estate agent with a big fake grin on his face.

"Welcome to 'Le Diable Rouge'. Come in, come in. Make yourselves at home." The man ushered them in impatiently, and slammed the door shut behind them. "My name is Bentley, and I would like to take this moment to quickly tell you that we do already have an offer on this house, but the owner would like to wait to see if you would make a better offer."

Bentley received a raised brow from Arthur. "Slow down there, mate. We have yet to even see the house."

Amelia rolled her eyes at Arthur before smiling at the estate agent. "If we like it, we'll make an offer to the owner."

"Brilliant, let's get started then." Bentley gleefully clapped his hands together and started walking.

Arthur followed his wife into the foyer, which had many doors leading to different rooms. A massive spiral staircase took up the majority of the space, with a chandelier delicately hanging from the ceiling, casting glittery shadows in the sunlight. As they walked to the kitchen, the wooden flooring beneath them creaked and groaned under their weight.

Amelia was the first to walk into the room; her eyes widened. The walls were painted a deep red. The cupboards took up most of the walls; their smooth varnished doors opened with small iron knobs. Amelia spun on her heel, taking in the Victorian themed kitchen. Apart from the appliances, which stood out from the rustic look, nothing seemed to have changed over the years. The ceramic tiled windowsill was lined with crusty brown leaves and a few dead bugs for decoration. Amelia turned her nose up when she noticed the dead bugs, but Arthur thought it was rather amusing that no one had found the time to clean the place before letting potential buyers view it.

In the centre of the room stood a grand kitchen table with old knife marks and dents that would take ages to sand out. Arthur examined it, knowing it would be the first thing to go. A door to the side of the kitchen led to a parlour that could be considered a small dining room. Amelia quickly went through each cupboard, hoping to find something left behind by the previous tenants. She discovered a clay bowl with a half-burnt roll of sage tied with string. She took it out and placed it on the table in front of the estate agent.

Bentley's face was filled with dread and Arthur thought he even caught a glimpse of recognition as he spoke.

"I'm not sure why that's there. It was most likely left by the previous owners. Once you've made your decision, I'll get rid of it."

"Do you recognise it?" Arthur asked.

"Of course not. Shall we continue?" Bentley walked away without hesitation; Arthur could tell he was lying.

Arthur cast one last glance at the sage before following Amelia and Bentley into the lounge. With the notable exception of a very large grandfather clock in one corner of the room, the lounge appeared normal and empty. Amelia approached it and opened the large compartment containing the gleaming pendulum. The clock was a work of art. Every surface of its wood had been meticulously carved with swirls and patterns. The only odd thing about it was the clock's face, which had numbers leading up to thirteen instead of the usual twelfth hour.

"How come there are thirteen numbers rather than twelve?" Amelia asked, pointing to the clock hands.

Bentley faked a smile. "The clock has been here since the house was built. It's part of the house."

"How old is this house?" Arthur asked.

Bentley began to pace up and down the room, irritated by Arthur's ridiculous questions. "It's from the Victorian era but I don't know the exact year."

"Do you know anything about this house, Mr. Bentley?" Amelia scowled.

Bentley paused his pacing and fixed his gaze on her. "The house was built around 1880. That's all the information the owner has given me."

As Arthur and Amelia walked around the lounge, taking in the beauty of the place, the room fell silent. Arthur adored the fireplace and imagined himself poking the fire while his children sat nearby, listening to his famous ghost stories. Amelia liked the large windows with sunlight streaming in; they gave the room a homey feel.

From the corner of Arthur's eye, he could see something black protruding at the back of the fireplace, where a brick was missing. He reached in, pulled it out, wiped the soot off and rolled it around in his hands. It was another bowl filled with burnt sage. He held it up for Bentley to see.

"Another one," he said. "This is getting kind of strange, don't you think?"

"Maybe the previous owners liked burning sage," Bentley replied, bluntly.

Bentley began to check his watch every few seconds, growing tired of their presence and eager to move on. He watched Arthur and Amelia together; she stood next to Arthur, her expensive suede skirt and matching blouse made him look like a washed-up sea urchin, with his ripped camos and wrinkled T-shirt that badly needed ironing. His unkempt hair and straggly beard couldn't compete with her flawlessly made-up face and curly, glossy hair. They didn't go together, and Bentley couldn't figure out why they were even a couple. His entire outfit looked to have been put together by a child, in stark contrast to his partner, who appeared to have just stepped off a catwalk. Bentley couldn't help but blush when she smiled sweetly at him.

Arthur huffed as he noticed Bentley's flushed cheeks and excused himself to explore the rest of the house alone. Having returned the bowl to the fireplace, Arthur went through each room, discovering at least one more bowl with a burnt clump of sage in a corner, hidden behind old newspaper. Something caught Arthur's eye in one of the downstairs rooms: a built-in library. It even had books on the shelves and a beautifully crafted desk in the corner. In that moment, he knew that he wanted the house, despite the strange findings. It looked as if the room had been renovated from a simple second reception room into the perfect library where there would be peace and quiet.

Amelia went upstairs and checked the bedrooms and bathrooms. The bedrooms were all the same, with a small fireplace in the corner and Victorian-style decoration. Arthur stayed in the library, eagerly flickering over each leather-bound book.

Arthur liked reading. He could enter a different world and drown out Amelia's annoying moaning, just by sitting in his favourite chair and opening a good book. His wife was not an avid reader, and she would always scowl at him when he would take a rest with a book in his hands. This library was filled to the brim with books just waiting to be read.

A large leather sofa sat in one corner of the room, beside the towering bookshelves, and across from it was a beautifully handcrafted pine desk and matching chair. Arthur couldn't believe his luck; it was all so beautiful. The crisp green curtains matched the soft green Persian rug. The floorboards were creaky, yet had character about them with their gnarled indents and scrapes that had been accumulated over time. The chandelier above his head looked dusty and had at least a year's worth of cobwebs and dead flies stuck to it.

That won't take long to sort out, Arthur thought as he sat on the sofa with one of the books. Although the library was an excellent surprise, he couldn't help but notice that each book was on the topic of the supernatural and in particular, exorcisms. His eyes scanned the titles and not one of them was a different subject. He found it rather peculiar, but then again, whoever had lived here before may simply have had a strange obsession with the afterlife. He shook off the eerie feeling and settled onto the sofa, quietly reading and waiting for Amelia to make up her mind about the house.

Amelia stroked the porcelain sink as she looked around the bathroom, taking everything in. She stood there, admiring the smooth surface. She adored the bathrooms because they were the most modern rooms in the house, and she knew Arthur would be much more at ease if he didn't have to dip into his savings to update them. The bathtub and sink were a sleek black, with gold taps that gleamed in the light. A mirror in a gold-painted wooden frame hung on the wall in front of her, and she smiled at it as she imagined herself taking a bath with hot steam coming from the bubbled water. That'd be the first thing she'd do after they moved in. One of the bathrooms even had a shower for her to use after her workouts.

She loved everything about this house and knew she had to make it her own.

"Amelia?" Arthur called up the stairs.

Amelia grinned as she popped her head over the bannister.

"Yes?"

"What are your thoughts?" Arthur asked, as he watched Amelia bounce down the stairs, her hand running along the smooth bannister.

"I love it, especially the bathrooms. I think we should put an offer in."

"We haven't seen the back garden yet. Don't get too hasty," he warned.

Her smile dropped into a scowl. "I don't need to look out the back. I've already made up my mind."

Arthur sighed loudly, before commenting as he walked away. "Well, I'm going to take a look—before you speak to Bentley. I want to make sure this place is safe enough for the kids."

Amelia crept towards Bentley, having watched Arthur disappear through the kitchen door. He was still waiting for them in the lounge, staring out of the window, and wishing that he was anywhere but there. He turned as she entered the room, and upon seeing her smile, he knew he'd make a sale today. He breathed a huge sigh of relief. There had been hardly any interest in the house, and he'd got lucky when this couple came to look at it. They appeared to have no idea about its history, and he wanted it to stay that way, so he kept his mouth shut. If they discovered the history after they'd purchased it, then they would have to deal with it and sell it themselves. He didn't want anything more to do with this place: the creaks and groans of the house grew more unsettling the longer he spent inside.

While watching her reaction, he nervously bit his nails. "So, what are your thoughts?"

"We'll take it. My husband is looking over the garden, but we are very interested in the house, and we're willing to offer you more than anyone else looking to buy it," she said with a smile.

"Brilliant! I'll set up a meeting to finalise the paperwork first thing tomorrow morning."

Arthur entered the room and noticed Amelia holding the pen as she wrote in her small pocket diary. In dismay, he shook his head.

"You couldn't possibly wait, could you?"

"What else can I say? I was simply too excited." She laughed.

"I'll see you both at our meeting tomorrow. I wish you a pleasant day," Bentley stated as he walked towards the door.

"Why are you in such a hurry? You're the one who's meant to be locking the house up after we leave," Arthur said, eyeing him suspiciously.

Bentley grimaced and nodded as he swallowed loudly. Amelia shrugged as Arthur looked at her, unsure what Bentley seemed so worried about. As Bentley locked the door, they noticed his hands shaking.

"What about the other couple, the ones you said had already put an offer in?" Arthur asked.

"Your wife offered to pay more," Bentley stated, flatly.

"Well, you can knock some off for the dangerous garden steps," Arthur replied through gritted teeth. He was annoyed with Amelia for not bothering to discuss the offer with him first.

Bentley ignored Arthur's comment and stepped back from the door. "I'll see you tomorrow to sign the paperwork," he muttered, brushing past them.

Arthur stood there in awe as Bentley descended the steps, narrowly avoiding the crumbling edges. They both watched as he yanked open his car door and practically threw himself inside. The car accelerated away noisily, leaving skid marks on the road. Even one of the neighbours looked out of their window to see what was going on because the exhaust was so loud.

"Strange man," Arthur muttered.

"For once, I must agree with you there," Amelia said.

She smiled as she held Arthur's hand, her fingers intertwined with his. He returned a faint smile, but his thoughts were elsewhere. He wasn't sure if Amelia's offer was the best option, and they weren't rich enough to just throw money at the house. This was his inheritance. She could tell he was deep in thought, so she dragged him down the stairs to their car and opened the door for him. He got in automatically and she slammed it shut. Arthur looked at the house, watching the sun glaring off the windows. Something caught his eye in the lounge window. It looked like a pale, white face staring straight at them, but when the car began to move, whatever it was vanished, leaving an empty but grubby window.

Although it felt warm outside for a winter's day, a shudder ran up his spine as the image of the face burned itself into his mind. He wasn't sure if his eyes were playing tricks on him, or if he actually did see someone in their new house, staring out of the window.

CHAPTER 2
Moving In

The piles of cardboard boxes cluttered both the entrance hall and Amelia's mind as she stared at the mess Arthur was bringing in. He stood at the front door, holding another stack of heavy boxes, his muscles bulging from the strain.

She glared at him and pointed to the lounge. "No more in here. Put the rest in there."

"You do realise how heavy these are," he muttered sarcastically, as he stepped around the other piles to reach the lounge door.

"I need these put away as soon as possible. My mother is arriving tomorrow morning," Amelia warned.

She leant against the wall, not bothering to lift a finger to help as she watched him struggle to open the door. The more she examined his features, the more irritated she became. She loved him deeply, but their relationship had recently taken a dark turn. She wasn't sure why, but everything he did was beginning to irritate her. Maybe she had too much going on in her life and didn't have the energy to work on their marriage. Maybe the kids were wearing her down, making her tired and weary from juggling her workload as well as trying to keep up with things at home. She crossed her arms and shook the thoughts from her mind.

When she looked down, she noticed small white scrape marks leading from the lounge to the bottom of the stairs. She knelt and rubbed her finger across one, feeling the rickety indent beneath.

"Arthur, could you please come here for a moment?" she called out.

She could hear him muttering from the lounge and stomping his feet as he came towards her. When he noticed her kneeling on the ground, stabbing her finger into the wooden flooring, he raised an eyebrow.

"What are you doing?" he asked.

She pointed to the markings. "What are these? I didn't notice this when we viewed the place. They look new."

Arthur knelt next to her, his knees cracking loudly. Amelia's lips twitched into a smirk, but she quickly wiped it away before he noticed. He knelt even lower, his musky aftershave wafting up her nose. She loathed that smell, and she despised it more every time he wore it, but still, he wore it every morning like clockwork, even though he knew it made her feel sick. She wrinkled her nose and held her breath to avoid inhaling it as she watched him inspect the deep groove marks in the wood.

"I don't actually know what those are. It looks to me like someone has dragged something across here," he said, as he crawled across the floor to the stairs, where the marks continued. "They're on the stairs too."

Arthur stood up, his knees cracking once more as he followed the marks up the stairs and onto the landing. Amelia followed him, intrigued by her findings and curious about where they would lead. She almost collided with him when he abruptly stopped outside their bedroom door and stared at them while stroking his stubbly beard in thought.

"They appear to lead into every room. Perhaps it was done by the delivery men as they carried the furniture up the stairs."

She rolled her eyes at him. "So, why are these marks leading into each room? They can't be from the furniture because they all look the same. Besides, I gave them strict instructions not to drag anything across the floor."

"Well, I don't know then. Why bring me up here if you don't want to hear my thoughts?" he spat.

"You came here of your own free will, I only asked you to look at the ones downstairs."

He sighed in exasperation and stomped down the stairs, leaving her up there alone. He didn't have the energy to argue with her, and he needed to finish unpacking the boxes before she began complaining again. In frustration, he walked into the lounge and kicked one of the boxes. There was simply too much to do and not enough time to complete it.

As Amelia's loud hip-hop music began to vibrate from upstairs, he glared at the ceiling above him. She always did this after an argument to get back at him; she knew he disliked loud music. He took a pair of earplugs from his pocket and inserted them to block out the noise. He had bought them for situations like this one, but she had no idea he had them. This made it even better, because she would now stay in her room thinking she was bothering him when, in reality, he loved the peace and quiet of her not being around him.

He began to hum a tune as he moved the boxes away from the grandfather clock, taking care not to tip it over. He looked over at it and smiled, admiring the craftsmanship that had gone into every detail. Amelia wanted to get rid of it because it made her feel uncomfortable, but he liked how it stood in the corner of the room and he knew the kids would like it as well. When he bent down to pick up yet another box, he noticed more white marks on the floor leading away from the clock.

He pushed the boxes aside to get a better look and discovered that the marks were leading out into the hallway, where Amelia had first noticed them.

"How peculiar," he muttered, staring down at them.

It would be simple enough to buff them out, but that didn't stop him thinking how odd it was having these scrape marks leading out from a grandfather clock. Maybe Amelia was right and this clock was creepy, or maybe the markings had always been there and they'd only just noticed them.

He opened the clock door and bent down to inspect the pendulum inside. A cold draught blew in his face as he searched both for the source of the scrape marks, and for the clock's failure to tick. He ignored the strange breeze coming from inside the clock as his mind was too focused on the jammed pendulum. He pushed his finger between the pendulum and the wood, causing the clock to chime loudly as it fell on the twelfth hour. He jumped, banged his head on the clock and fell backwards. With his heart racing and his head pounding, he stared up at it, watching the hands spin round and round. At least the pendulum was fixed, he thought as he brushed himself down.

He carried on arranging the boxes, pushing the odd markings to the back of his mind. His muscles ached from overuse; he was getting tired but he kept going, at least until most of the boxes were unpacked. It would have taken him a lot less time to finish the job had Amelia bothered to come down and help, but she didn't want to ruin her nice, perfectly pink, painted nails.

He stretched his back, it clicked loudly. He checked his watch, it was just after midnight. He couldn't understand where the time had gone as he looked around the room. He pushed the thought to the back of his mind and looked at the clock and then at his watch, realising that he had fixed the clock to match the exact time on his watch.

"I suppose that saves me from having to try to set it to the right time," he said to himself, although he still considered it odd.

He stretched once more before deciding to call it a day, leaving one last box in the corner of the room. He dragged his tired legs up the stairs to their bedroom and quietly opened the door, taking care not to wake Amelia. He undressed, tossed his clothes into a corner of the room, and climbed into bed beside her.

As Arthur tried to nudge her onto her side, she stirred slightly, her soft snoring abruptly stopping. He took out his earplugs and slid them into his bedside drawer, hoping the scraping noise of the draw wouldn't wake her.

"The kids will return early tomorrow. Keep in mind to thank the babysitter for having them," Amelia mumbled.

"Yes, my dear," he replied as he pulled the covers up over his body.

He slumped back, his arms and legs groaning with exhaustion. He knew he'd feel the burn from his muscles the next morning, which he wasn't looking forward to. He couldn't decide which was worse: Amelia moaning at him all day and the kids running around like headless chickens, or his muscles burning and causing him constant pain. He pushed his head deeper into the pillow and felt his muscles begin to relax one by one. The pillow was cool against his cheek, and the covers were just warm enough for him to fall soundly asleep.

CHAPTER 3
It Begins

In the early hours of the morning chains could be heard rattling across the wooden floor, while a strange clicking sound kept time with the grandfather clock. It was a short, sharp sound, powerful enough to vibrate the walls as it echoed throughout the house. It sounded like a cricket. The rattling chains continued, clanking together as if something was dragging itself across the floor.

Arthur stirred, but not enough to wake himself. Instead, the sounds infiltrated his dream, transforming it into a nightmare, featuring a dark figure with long, lank hair that covered most of its face, revealing only its pale white chin, which was covered with a web of black and blue veins. It dragged a massive, linked chain across the floor, hauling it over its shoulder. Despite its apparent frailty, it was strong enough to drag five bodies tangled in its chain behind it. The bodies all wailed for help, but Arthur could only stand there and watch as it approached, clicking with every movement of its skinny body. Before Arthur could see any more of the strange being, something startled him awake. He sat bolt upright in bed, the remnants of the nightmare fading fast as he rubbed his sleepy eyes.

Thump, click, scrape. Thump, click, scrape.

It was like a melody that grew louder and less muffled as Arthur woke properly from his slumber. Although his mind was foggy, his heart was pounding in time with the sounds. He wiped his brow with the back of his hand as he listened.

Thump, click, scrape. Thump, click, scrape.

There it was again. The clicking noise was the most disturbing, it penetrated Arthur's ears as he tried to figure out what could be making it. He didn't want to get out of bed, and he didn't want to wake Amelia in case she moaned at him.

Thud, thud, thump.

The noise grew significantly deeper, as if something were being dragged up the stairs. He sat, spellbound by the noise, unable to move for fear of what might be lurking in the shadows. Terror—a feeling he had long forgotten—was creeping up inside him, piercing through his skin like shrapnel, bringing beads of sweat to the surface and soaking the bed covers.

He eventually mustered the courage to investigate and dragged his weary legs out of bed. An icy sensation engulfed him, raising the hairs on the back of his neck as his mouth became dry, making it difficult for him to swallow. He crept up to the bedroom door, pressing his ear against the cool wood. A low moaning could be heard from the other side of the door, which confused and terrified him. He listened carefully, trying to figure out what it was, but all he could hear were soft groans.

"Arthur! What are you doing?" Amelia's voice rang out from behind him, making him jump and bang his head on the door. His body shook violently and his heart felt as if it was about to jump right out of his rib cage.

"I'm hearing strange noises," he said, shakily.

"It's most likely just the house creaking with age. Most old ones do," she replied, unconcerned by Arthur's unusual behaviour. "Just come back to bed, we have an early start tomorrow."

The noise stopped abruptly, leaving an eerie silence in its wake, and Arthur both shaken and startled by its sudden cessation.

"But there was something. I could feel it," Arthur grumbled as he climbed back into bed, rubbing the side of his head.

Amelia yanked him back with her hand and threw the blanket over him. "You'll forget about it by the morning. Just go to sleep."

He leaned back and rubbed his throbbing shoulder. He was sure Amelia didn't realise how strong she could be at times. His shoulder ached from her grip, which made him feel even more irritable. He rolled over, turned away from her—not wishing to put up with her snoring as well as everything else.

His heartbeat had only just begun to steady itself when he looked up to see a long, dark figure standing against the wall. He yelped in surprise and scrunched his eyes shut, not wanting to see anything else, but sanity prevailed, forcing him to pry his eyes open just enough to see the shadow of a tree outside making shapes on the wall. He turned over again, reassured that his mind was playing tricks on him. This time he snuggled into Amelia's soft, warm body, wanting some comfort from her. She pressed her body against his, allowing him to cuddle her, and, for the first time in a long time, they both held each other. Arthur took in her sweet scent and burrowed his head deeper into her neck, blocking out the moving shadows on the wall.

Behind Arthur, one of the shadows on the wall remained perfectly still, staring at them both from across the room, its knobbly spine protruding

from its arched back. Arthur and Amelia slept
soundly in their bed, unaware that something was
closely observing their every move.

CHAPTER 4
The Weak One

The morning sun shone through the dusty kitchen window, and birds sang their morning songs in a nearby tree. Arthur had forgotten the terrors of the previous night, as he sat at the kitchen table happily whistling to himself with Amelia opposite him, writing a list of chores to do that day in her note pad. She raised her head, a playful smile on her lips, she liked it when Arthur whistled. It reminded her of the first time they met, when he had whistled her favourite song to impress her. He noticed her smiling and stopped whistling.

"You alright?" he asked.

She nodded. "You haven't whistled in a very long time. I had forgotten how much I enjoyed it."

He looked surprised, and a wry smile twitched on his lips as he continued whistling, louder this time.

She flipped open her note pad and pointed to the first chore. "You should buff out those marks today, before the kids arrive, or they'll just get in the way."

"Good idea," he agreed and stood up to wash his dirty breakfast bowl. "I'll get started now."

He left the kitchen without another word and headed for the shed in the garden, where he had placed his tools the day before. They were still in boxes, and it took him some time to dig through them to find his electric polisher. He had looked through all of them but couldn't find it, until he looked up and noticed it was on the workbench, right in front of him. He picked it up and examined the neatly wrapped cord and the machine's polished appearance—*I don't remember putting this here.*

Amelia watched him come in through the back door, polisher in hand. "Wow, that was quick."

"Did you leave it on the workbench for me?" he asked.

She shook her head, confused. "I don't touch your stuff, remember?"

"For some reason, it was on the workbench. I don't recall putting it there," he said as he plugged it in.

"You've been working a lot lately. You probably don't remember doing it," she said matter-of-factly, shrugging her shoulders.

He thought for a moment, wondering if what Amelia said was right, and if he had forgotten about it. A vague memory resurfaced of him taking it out, but he couldn't remember why he did. He didn't want to think about it any longer, so he turned on the polisher and began buffing out the scratches.

Amelia helped out in the kitchen, unpacking the remaining boxes and making sure everything was in order before her mother's arrival later that day. Her mother's bedroom was all ready for her, and Amelia even found time to pick some wildflowers from the garden to place in a vase as a finishing touch.

Time flew by, and Arthur was almost done buffing out the scratches. He smiled as he turned off the polisher and looked at the finished product. The floor sparkled, and the scent of wax wafted through the air. A knock at the door jolted him out of his daydreaming, and he noticed shadows appear behind the frosted glass front door.

"It's open!" he yelled, as he wrapped the cord around the polisher.

The front door flew open, and two identical six-year-olds with a mop of dark, curly hair, and crimson cheeks squealed excitedly at the top of their lungs with a young woman behind them. An elderly lady followed them in, assisted by Amelia's sister, Flo.

Flo was a younger version of Amelia, yet her features were much softer, with big blue eyes and straight brown hair, styled into a sleek bob. She wore jeans with holes in the knees, and a tight black shirt with a band's logo on, which Arthur recognised as a band from the seventies.

Arthur smiled at Flo and moved to the side to allow them to pass.

"Dylan, Charlie! Will you please be quiet?" Arthur grumbled.

"Sorry, Dad," they replied in unison, as they scuttled off up the stairs to look at their new room.

Arthur turned to the young woman who had escorted them in. "Thank you, Annie. How much do we owe you?"

"The same as usual. I would love to look after them for free, but I have college fees to pay off." She chuckled.

He pulled out his wallet and began counting the notes. "And you don't mind the difference in location?"

"I don't mind at all. It's not that much further, and I also look after a few other children around here too. But for obvious reasons, I cannot look after them overnight. This was just a one off to help you."

He hesitated before pulling out another note from his wallet.

"Here's some extra for the fuel. Same again next week?"

"Of course! I'll see you all then. Say goodbye to the little tikes for me. I must rush, got another class to go to!" And with that, she was gone.

Amelia burst through the kitchen door and ran to her mother. She gave her a long hug, shoving Flo out of the way so she could support her mother into the lounge.

"Hello there, Dotty. It's wonderful to see you again." Arthur smiled at the elderly lady.

She looked up at him, a familiar expression on her face. "Oh, hello dear."

Arthur noticed Amelia trying to support Dotty and approached her to take her arm. He led her into the living room and sat her on one of the chairs. Amelia scowled at him.

"I have a special chair over here for you." Amelia indicated toward a recliner chair in the corner of the room.

Dotty shook her head vigorously.

"I'm already in a chair. I'm not moving again. My feet hurt."

Arthur raised his brow at Amelia, who stood there with a pitying expression on her face, staring down at her mother. Dotty's hands shook as she clutched her walking frame, as if unable to let it go. She remained silent and scared, her sad blue eyes watering. Amelia noticed that her silvery white hair was matted and unkempt.

"I'll take you out tomorrow to the salon to get your hair done."

Dotty gave Amelia a blank stare; she had a permanent pained expression on her face. What had once been a much-loved hand-knitted cardigan had now become ragged and hung loosely on her tiny frame. She was dressed in a flowery skirt that reached her pale knobbly ankles, and tatty shoes that vaguely matched the colour of her cardigan.

"I want to go home," she said.

"You can't go home, Mother. Your house has been sold and you live with us now. You're too old to live on your own," Amelia stated flatly.

Flo appeared, standing in the doorway. "Do you need anything else before I go, or would you like me to stay?"

"When will my mother's belongings arrive?" Amelia demanded, looking at her as if she were a cockroach that needed to be squashed.

Flo noticed her expression and turned away from Amelia's glares before adding, "she's *our* mother, Amelia."

"It needs to be done as soon as possible. I want her things here." Amelia said, ignoring her sister's comment.

Arthur glared at Amelia before responding to Flo. "What Amelia means to say is that will her things be arriving today?"

Flo handed him a note from her pocket.

"This is the company transporting Mother's belongings. They will be here later today. There isn't much to be brought here as my dear sister has sold most of the furniture and several other items."

"If you think you'll be getting any of the money from the furniture, then you're mistaken," Amelia yelled.

Arthur cast a disapproving glance at Amelia. "You don't have to be horrible. You can just say you've spent it on a new bed for Dotty. Flo has helped immensely, so please be a bit nicer to her."

Amelia shifted her gaze to Arthur.

"And why should I? The reason why my mother is here in the first place is because my dear little sister can't look after her. And from the way my mother looks now, she hasn't done a very good job anyway. Look at her! She's so skinny and frail."

"It's called growing old. Deal with it," Arthur muttered as he observed Dotty's hair and face.

"Arthur is right. I know it's hard to see Mum age and deteriorate, but you can't blame me," Flo elaborated. "I'm going travelling. It's something I've wanted to do for ages."

"I don't care. You should have done more for her," Amelia snapped.

As she looked at Amelia, Flo's face was filled with anger.

"I have done a lot for her. You're the one who decided to have her here, before I announced I was going travelling. I know what your game is. You've sold her house and belongings because you're bloody greedy and want a bigger inheritance."

"I did what was necessary for our mother." Amelia approached her sister and stood inches away from her. "This conversation is done. Get out."

Flo was unfazed by Amelia's anger. She knew she was in the right from the way her sister acted. She approached Dotty and kneeled beside the chair.

"I'll call you every week, Mum. And once I return, I'll come and visit you."

Dotty nodded and placed a hand on Flo's shoulder.

"Thank you. Goodbye, darling."

"I told you to go," Amelia snapped, growing impatient.

With a tear in her eye, Flo got up and left the room. "I'll keep in touch, and don't forget that the stairlift is being measured up tomorrow. They'll be here around midday," she mumbled to Amelia as she exited. "Tell the kids I love them."

The front door swung open and then slammed, causing the walls to shake. From across the room, Arthur glared at Amelia, disgusted at how she had handled the situation.

"You didn't have to humiliate her. She's your sister."

The awkward silence between Arthur and Amelia was broken by the sound of Dotty snoring. Amelia smiled as they both looked at the frail old lady. She fetched a blanket and wrapped it around her mother, immediately forgetting about her sister.

"She'll be safer here," Amelia eventually responded.

The sound of children playing in the back yard reminded them that they had the twins to care for in addition to Dotty.

"We'll manage," Arthur muttered as he looked at Dotty's serene expression.

Dotty stirred and began to mumble incoherent words.

"Taranock, Taranock, Taranock."

Arthur knelt beside her and rested his hand on her arm. "Are you okay?"

"He's awakened to feed on our souls." Her voice faded and she fell into a deeper sleep.

He remembered his nightmare from the night before as he looked at her near-translucent skin with its prominent blue and black veins. The image of the strange figure entered his mind; he gasped for air, shook violently and felt faint as an overwhelming sensation washed over him. He grabbed Dotty's walking frame and steadied himself, which caused Dotty to wake up and panic.

Amelia snatched Arthur's hand and yanked him away from the frame. "What on earth are you doing to my mother?"

The room began to spin, and Arthur swayed before collapsing to the floor, dragging Amelia with him. He felt the blood drain from his face before he blacked out, and Amelia's screams faded quickly to the back of his mind.

CHAPTER 5
Tick-Tock on the Clock

Arthur woke on the sofa, unsure how he got there. He rolled over onto his side, where he was met by an annoyed Amelia staring down at him. His brain felt as if someone had drilled a hole into it and the contents were slowly leaking out. His head pounded, causing his vision to become slightly blurred.

He couldn't remember why he had fainted, and the terrifying sensation he had felt earlier was rapidly fading from his mind. His heart beat more steadily as he lay there listening to Amelia rant at him about fainting on purpose, and how it wasn't fair for her to have to look after him as well.

"Did you put me on here?" he asked, eyeing her arms up and down in surprise.

"Well, once I made sure that you were alright and breathing properly, I dragged you onto the sofa."

"And how did you manage that?" he muttered.

"I am stronger than you think. Besides, you only fainted. It isn't a big deal." She smirked, then began complaining again, flapping her arms in his face.

He zoned her out, quietly taking in their lounge's surroundings. He noticed Amelia had been extremely busy while he was out for the count. The furniture had been rearranged, and while it looked better, he couldn't help but notice that the back wall was bare. The shadows from the rose bush outside the window moved along the wall like gnarled claws. It looked creepy. He knew his imagination would run riot, transforming each shadow into something more menacing to scare him.

"I think we should hang something or move some furniture there. It looks a bit bare," he commented, oblivious to the fact that Amelia was still questioning him about earlier.

As she stared at him, her eyes narrowed into slits. "Were you even paying attention to what I was saying?"

"My head is pounding, and I'm having trouble concentrating right now," he said.

Her expression softened as she slid her hand into his moist palm. "Should we hang a mirror on the wall?"

He nodded. "Yeah, I think that's a good idea. Where are the kids?"

"It's almost midnight. You've been out for the count for a while. Probably faking it just so you can sleep."

"I didn't sleep; I passed out. There's a difference," he muttered quietly, but not so quietly that she couldn't hear him.

"Just get yourself ready for bed," she snapped.

She snatched her hand back and strutted upstairs into the en-suite, slamming the door loudly behind her to express her frustration. Arthur got off the sofa and slowly made his way upstairs to their room. Still feeling slightly dizzy, he slumped onto the bed and snuggled down into his pillow, not bothering to get undressed. He didn't have the energy to move, nor did he want to leave his comfortable bed.

He could hear Amelia brushing her teeth vigorously through the door. He knew she was upset, but brushing her teeth so strenuously was a bit extreme, if not downright pathetic. In his opinion she was always going over the top. That's why their arguments always tended to take a rapid turn, especially when she was the one to start them.

He, on the other hand, hated arguments and rarely started them, even when she got on his nerves. He always tried to avoid them and even went so far as to apologise, even though most of the time he shouldn't have had to. He wiped the images of their fights from his mind, knowing that if he kept thinking about them, he'd become irritated.

He turned the other way and faced the wall, but he knew he'd be huddling up to Amelia at some point during the night. The wall in front of him looked desolate and depressing, with old nicotine stains ingrained into the cream-coloured paint that covered the walls and ceiling. It desperately needed something to liven it up. He didn't want to have to stare at it all night, with his imagination running wild and using it as a blank canvas, but there wasn't anything he could hang up there just yet.

He wasn't even tired, despite his head still pounding. He quickly turned off his bedside lamp, and pretended that he was already asleep, in order to avoid another argument. He could hear her footsteps and felt her creeping into bed, and then everything went dark with the click of her bedside lamp.

Amelia lay there contemplating tomorrow's chores and just how much they were piling up. As she drew the covers up to her neck, she could hear Arthur's nose whistling slightly. The temperature in the room was uncomfortably low, and her fluffy socks weren't doing their usual job of keeping her feet warm. She moved across to Arthur's warm body and pressed her feet against his legs to warm them up. They had left the heating on full blast and their windows were closed, so she couldn't figure out why she was so cold. It wasn't even that cold outside. Admittedly, there was a slight chill in the air, warning everyone that it would be freezing in a few months' time, but it wasn't cold enough to add an extra layer or two of bedclothes.

The grandfather clock downstairs chimed 1 o'clock, and Amelia opened her eyes to check the digital clock beside her. She couldn't figure out how she had squandered an hour in bed not sleeping, but no matter how hard she tried, she couldn't fall asleep. She considered turning on her light and reading a book for a few minutes, but then she heard a strange noise coming from downstairs.

A loud creaking sound echoed up the stairs, followed by a scratching noise, as if someone was trying to claw their way out of something. Amelia strained her ears to hear, remembering what Arthur had said about strange noises the night before. Maybe he was right, and there was something odd about the house. However, Amelia was a sceptic who could always debunk myths and legends before Arthur blew them out of proportion with his overactive imagination. But there was something grotesque about the sounds—something unnatural. It was enough to make Amelia's palms sweat.

Thump, click, scrape. Thump, click, scrape.

Amelia's heartbeat quickened, as she heard the strange repetition of sounds. She sat in bed, staring at the bedroom door, trying to figure out what was causing them. The noise seemed to be getting closer to the door, and she scrunched her eyes shut, terrified of what was about to come through.

Click, click, click.

The noise became increasingly loud until it was all Amelia could hear.

"Go away!" she shrieked.

Arthur suddenly sat bolt upright in bed and turned the light on. "What the hell, Amelia?"

He could see her terrified expression and instantly realised something was very wrong. She rocked back and forth in bed, screaming at the top of her lungs, waking up the twins, who were just across the hall, who in turn began to scream in unison with Amelia's shrieks.

"Make it go away!" Amelia squealed.

Arthur grabbed her hands and yanked them away from her ears, revealing a trickle of blood oozing out from each one. He fumbled around for something suitable and having found something, frantically dabbed at them to absorb the blood. Arthur could barely get a word in, so he began shouting over her.

"There's nothing here. Calm down!"

He was terrified by the fear and panic in her eyes. He could tell she was in pain, but he couldn't figure out what was bothering her so much. He grabbed a glass of water from his bedside table and threw it in her face, hoping to stop the hysteria. She sat there with her mouth agape and a dripping wet face.

"What is the matter with you? You've just woken up the entire family." Arthur sighed as he got up to check on the kids.

It was his turn to slam the door behind him in frustration. He went into the twins' room, comforting them until they eventually quietened down, their bodies curled up in his arms.

Charlie sniffed loudly, pointing to the back wall of their room. "A bad man came in here."

Arthur sat on the bed, cradling the boys. He watched the shadows on the wall move as if they were real people moving around inside the room.

He sighed and got up to close the curtains, shutting out the light from the streets lamps outside. The shadows on the wall disappeared, bar one. Within a split second it also vanished, leaving only the bare wall to see.

For a moment, he stared at the bare wall, confused as to where the other shadow had come from if it wasn't from outside. He shook his head before returning to Charlie's bed where the twins had cuddled up, leaving Dylan's bed empty.

He whispered sweet words into their ears, soothing them back to sleep.

"Hush, hush, it's ok. Daddy's here now."

He watched them for a while, just until their snoring became more noticeable, then he quietly crept away, hoping that they wouldn't wake up until the morning. He made his way back to his room and found Amelia sitting in bed, staring at the wall beside her. When she saw Arthur, her body quivered with fear, and her eyes welled up with tears.

"It's here," she whispered, as she pointed a finger at the wall.

Arthur examined the back wall, finding nothing but the cobwebs Amelia hadn't yet cleared away.

"What's here?"

"The Taranock." Her chin wobbled as she fought back tears.

As he sat on the edge of the bed, Arthur sighed. "What is the Taranock?"

"It's here, over there. Can't you see it?" she begged, her eyes full of desperation.

He returned his gaze to the wall, just to show Amelia that nothing was there. "All I see is an empty wall." He took her covers and gently helped her into them, and softly stroked her hair. "It's just a nightmare."

He leaned over and turned off the light. Amelia's eyes widened in terror as she pulled at Arthur's shoulder, urging him to turn around. He didn't bother to turn, and thinking it was Amelia's imagination, he instead got into bed and closed his eyes.

A tall figure with broad shoulders, a thin frame and long, gangly legs, was silhouetted against the pale wall behind him. Its rickety, elongated fingers clicked as they moved across the wall. Amelia's heart skipped a beat as she fumbled for the light switch, unsuccessfully attempting to turn it back on. It kept slipping through her sweaty palms, and in the end, she left it dangling by the bed.

She turned her attention back to the wall, but the figure had vanished, leaving only the pale wall and its cobwebs. She didn't want to believe that there had been anything there, but her gut told her something was wrong with this house. Her heart pounded. If it hadn't been for Arthur turning the light off, she would have dismissed it as a trick of the light, but she knew she had seen something, and what she had felt emanating from it was truly evil. The wall looked normal once again, with the only shadows cast by the trees outside.

Arthur tossed around in bed, feeling slightly guilty about telling Amelia that it was just a nightmare. His feet were still freezing from walking on the bare floorboards, even with the covers over him. He could sense that she was also awake, but she had turned over and faced the window instead of the wall. The name that she had said kept rolling around in his head—the Taranock. It was starting to give him the creeps and he couldn't seem to get it out of his mind. The twins had also said they saw something in their room.

He could hear her breathing beginning to calm down, but he could sense a tension around her. He could tell something had scared her, but he wasn't sure if he wanted to know. She was never scared of anything. Her only concern was that his inheritance money would run out. He could feel her hand slipping into his, and her touch was icy cold.

He felt her arm and it was frozen. "How come you're so cold?" He felt her shoulders shrug beside him.

"The heating must not be on."

"But it's hot in here. You shouldn't be so chilly. Put on a jumper or something," he said as he turned the lamp back on.

She gave him a weak smile as she looked at him. "I've got you to warm me up."

He looked surprised, but he obliged and wrapped his arm around her so she could snuggle up to him.

"Are you going to explain why you were screaming earlier?"

"I thought I saw something." She shrugged again, as if she was already bored with their conversation.

"Or could it have been a nightmare?" he asked.

She nodded. "If I did have a nightmare, then I don't remember it, but I remember the sensation it gave me. That's something I haven't had in years."

"Why did you say that word?"

"What word?"

"The Taranock."

"Did I? Everything feels fuzzy, I don't remember saying that."

"Try to get some rest." He snuggled up to her and kissed her on the cheek.

She yawned and stretched. The sound of her hip clicking startled them. It was a sound that triggered something in both of them, but they couldn't put their finger on why. The memory of earlier was fading quickly, leaving them both confused but aware that there was something about this house that seemed to be draining them.

"What time is it?" she asked, shaking the thoughts from her mind.

Arthur checked his watch.

"It's shortly after one."

"That can't be right. I swear I looked at the clock earlier and it was just after one." She checked the clock on her bedside table and saw that he was correct. "How strange. Perhaps I dreamt it. Who knows?"

She snuggled in closer, her hand on his chest, feeling his heartbeat beneath; she needed to feel the warmth of his body.

He could tell she was still scared, so he let her, despite his annoyance at her for waking up the kids. He leaned away and turned off the light. In the darkness, the wind thrashed against the window, the branches clawing at the glass as if someone was trying to break in. He lay there watching the swaying trees, deep in thought about the house. He hoped he hadn't made a mistake in buying it, because even if they wanted to, they couldn't afford to leave. They had no choice but to stick with it and make it work.

Maybe he was overthinking the strange noises and the nightmares, but even so, there was still that feeling he couldn't shake, no matter how hard he tried. There was a sense of resentment; it was the sort of feeling that could rip through someone's core and leave them bitter and disturbed, feeding the dark thoughts that were usually kept buried in their mind. That was exactly what was happening to Arthur. He was becoming irritable and bitter. He didn't think that a house could do that—perhaps something else could be messing with him. He didn't believe in ghosts, or the paranormal. He dismissed it as nonsense, but even so, he couldn't shake the feeling that something in this house wanted them out.

He closed his eyes and listened to Amelia's soft grunting as she slept peacefully in his arms. These were the kinds of moments that made having a family worthwhile. As he stroked her cheek, he could feel the softness of her skin beneath his fingers. He started to drift off into a dark, foreboding sleep where the Taranock clawed its way into his thoughts, invading them with horrific images of torture.

CHAPTER 6
The Arrival of Trish

The twins bumbled in and out of the lounge, full of mischief and mayhem. Amelia sat in her chair next to the open fire, trying to read, but all she could hear was banging from the hallway, where Arthur was hanging paintings and a large mirror. Workmen had already turned up to inspect the stairs to fit the stairlift. After they had taken all the information they needed, they had left, leaving Arthur to carry on banging nails into the walls.

A knock at the door interrupted her thoughts, and she sighed loudly as she got up to answer it. She knew Arthur wouldn't have heard it because he was wearing his large ear defenders to drown out the banging, which he was causing. She approached the door and opened it, half expecting someone to jump out at her as there was no silhouette visible in the frosted window. As it happened, someone had left a basket full of goodies and a note introducing themselves on the doorstep. She picked it up and examined the items, smiling when she saw her favourite chocolate tucked behind a box of muffins. She brought it inside and showed it to Arthur, who stood there looking at her blankly.

"It's from one of our neighbours!" she exclaimed.

He pulled off his earmuffs and followed her into the kitchen, where she set the basket on the table.

She ripped the note off and began reading it aloud. "Welcome to the neighbourhood. Love from Steve and Graham, at Number 2."

"I'm curious why they didn't stay," Arthur muttered, more to himself than Amelia.

"Well, it was nice of them to even bother. Should we go and thank them later on while your sister is round?" Amelia asked sweetly, fluttering her eyelashes in an attempt to persuade him.

"Yeah, but we can't just abandon Trish with the children. We need to keep her sweet so she can help us clean up the garden."

"We won't be long. I just want to thank them for the basket," she replied bluntly.

He knew he couldn't win and he didn't want to start another argument, so he gritted his teeth and nodded, once again giving into her—anything for a quiet life.

However, he also knew his sister was not going to appreciate being left alone with their children. Trish didn't like Amelia, and this would irritate her even more. She was only coming to help because he had asked her to, as she despised the idea of spending time with Amelia, and especially in such a confined space. He'd have to try to sweeten her up first—perhaps giving her a bottle of her favourite wine to calm her down before pushing the kids onto her. Once she'd had a glass of wine to unwind, she always became super nice to Amelia and would be much more willing to help out.

"I'll go to the store and get a few bottles of wine for her as a thank you." Arthur stated.

Amelia stopped what she was doing and locked her gaze on him. "Why do you always suck up to your sister? Why do you have to keep buying her things in order get her to do stuff for you?"

"She's helping us out. It's only fair that I give something back," he replied.

Her lips curved into a sneer. "What, by giving her bottles of alcohol to help with her alcohol addiction?"

His face turned red with rage as he stomped towards her, stopping inches from her face.

"Don't speak about my sister like that. She doesn't have an alcohol addiction." He took a step back, knowing deep down that she was right. He just didn't want to admit his older sister had a problem. He preferred to remember her as the brave and kind one when they were kids. He averted his gaze, not wanting her to see the guilty expression on his face. "I'm going to the shop. Did you want anything?"

"Just get something for the kids, but don't be too long as I have to take my mother to the hairdressers later. And something easy to cook for tonight because I don't want to spend another evening slaving away in the kitchen only to have everyone refuse to eat it," she snapped, turning her back on him.

He couldn't put his finger on it, but there was something about her that made him shiver as he left the room. He grabbed his wallet and keys from the side and headed out the front door, leaving the kids in the lounge. Their innocent little faces looked at him through the window, with their huge grins taking up the majority of their faces. Amelia had always wanted children, but she'd had difficulty conceiving over the years. The month they had planned to give up was also the month she had become pregnant with triplets, only for them to lose one at birth, leaving them with two beautiful boys.

After losing one of the babies, she had grown cold and bitter towards him, blaming him for the baby's death. The harrowing event had changed her, and what was meant to be a joyful time for them, had turned into mourning for the stillborn child. Amelia had refused to name the boy, so, Arthur had chosen the name Theo. She had him buried quickly; as far away from her as possible. Since then, she hadn't spoken of their third child, and refused to acknowledge that he had ever existed. The twins never knew of their other brother, and Arthur was hoping to tell them when they were old enough to understand.

Arthur smiled and waved back, and their eyes lit up with delight. They all shared Amelia's wild, curly hair, but their features were more similar to his, with small button noses and wide brown eyes. He wondered if Theo would have had the same complexion if he were still alive, but every time he imagined his third son, there was nothing but a hollow face in his mind.

The cold morning air felt clean and crisp, and he pretended to smoke a cigarette by exhaling puffs of white fluffy clouds. His fingers itched, he missed smoking, but he knew that quitting had been for the best. His lungs weren't as strong as they'd been in his younger years, and if he had continued, it would have killed him.

He skipped down the crumbling steps and out through the gnarled iron gate to his car. Something caught his attention. He turned to see one of his neighbours staring out of the window of their newly renovated house. He waved to her, and her smile seemed tinged with sadness as she returned his wave. She closed her curtains.

Getting into his car, he shifted into gear and drove away. He focused his attention on the icy road ahead, the houses blurring into one colour. As he opened the window, the wind whipped through his hair. He admired the scenery of his new neighbourhood, which appeared beautiful and equally quite glamorous, with its modern homes surrounded by lush greenery and immaculately manicured lawns. Vibrant colours stood out in clusters of newly trimmed hedges, with long green stalks looming over the grassy verges. There wasn't a weed in sight, and nothing was broken or chipped in any way.

That was the standard he had wanted for his new home. In comparison to the newly renovated houses with their sleek-looking white fences, his house appeared bleak and rundown. It was in desperate need of a lick of paint and some loving care.

He could smell the coast air wafting in through the open window, and he breathed it in, smiling to himself.

The closer he drove to the seaside town, the older it looked, with its eighteenth-century style buildings and quaint little shops. The roads narrowed, his car becoming increasingly close to the other cars parked along the side. He wasn't used to the country roads, and he had already noticed that many of the cars were large 4x4's or pick-up trucks, probably used for either fishing or for the farms nearby. He drove past the town and into the next one over, looking for somewhere more modern to shop. He went into autopilot, his mind drifting to what Amelia had said the previous night. He didn't understand why she had said that strange name, Taranock.

He rounded the corner, and there it was, at the far end of the busy street—the grocery store. Crowds of people walked along the pavements, with their heads buried in their phones, not looking where they were going. To him, they looked like robots, devoid of any expression or emotions.

While Arthur was at the store, Amelia was left at home to care for the children. The house was in disarray, and she knew Trish would notice and use it against her. She knew Trish had never liked her, she had made that abundantly clear the first time they'd met. Trish had stood inches away from Amelia within the first few seconds of meeting her; she had scanned her expensive-looking outfit and perfect bouncy curls. She was trying to find flaws, hoping to tell her perfect little brother that she was no good. Over the years, Trish had mellowed slightly, although she still only talked to her if she wanted something or if she had been drinking.

Trish, with her straight blonde hair and mismatched clothes, looked nothing like Amelia. She would never wear any jewellery, nor would she ever wear anything apart from trainers, while Amelia lived in her stilettos. She idolised them; they made her look more sophisticated, and she had noticed how when she wore them, people took her more seriously than when she wore flats. Trish had no boyfriend, and she didn't have many friends either. She was the complete opposite of Amelia, whose phone was always buzzing either with some juicy gossip or an invitation to a girl's night out. Amelia thought Trish was pathetic and had no life, but Trish loved being alone and would only make an exception for her baby brother. If Arthur needed help with anything, which was pretty much every week, then she'd be there.

Their parents had passed away a few years before, leaving Trish to be the only close family member Arthur had left.

Amelia tensed her shoulders as she stood at the kitchen counter, listening to the clock ticking from the lounge, taunting her with every passing second; getting slowly closer to when Trish would appear on her doorstep. She hoped Arthur would return before she appeared. Amelia didn't want to be stuck with Trish, having to ask polite questions to pass the time.

She tapped her perfectly manicured nails impatiently on the counter, in time with the ticking of the grandfather clock, waiting to hear his car pull up outside. He'd been gone for a while, and she imagined him stuffing food into his mouth, sitting in his car, waiting as long as he could, just to annoy her. Time was running out for her to take her mother to the hairdressers, and a pang of guilt surged through her body.

A high-pitched scream from the lounge brought her back to reality, with her mother's instinct leaping into action, at the thought of one of her kids being hurt. Three strides was all it took for her long, slender legs to cover the space between the kitchen door and the lounge. She barged through the door, scanning the room for any breakages or accidents that could have caused the scream. She stood there, hands on her skinny hips, staring down at the twins, who completely ignored her presence in the room and instead stared fearfully at the grandfather clock.

"What happened, boys? Tell Mummy."

"The clock moved," said Charlie, pointing his stubby little finger, his lip quivering with fear.

Amelia furrowed her brows as she opened the clock to examine the pendulum inside.

"It's just a clock. There's nothing wrong with it."

"There's a scary man in there," said Dylan, his voice squeaking.

She closed the clock door. "A scary man in the clock? What has school been teaching you?" She pulled Charlie to his feet, motioning for Dylan to join her and plonked them down on the sofa. "Come and sit down here. Auntie Trish will be here soon, and she's excited to see you all."

She glanced over at her mother sleeping in her armchair, oblivious to what had just happened. A book rested on her chest as it rose and fell in time with her quiet snoring.

A car pulled up outside and Amelia shot up to look out of the window. She could see Arthur taking the steps two at a time with a couple of bags full of groceries. When he opened the door, Amelia was waiting for him in the foyer, her arms folded and scowling at him with scornful eyes.

"Why has it taken you so long to get the shopping? I don't even have enough time to take my mother to the hairdressers. She's so disappointed." Amelia lied, knowing that her mother wouldn't care if she didn't go.

Arthur's good mood vanished, swiped from beneath his feet as he looked at Amelia.

"There were queues everywhere, so I had to wait. You need to relax and stop being so stressed out all the time. I'm here now, and Trish hasn't even arrived yet."

Amelia's eyes narrowed into slits as she jabbed a pointed finger in his gut. "You're the one who stresses me out."

"Don't start." He grabbed her hand and pushed it away before she could jab him again. "I want everything to be calm before Trish arrives, so you can schedule this fight for later."

She looked as though she had just been slapped across the face, her eyes wide in surprise and her mouth hanging open. She stepped back to let him pass and watched him walk into the kitchen to unload the groceries. He was beginning to stand up to her, which was strange as he usually just let her have her way. She couldn't figure out why Arthur had suddenly changed, but she didn't like it. She disliked being told what to do or even being told off by him. She was the lady of the house, and she always got her way, even if it meant going to extreme lengths. She wiped the scowl from her face and smiled, hoping to keep him sweet for later.

"Are you going to set up a wine glass for Trish?"

Arthur peered around the doorway, eyeing her closely. "Yes, why?"

Her stiletto heels rapped on the wooden floor, and Arthur noticed her fake smile widening as she approached him.

"Perhaps you should pour us one as well … before we go and introduce ourselves to the neighbours."

He grabbed another glass from the cupboard and set it down next to the first one. With the pop of the cork, the wine was poured into the glasses, slightly spilling over the sides.

Amelia grabbed a towel and mopped up the spillage. "Aren't you having one?"

"No, I'm not in the mood for one." He stowed the bottle and began preparing food for the kids.

Amelia stood at the counter, watching as Arthur's trembling fingers tried to pry open a packet of sausages.

"Why are you staring at me?"

"Sorry, I'll just stay out of your way," she muttered and left the room to see what the kids were up to.

Anger rose inside him. This woman was irritable, impatient, and impossible to even speak to, let alone live with. He couldn't remember why he'd asked her out in the first place, and now he was stuck with her. He couldn't divorce her even if he wanted to. She would take half of his assets, leaving him with almost nothing. These days his life was totally centered around her and her needs, and he was sick of it. From now on, she would have to follow his rules, not hers.

He stood there smiling to himself while chopping vegetables for dinner. He could imagine her in the lounge sulking or moaning to her mother about him, but he didn't care, as long as she was in there and he was doing his own thing—without her staring at him all the time.

There was a knock at the door.

"You can get that." Amelia called from inside the lounge.

In temper, Arthur slammed the knife down, nearly cutting into his leg as it fell to the floor, and stomped from the kitchen to the front door, yanked it open to find Trish there with a big smile on her face. Her ridiculously oversized sweater hung down to her knees, and made her look like a giant fluffy marshmallow. Her hair was scraped back into a tight greasy bun, and there wasn't an ounce of makeup on her perfectly framed face. Her black leggings scrunched at the knees and her trainers looked as if they had seen better days, but still, she was here to relieve Arthur of all his duties and help him with the house.

"Arthur, darling!" she gushed, as she drew him into her chest for a tight hug.

"Hello, Trish. I'm glad you could make it. Come in. I've already poured you a glass of wine." He stepped aside to let her in, and her smile broadened when she spotted the glass of her favourite wine sitting on the counter in the kitchen.

"Oh, my sweetheart. You shouldn't have done that!" She chuckled as she threw her suitcase into the lounge, almost colliding with Amelia's legs. "This place is absolutely stunning! It's fantastic. I love it! Amelia is so lucky to have you."

She skipped into the kitchen after Arthur and grabbed the glass of wine. With one long swig, half the wine had completely disappeared into her mouth. "That's better. Speaking of the little witch, where is she? Hopefully signing the divorce papers as we speak."

"She's in the lounge." Arthur tried his hardest to hide the smile from his face. "Keep your voice down, otherwise she will hear you."

Her face screwed up and she took another swig of her wine. "I hope she does hear it." She looked around the kitchen and shook her head. "No, no, this colour will not do. You need something a lot brighter in here. Don't let Amelia choose the colour, otherwise you'll be looking at pink walls."

Trish turned around when she heard a cough from the doorway. "Oh, there you are. Hiding from me, were you?" Her eyes scanned Amelia's tall, skinny frame and smirked. She held out her hand, and Amelia grudgingly took it. She eyed Amelia's soft, feminine hand, with its elegant fingers and shiny, gold rings. "They must have set my brother back a bit."

Amelia yanked her hand away from Trish's grasp.

"He was the one that chose them, not me."

Trish looked amused for a moment. "Oh, darling, I was only joking. Anyway, I want to see my nephews."

She barged past Amelia, nearly tripping her up, and headed straight for the lounge where she could hear the kids laughing and playing. Amelia shot Arthur a look before following her slowly, visualizing Trish falling over and breaking at least one of her bones.

She despised Trish to the core, and wished the earth would swallow her up so she wouldn't have to see her again. Even her perfume was overpowering, filling every room in the house with Eau de Trish, and her irritatingly positive outlook on life. She hated the fact that Trish could get what she wanted simply by being in the right place at the right time. All the time. It was as if she was just a lucky symbol, attracting everything that she had ever desired into her life. Trish was wealthy, but she didn't appear so. She resembled a tramp more than a millionaire, but she'd always ask—*Why do I need to look rich when I'm already rich? It's a complete waste of money.*

Amelia wanted the money that Trish had. She desired Trish's good luck attitude, as well as the men who would flaunt themselves at her, attempting to catch her attention. She was a successful businesswoman, dabbling in the stock market, and made her millions by choosing which stock to get her nails into very carefully. The money she had made from the stock market, she had put into a cosmetic business, making her own beauty products, making even more money. Trish had everything, and Amelia had only a taste of it, but she was hungry for more. Trish had lent them a large sum of money to renovate the house, but only in Arthur's name so Amelia couldn't touch it, Trish had known that would irritate her. She watched Trish's eyes light up as she entered the lounge, she knew that she had the one thing Trish was longing for; Trish wanted children of her own. She watched Trish interrupt the kids playing and cuddle them.

"Oh, my little darlings," Trish gushed, staring at the twins. "I could just eat you both up!"

In some ways, Amelia felt sorry for her, but deep down she thought Trish was an evil cow, desiring her children and jealous that Amelia could and did have them while she was unable to.

She watched Trish as she tickled one of the children, making them both giggle with pleasure. Amelia left her to it and went into the kitchen with Arthur. He was almost done with the casserole and was chopping the last few carrots.

"Has she settled in?"

Amelia nodded and took a sip of her wine. "She certainly has. How long will dinner be?"

"A little while yet," he said, looking at his watch, "but we can stop by the neighbours and be back in time for dinner."

Amelia gave him a dark look. "All right, fine."

Arthur sighed, knowing she wasn't pleased with the plan, but he didn't care what she thought any longer. "It's either that or we wait until after dinner to go, but it'll be a while before its ready. Is that better than going now ... did you really want to spend more time with my sister?"

"No, I don't want to spend another minute with that woman." She looked at him wearily and willed herself to remain as calm as possible.

"Well then, I suggest you get yourself ready and then we'll leave," he said.

She nodded and disappeared through the door, her footsteps echoing up the stairs. He cleaned up the kitchen and laid out the dinner plates before going into the lounge, where Trish was happily playing cross-legged on the floor with the kids beside her.

"Trish, is it okay if Amelia and I go out to see the neighbours quickly? We want to thank them for the basket they sent us," he asked, a little too nervously for Trish to ignore.

She smiled as she looked up at him, watching him twiddling his fingers as if about to ask a parent for something massive.

"Of course, you can. How long do you think you'll be?"

"An hour or so," he said.

Before responding, she paused for a moment and clucked her tongue on the inside of her cheek.

"That's perfectly fine. I'll keep an eye on the dinner too. Go now, and it'll be ready for when you return. Dotty won't be any trouble either." She smiled Dotty's way, watching her sleep peacefully in her chair.

His mood lightened as he left the room with a spring in his step. He'd expected Trish to complain and force them to stay, leaving him with two moody women to deal with instead of the usual one. He tapped the bannister and yelled up the stairs at Amelia.

"Are you ready yet?"

"I'm coming!" she hollered back as she descended the stairs.

He watched as Amelia, with her flawlessly made-up face and curly, glossy hair, came bouncing down the steps in a new pair of ridiculously tall high heels and a different outfit. He couldn't understand why women had to dress for every occasion. There had been nothing wrong with her previous outfit, but for some reason she had changed into something much more formal, as if she were a model about to step onto a catwalk.

Her feet barely touched the steps, and her perfect mood had returned. She hoped that these neighbours were as attractive as she was, so she could make some more appropriate friends, instead of hanging out with Arthur and his low-class buddies, all of whom drank beer from a can and not from a glass.

She yearned to live the high life and to have more friends who shared her viewpoint, rather than having to live below her standards on Arthur's pitiful wages. Although Amelia had a job, it earned her nothing compared to the amount of money Trish earned, and Amelia couldn't understand why Trish wouldn't dress the part, as she would if she had that kind of money lying around. She was looking forward to meeting her new neighbours, and judging from the basket full of goodies, she felt they would have impeccable taste, and she hoped there would be someone there more suitable for her than Arthur. She longed to run away with someone who was handsome and wealthy, even if it meant having to move country.

Arthur took her hand in his and escorted her to the front door. A cold breeze washed over him, and he had the impression that he was being watched. He looked around the lounge and saw that everyone was busy. There was no reason for him to feel that—so why did he? He could tell Amelia's mind was elsewhere because she was eager to leave, so he didn't bother mentioning it to her. He looked around the hallway and noticed a dark shadow peering over the bannister at them from the top landing of the stairs. Its long, lank hair obscured much of its white face. A small whimper escaped his lips, and the thing vanished in an instant. Amelia raised her eyebrows at him, wondering what he was up to, but Arthur didn't budge. He stared long and hard at the spot where it had been, attempting to erase the image from his mind.

"Come on, Arthur," Amelia snapped, pulling him out the front door. "What is wrong with you? Snap out of it!"

"I think I've just seen a ghost," he muttered as she pulled him down the steps of the front garden.

"Don't be a moron." Her hoarse laugh echoed through the evening air, frightening some birds that were nesting in nearby trees. "There is no such thing. Come on, we don't have much time as it is, don't want you wasting it."

He looked back at the house, and he could have sworn that the curtain twitched in the upstairs bedroom window. What if they had bought a haunted house? What if something truly evil was living with them?

He caught a glimpse of Amelia out of the corner of his eye and hoped that she would be the first to be eaten by it, just in case it needed something to gnaw on. He knew he shouldn't be thinking such things, but it made him feel better to think that if there was something evil living with them, he'd be able to throw Amelia at it first, so he could take the kids and run.

CHAPTER 7
Secrets Unfold

A man answered the door, flashing an enormous toothy grin, and ushered them inside.

"Hello. Hello, welcome. I'm Steve and this is Graham."

Graham and Steve's house was right across the road. The house was gorgeous from the outside with a flawless, neat lawn, gleaming windows, and the perfect, suburban layout. It was identical to the house next door, yet it felt that it had more life to it. It looked as if it had just come out of an estate agent's catalogue for the perfect family home.

Steve's flamboyant-looking friend stood next to him, welcoming them to their home. The house was just as bright and unique as them, with dashes of different colours mixing in with vibrant paintings on the walls. Amelia's face dropped as she entered. This was the complete opposite of what she would want in a friend. These men had no taste whatsoever. Everything was so brightly coloured that it started to hurt her eyes. She looked away and focused her attention on their impeccably white smiles.

"Thank you for the basket. It was very nice of you."

Graham nodded, taking Amelia's hand and dragging her into the starkly furnished lounge, where there was limited seating, and everything looked as if it was from an alien spaceship. Arthur could tell Amelia was feeling uncomfortable, which made him smile even more, glad to see that there were other people like him, who she didn't want to be around.

Steve and Graham looked polar opposites. Steve looked fashionable, yet manly, with his rustic, gentleman's look, while Graham looked like a flamboyant peacock, with an overpowering campness about him. Amelia wasn't sure if they were an item or just friends, but to her, they looked ridiculous.

"I love the place. It's very unique," Arthur said, hoping that his remark would irritate her.

She scowled at him before smiling at Steve and Graham. "You have a beautiful home," she said through gritted teeth.

Graham laughed. "It took us years to find the right furniture and artwork, but it was all worth it in the end. We adore our home, and we're delighted that you do as well. I have a feeling we'll get along just fine."

He motioned for them both to take a seat before opening a cabinet beside him. He took an expensive-looking bottle of wine and popped the cork loudly, narrowly missing Amelia's head.

"Darling, can you get four glasses from the kitchen?" Graham asked Steve.

Steve nodded and walked away, his gleaming black Gucci shoes gracefully clapping against the marble floor while Graham swayed his hips to the soft jazz music coming from the corner of the room. Steve reappeared moments later, carrying delicate crystal glasses, aware that if he dropped them they would shatter into tiny pieces. He handed them to Graham and sat next to him, his tight, white jeans creasing up around his hips, making his legs appear longer than they were. The seams on the side were stretching with the pressure, and Arthur hoped they wouldn't split open while he was there.

Graham poured them a glass of white wine that glistened in the setting sun. Arthur and Amelia sat awkwardly, unsure of what to say—or do.

"So, are you two together, or just housemates?" Amelia blurted out.

Steve laughed loudly. "No, we're not together. We've been friends for a very long time. We met about fifteen years ago at our old workplace in London before moving here for a quieter life. I love the countryside and Graham adores the sea. This place has its quirks with the old buildings and fishermen, but we've slowly been building more modern-style houses to brighten up Whitely Bay. It's brought more families in, which means more profits for small businesses."

"Yes, that's right," Graham said. "We created a business after my poor nana died. She left me some money, and I asked Steve to help me to put it to good use. So, we build houses. This house we had built from scratch and many of the houses around here were built by Steve and our team. I do the designing and decorating, and Steve does the manly stuff. It's a nice, easy-going business."

"My dad used to be a builder and taught me his trade. I also studied it in college." Steve said.

"And I studied architecture. It just made sense for us to start a business. We were going to move out of this house after it was built, but we liked it so much that we stayed."

"That is, until I find a girlfriend who will whisk me away." Steve cut in.

A sad look spread across Graham's face as he took a sip from his glass. "And I'll probably stay here, lonely and gay." He hesitated for a moment before looking up at Arthur and smiling. "So, what do you two do?"

"I work in finance, and Amelia swans around, barking orders at clients." Arthur smirked.

"In other words, I'm a psychologist. Only entry level though. Although, that will have to be put on hold while I take time off to look after my mother," she stated flatly.

The room fell into an awkward silence as they sipped their wine. Steve cleared his throat; a knife could have sliced through the tense atmosphere.

"So, why did you buy the house of weirdness? Is it the rustic appearance, or were you just desperate?" he asked.

Graham laughed next to him, sipping his wine, and licking his lips, as he relished the sweet, tangy flavour.

"That property has been on the market for some time. Nobody has been interested in buying it," Steve said.

Arthur perked up, eager to hear more. "What do you mean by the house of weirdness?"

Steve gave Graham a sidelong glance before proceeding. "You must know about its history, right? It's one of the reasons why we never renovated that place and built this one instead."

Amelia shrugged her shoulders as she looked at Arthur. She had no idea what they were talking about. "I don't know if I want to find out, to be honest with you," she said.

"I think you should know about the house if you're going to live there. I wouldn't want to live in a place where a family went missing, without knowing what had happened before..." Graham's voice trailed off. He noticed the shocked expression on Amelia's face, as she clearly mouthed the word no at him.

Arthur ran his fingers through his scraggly, unkempt hair, fixing Amelia with a bewildered stare. "I don't believe this," he said. "You knew all along about the house?"

He could see the humiliation on her face. Her cheeks flushed bright red and her face flustered as she stuttered.

"Well, no. I assumed something had happened, which was why the price had been dropped so low, but I didn't know what."

Arthur's jaw dropped. "So, you basically knew, and you didn't think to tell me what I was buying with MY money?"

"No. I didn't know, I guessed. And there was nothing stopping you from researching the house before paying the very low asking price with YOUR money," Amelia retorted.

Steve and Graham sat there watching the argument unfold in their house.

"Maybe we should get some popcorn," Steve said to Graham.

"Good idea," Graham replied. "You know I love a snack when I'm watching strangers air their dirty laundry in my own living room."

Arthur and Amelia turned to Graham, shocked and slightly embarrassed.

"Well ... there's no need to be rude," Amelia snapped. Arthur shifted in his seat uncomfortably, feeling the heat from the rage radiating from Amelia's body next to him. He couldn't help but smirk as she looked at Graham, dumbfounded.

"Oh, don't worry about Graham. He has no filter and tells it like it is," Steve said as he took another sip of wine.

Amelia couldn't believe she was being spoken to in such a manner, and her cheeks flushed even more as Graham's piercing blue eyes locked on hers.

"So, going back to the family disappearing, what happened, exactly? Were they ever found?" Arthur asked, breaking the awkward silence between them.

Steve's eyes lit up excitedly. "Oh, I just love telling new people the history of the house. It's a good spooky story!"

"Do you know what 'Le Diable Rouge' means?" Graham spoke up.

Arthur tilted his head. "I know it's the name of our house, but I'm not sure what it means."

Steve's lips curled into a cruel grin. "It translates to 'The Red Devil'."

Amelia's eyes widened in surprise. "How come it's called that?"

"It was named that after the first family went missing shortly after it was built in the eighteenth century," Graham explained. "People went missing in that house all the time and over the years it became a good ghost story to tell the kids on Halloween night. I didn't believe any of it until the last family who lived there vanished one day, leaving behind all their belongings, including the dinner table, which had been laid for supper." Graham finished his wine and poured himself another glass before continuing. "They were never found. Their car remained where it was parked, on the road outside, and there was no evidence of a break-in. Some say they ran away and took the kids because they were in debt, which may have been true, but even so, I can't imagine them leaving all of their belongings behind, especially if they were short on cash."

"I thought the investigation was still ongoing. I'm surprised the house's owner, the family's grandmother, hadn't told you. She really should have," Steve stated.

"And everyone else knew except me?" Arthur asked, clearly irritated as he glared at Amelia.

Graham's stare caused Amelia to shift uncomfortably in her chair. "It appears so."

"That's fantastic, to say the least. Is there anything else I should be aware of?" Arthur asked.

Graham took a cautious look at Steve before speaking. "I suppose you should just be on the lookout for anything unusual. I'm not a believer in the supernatural, but I can't think of any reasonable explanation for their sudden disappearance."

Arthur stood up and started pacing the room. "How long ago did all this happen?"

Steve could tell Arthur was angry, and he didn't want to make it any worse than it already was. "It was about a year ago. The grandmother put it up for sale a few months after their disappearance, which is, to say the least, unusual. I would have thought she would have waited for them to be found, but she didn't. She put it up for sale and put all of their belongings in storage. We had no choice but to help her, the poor dear, because no one would go near the place. Nobody wanted it until you showed up."

"Hold on a sec. The estate agent told us that someone else had already put an offer in when we were viewing the place," Amelia piped up.

Graham laughed. "That is something they always say. It's intended to put you under pressure to make an offer."

Arthur slowed his pace and rolled his eyes. "Amelia, of course you'd get sucked into their little games. It's you all over."

Amelia's eyes bulged with anger. "What's that supposed to mean?"

With his hands on his hips, Arthur's nostrils flared as he stared down at her. His brow furrowed and his lips tightened. He seemed to want to say something, but he kept his mouth shut and moved away from her.

Graham sat there sipping his wine, looking amused. He was enjoying the drama, but the tense atmosphere around them made Steve uneasy. He could tell by the way Arthur and Amelia acted around each other that their relationship was already on shaky ground, and Graham was only making matters worse.

He got their attention by clearing his throat loudly. "But the house is lovely," he said, "and you have the largest garden in the neighbourhood. You'll realise how big it is once you've cut back most of the bushes. I don't believe there is anything to be concerned about." Steve smiled as he slapped Graham on the back. "Do you want us to come over sometime and help with the renovations?"

Amelia threw a sharp sideways glance at Arthur as he slurped loudly on his wine, ignoring her. "If you like, we don't want to cause any bother if you're both busy."

Graham threw his hands in the air, delighted. "We shall be over first thing tomorrow morning."

"But what about your jobs?" Arthur asked.

"We always book some time off around this time of year, you know, just to rejuvenate. And we are the owners of our business. We can do what we want." Graham explained.

Steve agreed and the room fell into a comfortable silence as they finished their wine. Arthur could see his house from where he was sitting, and noticed Trish moving around in the kitchen. "Apologies," he announced, "but I've just remembered that I left the dinner on."

He turned to look at Amelia. "We should go."

Amelia looked relieved as she stood up and placed her glass on the glossy pine table. "Yep, let's leave."

She left without another word, not even bothering to say goodbye. She was relieved to be out of there and away from Graham's menacing stare. She couldn't understand why everyone treated her that way, even a complete stranger she had just met. She knew she wasn't trash, in fact, she was far from it; she had the best, and most stylish clothes. Her hair and nails were impeccable—a chipped nail would be a total disaster and necessitate an emergency manicure appointment to fix. Her skin was flawless, and she always made sure to wear her most expensive Chanel perfume. She was perfect, and she knew it. So, why did everyone treat her with such disrespect?

She wanted to ask Arthur, but daren't, given the way he had glared at her before saying goodbye to the two ridiculously overdressed neighbours. As she walked down their impeccably neat lawn she looked across the road to the other houses, hoping that at least one of her neighbours would be like her and enjoy her company. Arthur raced ahead of her, leaving her trailing behind, deep in thought. Perhaps she should ask a few questions as to why no one liked her; she was desperate to find out, and moody or not, he was the best person to talk to about it. He would tell her the truth, even if she didn't like it.

"Arthur, wait! I want to ask you something," she panted. "I want to know why everyone treats me like crap."

He stopped and looked at her, surprised. "Why are you asking me that?"

She placed her hand on his and forced a smile. "I just want to know, so I can do something about it."

"Well, I suppose it's the way you speak to people." He sighed deeply, not really wanting to get into it. "You are very abrupt."

It was her turn to look surprised, her hand slipping from his and falling to the side. Arthur wished he had kept his mouth shut. He understood why everyone disliked her: she was a difficult person to get along with. He noticed a vein on her forehead throbbing and her eyes narrowing into slits, causing his heart to double flip.

"I'm not rude."

"You asked," he said sternly, moving away from her and inching closer to their house. "I speak the truth and if you don't like it then I suggest you stop asking me questions that you don't want to know the answer to."

Her shoulders tightened and she clenched her jaw. "You could have said it in a much more civilised manner."

He threw his hands up in frustration and stomped away from her. "This is exactly what I mean!" He glanced over his shoulder and saw that

Graham and Steve were staring at them through the window.

Amelia stood at the top of the path with her hands on her hips, tapping her foot heavily on the ground. It was her favourite pose whenever she was angry.

"Come along," said Arthur, "we have dinner to prepare."

He didn't wait for her, instead he continued across the road, narrowly missing an oncoming car that was going way too fast. He cursed them as he walked slowly through his garden and up to his front door.

Trish had already dished up by the time he walked through the door, leaving the last of the dirty crockery in the sink to soak. While the twins and Dotty sat in their chairs waiting for their food to cool, she hummed to herself. The boys giggled, pushing a toy car to each other from across the table. As he watched his children play, Arthur couldn't help but smile. The sound of Amelia's heels echoed down the foyer and as he watched his children, he wondered if they were the only good thing that had come from her. Maybe she was starting to realise that she needed to change her ways if she wanted people to like her.

Trish smirked as Amelia walked into the kitchen. "What's the problem, Amelia? Are your neighbours not up to your expectations?"

"I'm not at all sure what you mean." Amelia gave her a look and took a seat at the table.

Trish's grin widened. "I saw them in their garden before I came here. They're quite flamboyant, aren't they? That's not really your style."

Amelia folded her arms in disgust and stared at her sister-in-law, looking up and down. "At least I have a sense of style. You always wear plain clothes. You don't even wear perfume to hide your musky scent."

"Please, ladies. That's enough." Arthur muttered wearily. He glanced at Amelia's screwed-up face as she glared at Trish from across the table. Trish didn't seem bothered by Amelia's remark and continued to serve dinner.

She practically threw the bowl in front of Amelia. "Make sure you don't choke on your own venom."

She smiled as she placed a bowl in front of Arthur. "A perfect meal for my perfect little brother."

Amelia sighed and rolled her eyes. "Thank you," she murmured through gritted teeth.

She couldn't bring herself to argue any longer, she was exhausted and couldn't wait to get into bed. She had no interest in staying up late listening to Trish and Arthur talk about irrelevant family matters that had nothing to do with her, knowing that if she did stay up with them, Trish would hurl even more abuse at her. She ate her meal and waited patiently for the twins to finish theirs. When they were done, she yanked them from their seats and took them upstairs, leaving Trish to clean up and Arthur to take her mother upstairs.

The bath was warm and bubbly as she watched them lower themselves into the water.

"We need to wait for Theo," Dylan said, moving up in the bath to make room.

Charlie nodded in excitement. "Yes!"

Amelia looked at them, confused. "Theo?"

"He's our new friend. He plays with us," Dylan explained.

"Your new friend? How sweet," she said, playing along, amused. "And, where is he now?"

"He's standing right next to you," Charlie shouted excitedly, pointing to the empty space beside Amelia.

She jumped back in mock surprise. "Wow. He snuck up on me. Shall I put him in the bath next to you?"

The boys nodded eagerly, watching Amelia pretend to pick their friend up and place him in the bath.

Charlie shook his head. "Theo said that he can get into the bath himself, Mummy. He's as old as us and has the same birthday."

Amelia stared at the empty space in the bath, taken aback. "Really?"

"Yes, and he looks like us too." Dylan chimed in.

The memories of the stillborn boy entered Amelia's mind, bringing a tear to her eye. She sniffled, swallowing the shame she felt and forced a smile. "Well, that's nice that you both have a new friend to play with, but playtime is over and it's nearly bedtime."

She couldn't be bothered to wash herself, but she bathed them until they were both squeaky clean. After a quick change into their pyjamas and a bedtime story, they were both tucked tightly into their beds.

"Mummy, you didn't tuck Theo in." Charlie said, pointing to the doorway.

Amelia sighed, exhausted with the game. "But where is he going to sleep? He doesn't have a bed."

"He sleeps in the clock downstairs," they said in unison.

Amelia shuddered at the thought of the clock. "Really, why?"

The boys both looked at each other and then at the empty space in the doorway. "Because that's his home. He likes it there."

"But tonight, he wants to sleep with us. He says we're his new friends." Charlie giggled. He moved up in his bed and patted his pillow. "He can sleep with me."

Amelia felt a cold wave wash over her as Charlie tucked the covers up to his pillow.

"There. He's nice and cosy. Goodnight, Mummy."

"Goodnight, Mummy." Dylan said, snuggling down under his covers.

Amelia stood there for a while, staring at the strange lump in the covers beside Charlie. It was as if something was really there. But as she patted the lump down, it suddenly disappeared, leaving an indent of where it once was.

She wasn't sure if she was imagining things, but she could have sworn she felt something beneath the covers. Her mind was tired though, and she knew that it could play tricks on her at times.

She quietly shut the door and dragged her tired legs to her bedroom, where the bed welcomed her exhausted body.

CHAPTER 8
Was it a Dream?

Amelia crawled out of bed to get a glass of water. The wine Graham had given her had completely dried her mouth out—like the Sahara desert. The room was dark, but she could see that it was just after one on the clock on her nightstand. She checked to see if Arthur's side had been slept on. His pillow remained plump, and the covers had not been pulled back.

She could hear voices from downstairs. They were giggling, which immediately put her on edge. So, they were both still awake, and she could tell they were drunk. She crept downstairs and snuck quietly to the lounge door. The giggling and whispering stopped as she peered through the crack in the door, and was met by the sight of her husband and his sister, whose legs were entwined in an embrace. Two glasses of wine were placed on the table next to the sofa, along with half a bottle of wine.

Amelia's mind was filled with shock and disgust and she let out a scream of terror and rage. She closed her eyes and clutched her ears, attempting to clear her mind of the image.

"You're sick! You're sick!" she screeched, over and over again at the top of her lungs.

Trish, alarmed by the noise, followed Arthur to the top of the stairs.

"What the hell is going on here?" Arthur hissed.

Amelia looked up the stairs at them both staring down at her, puzzled and terrified. She stuttered, unable to get her words out, reluctant to explain what she had just witnessed. Arthur dashed down the stairs to her aid, unsure whether or not she was still asleep or having a nervous breakdown. He could feel her body trembling in his arms, and even Trish looked concerned.

They were both in their pyjamas, which were a little ruffled from sleep. Trish had a heart-covered pair of pyjama shorts on, and her hair looked like a bird's nest on top of her head, tied into a messy bun. Arthur didn't look much better with his coffee-stained grey t-shirt, and tight boxers.

"What happened?" he asked, while smoothing her hair.

Amelia was at a loss for words. She couldn't accuse them both of something which may, or may not, have occurred. She didn't want to appear completely insane. She looked around the lounge, noticing that it was dark, and that there were no glasses of wine, and that Arthur and Trish weren't even in there. With terrified eyes, she looked at Arthur.

"I thought I saw something ..."

"She's obviously having a breakdown," Trish interjected, as she dashed down the stairs to Amelia.

Amelia scowled at her for interfering. "No, no, no. I saw—" She was interrupted by a crashing sound coming from the kitchen.

"What in the name of God was that?" Trish hissed as she clutched Arthur's arm.

Amelia noticed and drew Arthur away from her, unable to shake the image of the two of them from her mind. She wasn't sure if what she had seen was real or if her mind was playing cruel tricks on her, but the feeling of disgust remained.

"I'm not sure. You ladies wait here while I go investigate," Arthur muttered, not wanting to leave, but knowing that if he didn't, Amelia would, as she always did, call him a 'pussy'.

He had to pry Trish's hand from his arm as he made his way toward the kitchen door. He could hear his heartbeat pounding, and his hands trembled as he gripped the doorknob, turning it as quietly as he could.

As he stepped inside, the darkness enveloped him. He quickly turned on the light and scanned the kitchen. Nothing seemed out of place. He couldn't find the source of the loud crashing, but something caught his eye to the left of the kitchen counter.

"Guys, come here and take a look at this."

"What is it?" Trish called from the foyer. As she spoke, Arthur could hear the fear in her voice. "Is it scary?"

Arthur groaned. "Just get in here!"

They both walked in hesitantly, watching Arthur trace his finger along a set of sharp scratches on the kitchen counter. There were five deep indentations in the surface of the wood. It was as if an animal had clawed it. Arthur couldn't understand how anyone could have done this without being seen.

"This wasn't here before, was it?"

"No, it wasn't there." Amelia's voice trembled as she went on. "I don't understand. What could make that? It looks like massive claw marks."

"For the first time in my life, I have to agree with Amelia, it seems that something large and fierce made these scratch marks," Trish said, while clutching Amelia's hand.

"It's hardly minor scratches either. It's ruined the entire counter. Amelia, did you see anything else down here?"

She shook her head. "I don't think so."

"This is completely messed up. Is it possible that it's a ghost?" The look on Amelia's face as the words left Arthur's mouth told him that he had made the mistake of mentioning the paranormal in her presence.

"Don't be stupid!" she exploded.

Trish glared at her, irritated by Amelia's tone of her voice when speaking to her brother. She dropped her hand in frustration. "Well, what else could it be?"

"It has to be an animal, perhaps a dog? There are always stray dogs around," Amelia stated.

"Suppose it was a stray dog, where has it gone? We would have seen it." Arthur went to the back door and rattled the doorknob.

"The door's locked, so it can't have been a dog. It's got nowhere else to go apart from here, and I'm sure I would have noticed it. Besides, look at the claw marks. They are too large to be a dog's."

"Let's go into the lounge. I don't want to be in here a second longer," Trish said, dragging Amelia by the arm into the foyer. Arthur followed them, his mind racing with questions. He was tired, yet his mind was filled with images of ghouls and ghosts. This didn't happen in real life, but as he took one last look at the claw marks before closing the door, he couldn't help but think that something weird was happening. He pulled Trish to the side before she could enter the lounge and hissed in her ear.

"What do you think?"

She looked at him, her face twisted with fear and confusion.

"I don't know what to think right now."

Amelia watched them closely from the sofa, observing Trish's movements towards Arthur. She still couldn't shake the feeling from earlier, and she was certain Arthur hadn't been in bed when she had awoken. Nothing made sense, and her mind was overworked to the point of exhaustion. She rubbed her eyes as she waited for them to take a seat. Arthur looked over at the empty space next to Amelia, but decided against it and sat next to Trish instead.

Amelia's hurt expression made him feel a little guilty, but his mind was on other things.

"As I said, if it is a ghost—"

"Please stop this nonsense." Amelia shot him a look from across the room, stopping him in his tracks. "There's no such thing as ghosts, or the afterlife."

"So, this is it then, is it? We live and then we die, we simply cease to exist?"

Amelia looked amused at his remark. "Yes, that's right, and the funny thing is, you're spending all of it with me."

His face dropped. "Great."

Trish smirked as she watched Amelia's expression shift from hurt to anger. "I don't think we'll be able to reach an agreement here," she said. "All I can say is that perhaps we should do some detective work and set up a few cameras around the house to see if we can catch anything. If there is a ghost here, we'll be able to capture it on camera, and Amelia will have to accept that there is life after death."

Arthur nodded. "I agree. I'll go and get some tomorrow morning and wire them in."

"So, I'm going to be spied on in my own home?" Amelia snapped.

"It's not about you, Amelia. For once in your life, stop making it all about you, and realise that the world does not revolve around you," Trish scolded, her eyes piercing Amelia's.

Amelia shifted her gaze away, muttering something incoherent under her breath. Arthur let out a yawn and stretched his arms. He groaned as he looked at his watch.

"Let's get some sleep. It's just after one, and we need to recharge our batteries for tomorrow."

"What? Just after one? I woke up at one and we've been here at least an hour. That can't possibly be the time," Amelia stammered as she stared at the grandfather clock.

Arthur double-checked his watch and then examined the grandfather clock. "My watch and the clock both show the correct time. Perhaps you had another nightmare."

"I remember it clearly, Arthur. It was just after one when I came down here and found you two rollicking together on the sofa," Amelia blurted out.

Arthur's eyes bulged. "I'm sorry, what now?"

Amelia realised what she had just said, her cheeks turned crimson as she averted her gaze away from their stunned expressions.

"I mean ... I mean ... I mean ..." she stammered.

"You mean what? You're accusing me and my brother of incest? That is a revolting accusation. What on earth is wrong with you? Why would you say that?" Trish squealed. "I knew you were jealous of our family, but this is taking the piss!"

Amelia got up and ran out of the room, leaving Arthur and Trish in silence. They listened to her footsteps thumping up the stairs followed by the bedroom door slamming, before Arthur finally spoke.

"I have no idea what's gotten into her recently."

Trish pursed her lips. "In all seriousness, Arthur, I think she needs to see someone. She's accusing us of incest. That's just the lowest of the low."

Deep in thought, Arthur stroked his scraggly beard. Trish noticed goose bumps appearing on his bare legs, but he remained silent, quietly thinking to himself. She kept talking, hoping to persuade him to send Amelia off to therapy.

"Look, we both know something isn't right with Amelia right now, and I know I don't particularly like her, but I am concerned about her, and her actions. You don't want the twins to see their mother's strange outbursts—they might say something inappropriate in school. She acted a bit like this when you lost the baby. Think about it for a minute." She reassured him by patting his knee. "Why do you think she's accused us of incest? Jealousy perhaps?"

"I don't really know. I'm just too tired to even think about this right now."

She gave a sympathetic nod. "Let's go to bed and discuss this in the morning."

She pulled him up and led him upstairs to his room. The door was still closed, and they could hear Amelia sobbing quietly inside.

"Would you like to sleep in the guest room while I go into the twins' room? I think she needs to not be disturbed for now."

He nodded at her; his shoulders slumped from exhaustion. "Alright, thank you. I'll see you in a couple of hours." He pulled away from her and dragged his feet to the guest room.

She watched him close the door before entering the twins' room, looking at which bed was big enough for her to get into. She smiled to herself as she watched them sleep peacefully, snuggled under their covers. She yanked Charlie's cover back and wriggled in until she was completely on the bed. Charlie stirred slightly but remained sound asleep as she wrapped her arms around him. The bed felt freezing beneath her skin but as she felt the side Charlie was on, it felt warm and cosy. She moved closer to Charlie and dozed off, unaware that there was something shuffling around downstairs.

The commotion could be heard throughout the foyer. *Thump, click, scrape, thump, click, scrape,* until it gradually disappeared into the lounge where it stayed for the remainder of the night.

CHAPTER 9
Amelia's Fight

The sun rose over the neatly trimmed hedges and in through the kitchen window, where Arthur and Amelia sat on opposite sides of the table glaring at each other. The atmosphere was tense, and neither of them wanted to speak first, their stubborn behaviour wreaking havoc on their already crumbling relationship.

Arthur kept glancing over at the claw marks on the counter, recalling the strange events from the previous night. He might have considered it was nothing more than a disturbing nightmare if it hadn't been for that evidence. While Amelia ate her cereal, he flipped through the pages of the morning newspaper, ignoring her intense stare. When Trish entered the kitchen, dressed and ready for the day, he let out a huge sigh of relief.

"Good morning, everybody!" Trish exclaimed joyfully. She hummed cheerfully to herself, and Amelia scowled at her—how could she be so happy after the previous night's events.

"Good morning, Trish," Arthur mumbled, dropping his paper and turning his full attention to her. "Have the twins woken up yet?"

"You bet they have! I'll get them in a minute," she replied, placing a bowl of cereal in front of him. "Now, eat something. We have a busy day ahead."

"There was a lot of commotion last night, I heard strange noises," Dotty announced, staring at her bowl. "I keep hearing this name in my head, the Taranock. I don't know what it means."

A deathly silence descended as everyone exchanged glances, unwilling to speak first. The awkwardness between them was so palpable that even Dotty noticed.

"What's the problem? Cat got your tongue?"

"What *exactly* is the Taranock?" Trish finally questioned.

"I don't know. It keeps popping into my head," Dotty answered, as she shoved a spoonful of cereal into her mouth.

"What do you mean, Dotty?" Trish wasn't sure what Dotty was talking about, but something deep inside her wanted to know more about the Taranock.

"The name does ring a bell," Amelia said, finally.

"You've heard it before?" Trish asked, intrigued.

Amelia looked deep in thought. "Somewhere, but I can't remember where from."

"You said it the first night you were here," Arthur chimed in.

"She did? But why?" Trish asked, taking a seat next to Dotty.

"That's all there is to it." Amelia snapped. "I can't remember! Besides, it's just a name. There's nothing more to it."

"Has it not occurred to you that there could be a reason for you thinking strange things? There's something weird going on in this house. Or it could all be a coincidence and you may need to see a doctor," Trish snapped, pointing to the claw marks. "But the evidence is on this counter here. They didn't just appear, you know. They were caused by something, and that something is possibly still here. And if your mother is also saying the name, then it must mean something.”

“I am hearing the name.” Dotty spoke quietly as she pushed her bowl away.

“Trish, just shut up.” Amelia slammed her hand down in frustration. “Everything that comes from your mouth is garbage.”

“At least it’s not venom,” Trish fired back.

“I’m warning you,” Amelia screeched, putting her face as close to Trish’s as possible, “keep your trap shut, or—”

“Or what? You’ll scratch my eyes out with your perfectly painted nails? I’m sure you wouldn’t want to waste my brother’s money on another manicure, would you now, darling?”

“That’s enough, ladies. It’s too early in the morning for this. Just simmer down,” Arthur interrupted.

Trish looked up at the window and frowned, making everyone turn their heads to see what she was looking at. Steve was standing at the window with his nose pressed against the glass, while Graham stood behind him, waving gleefully.

Arthur motioned them to the front door so they could be let in. Trish smirked at Amelia before leaving the kitchen, knowing that she wasn’t pleased about their sudden appearance. She was only gone for a few seconds before returning accompanied by Steve and Graham.

“Morning, guys! What a beautiful day.” Graham clapped his hands in excitement as he eyed Arthur’s bowl of cereal. “Still having breakfast, are we? Mind if I grab a bite before we start?”

“Help yourself,” Arthur mumbled while chewing on a mouthful of cereal.

Amelia gave him a disapproving look, unaware that Trish was watching her. Trish obliged, handing a couple of bowls to Steve and Graham.

"The milk is in the refrigerator. We have a selection—just in case."

Amelia looked up at Trish. "We?" she commented, spitefully.

Trish rolled her eyes, ignored Amelia's remark, and pointed to the pantry. "In there, boys."

"Thanks, guys," Graham yelled from the pantry.

Amelia sat there twiddling her fingers, desperate to say something, but instead, kept her mouth shut, avoiding yet another argument. She wasn't happy about them taking her cereal, but if she said anything, then the others would have a go at her.

Graham smiled at Trish through a mouthful of cereal. "So, who are you and what do you do for a living?"

Trish looked slightly taken aback by Graham's abruptness, but she covered it with a smile before responding. "I'm Trish, Arthur's older sister, and I own a beauty business. I make my own cosmetics. I also dabble in the stock market as a side business."

Graham's eyes widened in surprise. "Oh, wow! That's brilliant. Good for you. How long have you been in business?"

"Approximately ten years. I have shops all over the country now, but it all started in my parents' basement."

Amelia muttered something under her breath, and Arthur mouthed at her from across the table.

"Behave yourself."

"It's alright, Arthur. I can sense the jealousy from her." Trish placed her hand on Amelia's shoulder, squeezing it lightly. "She reeks of it. I'm used to women like her making comments about the way I look despite owning a beauty business. I suppose the industry does have a standard, but luckily for me, I don't need to be pretty as my products speak for themselves."

"What's wrong with the way she looks, Amelia?" Graham asked.

Amelia was stunned at Graham's response. She thought that he of all people, with his flamboyant look, would agree with her.

"Umm ... Err ... Nothing, really. It's just a bit plain."

"A bit plain?" Graham scanned Trish up and down and smiled. "I think she looks fine."

"All I'm saying is that Trish does not appear to be the type of person who would own a beauty salon," Amelia elaborated.

"And, why not?" Graham demanded.

Amelia could see the wickedness in his eyes as he stood over her, munching on his cereal like a greedy child. A cold sweat crept over her, and she realised she was digging herself into a hole from which there was no escape.

Graham was not about to drop the subject. He was enjoying watching Amelia squirm. It served her right. He'd seen people like her before, always turning their noses up at others, as if they were beneath them. Even though he had only met Amelia once, the evening before, he was already fed up with her attitude. She needed some of her own medicine, and he was happy to give it to her in the largest dose possible.

"Is it because you think she looks too plain to have a successful business; that she doesn't dress the part?" he asked through a forced smile. Amelia looked at him like a deer caught in headlights. "Because, let me tell you, I know a lot of successful businesspeople, and they all have one thing in common—none of them dress the part. They don't need to flaunt their wealth. Money isn't everything, and I'm sure Trish feels the same way."

"That's easy for you to say!" Amelia jumped up from her chair in rage and glared at Graham. "Clearly, Graham, you have never gone without, but I've never had much money. Some of us come from a lower-class family. I had to wear my mother's old clothes because she couldn't afford to buy me new ones."

Dotty shot her a look from across the table. "Simmer down, dear. Your father left us. What did you expect? I was a single mother bringing you and your sister up. Have some respect."

"Yes, he left us. So what?" she spat. "You could have tried harder to give me a better life."

Dotty stood up from the table. "We're not having this argument."

She turned to Graham and Steve and smiled. "Very nice to meet you both, but I'm going to take a nap in the lounge. I'm old and tired, and I need to rest."

Before she left, she turned back to Amelia. "I tried my best for you and your sister. Remember that."

"You didn't try hard enough." Amelia muttered under her breath as her mother shuffled out of the kitchen with her walking frame.

Graham laughed, amused by Amelia's outburst.

"Then, you of all people should know that money isn't everything. You had a good childhood, yes? You have happy memories regardless of the lack of funds, yes? Your mother kept you safe, warm, and fed, yes?"

"Well, yes, but—"

"But what? You've had a much better childhood than I ever did. I was thrown out onto the streets by my father and then put into care because no one wanted me. I could go on and on about my depressing past, and hate everyone around me because I never had anything to call my own. But let me tell you this, you make your own future. I could have wallowed in my own self-pity and let the depression consume me, but I didn't. I dragged myself out of it and found work. I got through college, got a degree, made a successful business, built a nice house with the help of Steve, and now I'm living the high life. It is up to you what you do with your life, but don't start looking down on others because your past was not filled with glitz and glamour."

Amelia sat stunned, chewing over Graham's words of wisdom. Graham could tell by the look on her face that he'd struck an emotional nerve. A tear ran down her cheek, which she quickly wiped away and stood up to leave, but before she could walk away, Graham grabbed her and hugged her tightly. She sagged against his chest, bawling her eyes out and drenching his pink cashmere sweater.

"Shh ... Shh ... That's it, girl; you cry your heart out. You've been carrying this around with you for a long time. Just let it all out."

Arthur looked at both of them in disbelief, and Trish appeared to be on the verge of crying; neither of them had ever seen Amelia cry before.

As he stared at the tears streaming down her cheeks, his rage and resentment for her vanished. He stood up and went to her aid, tightly hugging her from behind. Trish excused herself, muttering something about getting the twins ready for breakfast.

Steve was still eating his cereal next to them with a huge grin on his face. "Well, that conversation took an unexpected turn."

Amelia smiled weakly as she looked at him through tear-stained eyes. "I guess I needed it."

"Oh, you definitely needed it, girlfriend," said Graham. "How do you feel? Lighter? Better?"

"Surprisingly enough, I feel a lot better."

Graham gave her a warm smile. "Good. Let's put this all behind us and start afresh."

Steve stepped back, placed his bowl in the sink, and caught sight of the counter. He traced his index finger across the long scratch marks, suddenly jumping back in surprise as if a jolt of electricity had shot up his arm.

"What the hell is that?" Everyone turned to see Steve pointing shakily to the large claw shaped scratch. "When I touched it, it shocked me."

"We don't actually know what that is. It appeared last night," Arthur muttered, not really wanting to talk about it.

"It just appeared?" Steve asked, baffled.

"Yeah, we heard a huge crash in the kitchen, and when I went in to investigate, that's what I found—claw marks on the counter. We're not sure what caused it because there was nothing else in the kitchen and the back door was locked," Arthur explained, becoming more jittery by the second.

Graham and Steve exchanged glances.

"It sounds, and feels like, something out of a horror movie," Steve said. "That felt like an electric shock ... but ..."

Graham clapped his hands again, garnering everyone's attention. "Don't worry, we'll sand that out. Steve has an electric sander in the shed."

"I've been looking for an excuse to use it—it's still in the box but it'll be ideal for sanding that out. What do you think caused it? Perhaps you should hang cameras around the house to see if you can catch anything."

"That's exactly what I'm going to do. I reckon I'll need four or five cameras," Arthur added.

"Wait a minute! Do we still have that security system that we never got around to installing?" Graham asked Steve.

"I believe so. That's probably in the shed too. I just need to read the manual again so I can properly set it up."

"I don't want cameras all over the place." Amelia said, her eyes pleading timidly with Arthur.

"How else are you going to figure out what caused that mark?" Graham questioned.

She shrugged her shoulders. "I'm not sure, but I don't want to be filmed in my own home. What if I'm just in my knickers?"

"I understand, but it will be just me and you watching the footage at first," Arthur elaborated.

"Don't worry, girl. No one's going to see your pale, white cheeks." Graham laughed.

Amelia sighed. "Okay, fine, but if anyone else sees my pale, white cheeks, as you put it, I'm not going to be happy. At the very least, I deserve some privacy."

"We'll keep your secret safe." Steve laughed holding his hand over his heart.

Just then, Trish walked in with the twins trailing behind her. They spotted Arthur and Amelia and bounded straight for them.

Arthur grinned as he hugged Charlie. "How are we this morning, my boys?"

They both began talking at the same time, chatting away while Graham stared longingly at them.

"Oh, their sweet little hearts. They're gorgeous. You're both extremely fortunate."

"They are, indeed," Trish whispered to herself.

"Graham, pull yourself together," Steve said, watching a small tear trickle down Graham's cheek.

Graham wiped it away. "You know what I'm like with children; they are the most precious things on this earth."

"And you'll have them someday with someone, but for now, keep it together please."

"Right, so I'll fix the kids some breakfast while you guys get yourselves sorted. We'll start in the kitchen first, and then make our way to the lounge, depending on how long it takes," Amelia said, abruptly.

For once, everyone agreed with her and went about their business, leaving her alone with the children at the kitchen table. She moved quickly, preparing the boys' breakfasts while chewing over the argument she'd had with Graham earlier on that morning.

Perhaps she was overly sensitive. Perhaps she did look down on others, but so what? She had spent years in poverty as her mother gradually lost her mind, leaving her to fend for herself, and now that she had money, she no longer needed to associate herself with poor people. She aspired to be among successful businesspeople. She wished to attend lavish parties and dress up. That was nothing to be ashamed of. She shouldn't have to defend herself in front of people like Graham. The more she thought about Graham's words, the angrier she became. She'd let her guard down and allowed Graham to make her cry. She never cried. She was taught that crying was for the weak, and she was far from weak.

"Need any help?"

The sound of Trish's voice coming from the doorway startled her. "No, I'm fine, thank you. If you want, you can go help Arthur."

Trish entered the room regardless and joined her at the sink. She appeared nervous and awkward as she struggled to find the words to ask a question.

"You haven't really told us what happened last night. I'm concerned about you. We both are."

"Don't be. I'm fine." Amelia averted her gaze, not wanting to dwell on the events of the previous night. "It must have just been a nightmare, as Arthur suggested."

Trish nodded. "It could well have been, but we found you in the foyer, and you looked terrified."

"You would have been if you saw your partner and his sister going at it," Amelia snapped.

Trish held her hands up in defence. "But, it never happened. Last night was weird for all of us, not just you. You have to admit that there's something strange going on in this house."

"Yes, I admit it, and we'll find out when Steve sets up the cameras."

"I don't really believe in ghosts or ghouls, but I have a feeling we'll find something on camera."

"Let's not bring it up in front of the kids. Leave it until after they've gone to bed," Amelia warned, peering over her shoulder at the twins eating their cereal. Trish agreed and left her to clean up the kitchen alone.

Charlie suddenly looked up from his bowl and smiled at the empty chair across from him. "Mummy, Theo wants you to clean the clock today. He said it's getting a bit dusty in there."

"Why can't he do it?" Amelia asked, not bothering to look up from the sink as she washed the dishes.

"He says because you're special and he's chosen you to do it." Dylan said.

A sharp shiver ran up Amelia's spine as she whipped round to face the twins. "What do you mean by that?"

"He wants you, Mother," they said in unison, both smiling like Cheshire cats.

Amelia stared at them both cackling to each other, amused by their inside joke. "Right, that's enough. I don't want to hear about this *Theo* anymore," she said, trying to keep her voice steady.

Their smiles dropped, and they pushed their bowls away.

"We're finished," they said, getting up from the table. They turned toward the door and before they left, their grins returned, wider this time as they looked at her. "He said don't keep him waiting. He wants his clock cleaned, but only by you. No one else is to touch it."

They skipped out of the room and into the lounge, leaving Amelia staring at the door, open-mouthed. Her heart raced with a mixture of confusion and apprehension as she watched her twins leave the room, their words hanging in the air like an ominous warning. The mention of Theo and his insistence that she clean the clock sent a chill down her spine, stirring a sense of unease deep within her.

CHAPTER 10
Countdown

A few weeks had passed since the claw mark appeared. Steve had sanded it out like he said he would, leaving the counter as good as new. The house was coming together, and the aids and supports for Dotty had been put in place.

Her belongings had been put away neatly in her room, and Amelia had made sure everything was in place and that her mother's room had been set up to her liking. A calendar had been hung up on the kitchen wall showing all Dotty's appointments. She had settled in nicely. There had been no more strange noises or nightmares, and everything was beginning to come together.

The house was a hive of activity. Steve was sitting in the lounge, surrounded by boxes and wires, reading the camera manual quietly, his face set in deep thought. Graham was helping Arthur paint the foyer walls a cream colour while chatting about Graham's life and what he did for a living. Trish was entertaining the kids and Amelia was varnishing the bannisters.

Dotty had carved out a little space in the corner of the lounge to knit quietly. Her face was solemn as she stared at the wall ahead, her hands unconsciously weaving in and out of the wool. Her pale features blended into the white wall behind her, and if it hadn't been for her knitting, Steve would have assumed she was dead.

"You alright, Dotty?" he asked, noticing her staring at the wall.

She didn't bother looking his way; instead, she remained focused on the wall in front, her knitting needles click-clacking away. Steve watched her for a while, she didn't move anything other than her hands, she didn't even blink. Her hand movements became more rapid, and the balls of wool grew smaller with each stroke.

Steve became nervous as he realised her hands were moving a bit too quickly for such an elderly lady.

"Arthur, Amelia! Quick! Dotty's behaving very strangely!"

"What do you mean?" Arthur called from the foyer.

"Just get in here!" Steve shouted, as Dotty's hands sped up, faster and faster.

Arthur and Amelia appeared, followed by Graham, who frowned at Dotty when he saw what Steve meant.

The friction of her knitting had caused blood to seep from her hands. Her blue eyes had grown paler and began to water, as a result of her inability to blink. She was missing the stitch with every stroke of her knitting needles, instead plunging them into her paper-thin skin.

"Mum, Mum!" Amelia screamed, rushing over to her and trying to prevent her from impaling her hand with the knitting needle. She snatched the needles and hurled them across the room. "Mum, can you hear me?"

Dotty remained motionless, silently looking past Amelia towards the far wall. Amelia gently shook her, attempting to bring her out of her trance, but nothing worked. Amelia turned to face the others, who were staring in horror at Dotty as the blood seeped from her hands and dripped slowly onto the floor.

"I think she's having an episode," said Arthur. "Perhaps we should call the doctor." He approached and knelt beside Dotty. When he put his hand on her leg, she flinched, her gaze focusing on Arthur in front of her.

"Yes, dear?" she squeaked as she stared into his eyes.

Amelia grabbed her mother's blood-stained hands and showed them to her. "Mum, you were hurting yourself. Why have you done this?"

"Oh dear." Dotty lowered her gaze to her hands, unconcerned by what she saw. "How did that happen?"

Amelia exchanged puzzled glances with Arthur.

"You don't remember?"

"No, dear. I was just enjoying my knitting ... my knitting ... where is my knitting? What have you done to it?" Her voice became increasingly shrill, until she was screeching in Amelia's face, repeating herself over and over again. "My knitting ... where is my knitting?"

Amelia stood up and slapped her across the face to shut her up. It worked. Dotty fell back into her chair, dazed, staring up at Amelia in shock.

"Why did you slap me? Amelia, you don't slap your own mother. Go to your room now," she cried, and touched her reddened cheek.

"Mum, I think you need to rest. You look tired."

She focused her attention on Arthur. "Would you mind taking Mum upstairs and putting her to bed? There are some plasters in the kitchen cupboard. I'll go and get them."

Arthur nodded and assisted Dotty in getting to her feet. She was trembling and unsteady on her feet, so Arthur positioned himself behind her in case she collapsed. It took him a long time to get Dotty upstairs. She continued to lean back on him, causing him to stumble as well.

Every time she leaned back on him, she would quietly mumble to herself, "what powerful arms you have."

Dotty was starting to irritate him, so he pushed her up the stairs with more force, until she was on the landing. Her ice-blue eyes were full of mischief and it was even harder for Arthur to persuade her into her room.

"I don't want to go to bed. The Taranock will find me there."

He froze when the name came out of her mouth. "Why did you say that?"

"It dwells within this house."

"What do you mean? I don't understand."

"Taranock. Taranock. Taranock," she repeated.

"Dotty, stop with this Taranock nonsense. There is no such thing as the bloody Taranock!" he growled, shoving her gently towards her bedroom.

Dotty's face contorted into an angry scowl. She squinted her eyes and jabbed him in the gut with her finger. "You have no idea what you're talking about. He is real. I've seen him."

"It's all in your head, Dotty. I know this is hard to understand, but you're getting older. You're slowly losing your memories, causing you to become confused," Arthur explained.

Dotty grabbed Arthur's arm and dug her nails in. Arthur could see the veins in her forehead throb as he tried to yank his arm away from her, but she was surprisingly strong. Too strong, in fact. She had a firm grip on him and refused to let go.

She drew him closer, until her nose was inches away from his. "I know exactly what I saw, boy. You will find out soon enough, especially Amelia. It wants her," she hissed.

"Amelia! Get up here and help me. Your mother's gone mad!" Arthur yelled.

Dotty dug her nails even deeper into his arm, amused by his pained expression. Her lips curled into a cruel smile, and her pale blue eyes darkened as she stared into his.

"He'll be back tonight. If you want to keep Amelia, I suggest you keep a close eye on her."

"Why does he want Amelia?" Arthur asked, his gaze drawn to her now obsidian eyes.

"She did something bad. Very bad." She giggled.

Amelia appeared, catching sight of the blood dripping from Arthur's arm.

"What's going on here? Mum, what are you doing to Arthur? Get off him!" She yanked Dotty's hand away from Arthur and pushed her backward. Dotty tripped, falling into a small table with a vase of flowers on it. The vase smashed into her head, knocking her unconscious.

Amelia and Arthur stared in shock, rooted to the spot and unable to move to help her.

"I ... I didn't mean for her to fall," Amelia stuttered. "She was hurting you and I had to do something."

Arthur slowly knelt beside Dotty and felt her wrist for a pulse.

"She's still alive. I think we should get her to the hospital."

Amelia shook as Arthur placed Dotty in the recovery position.

"But, what will they say? They'll think we've been abusing her by the cuts on her hands and the gash on her head."

"Well, what if she has concussion? We can't leave her like this. She's your bloody mother. She could die if she doesn't get help."

"Would that be such a bad thing?" Amelia quietly asked, more to herself than to Arthur.

"What?" Arthur's eyes bulged with rage.

"I'm just saying this could be a good thing. She's been deteriorating rapidly for months and now she's injured your arm. Instead of watching her suffer every day, perhaps it is best if she is put out of her misery."

"I can't believe what I'm hearing." Arthur rose to his feet and took out his phone. "I'm calling an ambulance. I'm not going to carry your mother's death with me for the rest of my life just because you think it's easier to be without her. If we don't call an ambulance and someone sees her in this condition, we will get into trouble."

"She's my mother, not yours." Amelia grabbed Arthur's phone and threw it down the hall before he could dial. "I know what's best for her."

"Then I suggest you take her to her room by yourself, and if anything happens to her, I will tell the truth. It will be your fault, not mine."

He stomped down the stairs, leaving Amelia to clean up the mess.

Graham and Steve were looking at Arthur for answers as he entered the lounge. They had both been deathly quiet, trying to listen to the argument upstairs, but they'd only managed to catch snippets of it.

"What's happening?" they asked in unison.

Trish appeared behind Arthur and grabbed his bleeding arm. "Who did this?"

"Dotty had an episode upstairs and dug her nails into my arm. Don't worry, Amelia's sorting it now."

"Does she need any help? I heard a crash earlier," Trish asked, expressing her concern and looking at Arthur's wounds.

"No. Leave them be. Amelia can handle it. I wanted to call an ambulance for Dotty, but she doesn't want to, so she can deal with it," Arthur said bluntly, trying to ignore everyone's stares.

"Okay, but please let me get some plasters for those cuts. They're still bleeding. What happened to Dotty?" Trish went to get the plasters, while Steve and Graham sat Arthur down.

"She fell and smacked her head," Arthur muttered.

"Maybe we should call an ambulance then," Trish said.

"I've already tried. Amelia doesn't want to. She said that it might be better if her mother died, so then she wouldn't burden us. I can't believe she said that. So, she can deal with the mess she's gotten us into."

"She actually said she wants her mother dead?" Graham asked, shocked.

Arthur nodded. "Yep. She sounded so callous when she said it."

"That is harsh, man," Steve said.

Arthur looked down at the ground, visibly upset. "I don't want to talk about it anymore. Amelia can sort it out if her mother dies."

"On the plus side, I've sorted out the cameras. All I have to do now is place them in each room. They're discreet, so no one will know they're there and you won't notice them. They are basically like 'nanny cams', inserted into ornaments or stuffed toys, that kind of thing. I'll leave Dotty's until last, so we don't bother her." Steve smiled, changing the subject.

"That's probably the best idea. I don't want Dotty to be disturbed. She needs to rest." Arthur looked down at his hands, picking at a small scab on his finger, and still trying to ignore their stares and hoping that no one mentioned Dotty's strange behaviour. "I think it would be best if we started in the kitchen and worked our way backwards. How long do you think it will take?"

"I'd say no more than a few hours. It's simple enough." Steve cleared his throat as he handed the manual to Arthur. "You will also need to download the app, which connects to the cameras and allows you to see what's happening at all times. It also records, but you can delete recordings if there's nothing of interest."

"That's fine. Let's get started." Arthur stood up and stretched his legs.

While the men got to work and Trish played with the twins, Amelia was upstairs in Dotty's room dabbing a wet flannel on the small gash, before rinsing it in a bowl of deep red water on the bedside table. She would have assumed her mother was dead if it hadn't been for her soft breathing. Amelia was trying to gently wash the blood out of her mother's silvery hair with the flannel whilst glaring at her with venomous anger. Bringing her here, to this house, was a mistake. She was too much of a liability. Perhaps she should send her to a nursing home so that someone else could care for her.

Amelia's attention was drawn to the phone on the nightstand, and her fingers twitched, she desperately wanted to grab it and dial the care home's number in the next town over, but considered their financial situation and decided against it. She didn't want to spend any more money on her mother. Despite the fact that her mother had quite a bit stashed away, she didn't want anyone else to touch it; after all, it was her inheritance, so why should she spend it on her mother's care?

Maybe, her mother should die and give everyone a bit of peace and quiet. It would be much better if she would just pass away tonight. If her mother died, it would be as if a huge weight had been lifted from her shoulders. Amelia sank deeper into thought, thinking of ways to hurry Dotty on to the afterlife. Maybe she could suffocate her with a pillow? She's old; no one would bat an eyelid. However, Arthur might, based on their earlier conversation. He'd be the first to point the finger at her. Even though her mother had only just arrived, she was already fed up with having to look after her.

She should leave it for a while, just long enough for Arthur to forget what she had said, and then she could strike. It was in everyone's best interests, including her mother's. After all, she must be in pain, but perhaps due to her frailty, she was unable to express it properly. That had to be it. Her mother was in pain, and she would only be helping her.

"It will soon be over, Mother." Amelia stroked Dotty's hair, giggling at her own wickedness. "You will never have to suffer, ever again."

CHAPTER 11
The Rattling of Chains

It took Arthur a few days to figure out how the cameras worked, but once he did, they recorded every second of their lives. Amelia had been skulking around in a foul mood ever since Arthur had left her to care for her mother. Likewise, he'd avoided her, not wanting to be near her after her disgusting remark about little Dotty. He was beginning to seriously consider who he had married and whether a divorce was on the cards.

Amelia had managed to patch up her mother's head quite well, leaving only a small indent which wasn't noticeable to anyone visiting her. Indeed, Flo hadn't noticed anything amiss when she had come to say her goodbyes before setting off on her travels around South-East Asia. She had been full of excitement about her first stop at a retreat in Thailand, where she would be unable to contact anyone for at least a month. Amelia had cunningly got her mother ready for bed, hiding the marks on her arms and hands with her nightie and bed covers. Flo, with her mind focused on her own plans, hadn't noticed anything strange about her mother.

Arthur wanted to tell a doctor what had happened to Dotty, but Amelia watched him like a hawk, making sure he couldn't phone anyone. Amelia's words had been bouncing around inside his head, as well as Dotty's warning about the Taranock wanting Amelia. And just what did Dotty mean about Amelia's past? Had she done something horrific? She'd never told him much about her past, and nothing about her childhood, but Dotty's words weighed heavily on his mind.

Trish had gone home to run a few business errands, promising to return by the end of the week. Steve and Graham had been avoiding Amelia like the plague since Arthur had told them about her wishing her mother dead. Steve had given him a long lecture about keeping a close eye on her behaviour, and Arthur had to admit that Amelia's behaviour had been even stranger since they'd moved in. He certainly didn't like the spiteful comments she was making.

Amelia had distanced herself from the twins, leaving Arthur in charge of their care. They were scaring her with their bizarre behaviour. Dotty had been on bed rest since her fall, with Arthur poking his head in every now and then to check on her. Amelia stayed away from him as much as she could, but watched him from afar, making a few snide comments or the occasional lopsided sneer. She was up to something, he could feel it, he just wasn't quite sure what.

Arthur started his bed time routine, turning off all the lights downstairs and checking his phone app to make sure the cameras were recording. Although the noises had continued each night, Arthur had been surprised to find that they had captured nothing at all so far. The twins were already fast asleep in their room, and he was the only one left awake. He crept past his bedroom, dodging the now familiar creaks of the floorboards as he made his way straight to Dotty's room. He could have sworn he had closed the door properly, but it had been left ajar. As he crept closer, he could hear whispering coming from inside her room.

Something didn't feel quite right. He poked his head in to see where the whispering was coming from; the air felt dense and heavy.

Dotty was sound asleep and groaning softly. The moonlight streamed in through the window, casting peculiar shadows on the wall. He lingered for a while, watching her sleep. It was just after one in the morning, and he could feel exhaustion overwhelming him. He couldn't see anyone else in the room and was about to leave when something in the corner of the room caught his eye. A shadow appeared with a white object in its hands. As it grew closer, he noticed it was holding a pillow. The shadow moved silently to the other side of the room and faced Dotty's bed with the pillow above her peaceful-looking face.

Arthur moved as soon as the figure slammed the pillow down, covering every inch of Dotty's head. He grabbed the figure by the shoulders and tried to push it back, but it was incredibly strong. The figure still holding the pillow, turned, and the moonlight caught its face. It was Amelia. Arthur gasped in shock as Amelia cackled wildly, her eyes were menacing and black. Dotty's arms flailed in an attempt to remove the pillow from her face so she could breathe.

"What are you doing?" he screamed. He went after her again, this time yanking the pillow from her grasp. He hurled it across the room and shoved Amelia against the wall.

"What the fuck are you doing?" Amelia yelled from behind him.

He whipped round to see her standing in the doorway in her pyjamas with a horrified look on her face. She had turned the light on, and he could see the room properly now. There was no one else with him, apart from Dotty. When he looked down at his hands, he saw that he was holding a pillow over her face. In shock, he let go and backed away into the corner of the room.

"What ... what just happened?" he stammered, staring down at his hands. "You were just in here. I was trying to stop you from ... from suffocating your mother."

Amelia rushed up to Dotty and touched her neck, feeling for a pulse. Her eyes wide with terror and after a brief moment, sadness.

"She's dead. You've killed my mother, Arthur. You've killed my fucking mother!"

There was a ringing in Arthur's ears, which became so loud he couldn't hear what Amelia was saying. His legs began to shake, and he knew he'd pass out if he didn't sit down soon. He slid down into a foetal position on the floor, grabbing the wall for support.

"It wasn't my fault ... it wasn't my fault," he repeated over and over.

"It was you! I saw you!" she shouted in his face. "What are we going to do now, eh? We have a dead body in the house!"

Arthur looked up into her eyes and remembered what he had just seen. He had seen her with black eyes, but here she was, with her pretty blue eyes, yelling at him for murdering her mother. He couldn't blame her, and the horrific situation hadn't fully dawned on him because he was still confused by what he had seen. One minute he had been fighting her to get her away from her mother and the next minute he was suffocating Dotty. He had just murdered an elderly lady who had done absolutely nothing wrong.

The time hadn't changed, it was still just after one in the morning. Arthur was confused. Did any of it really happen? But as he looked at Dotty's lifeless body, he knew it must have happened.

Amelia turned away from Arthur and smiled cruelly as she stared at Dotty's lifeless eyes and wide open mouth.

"We'll leave her here for the night and figure out what to do in the morning."

"But I murdered your mother. You must call the police," Arthur sobbed.

Amelia tilted her head. "No, I'm not going to do that. We're in this together. You're my husband. Come to bed, and we'll figure it all out in the morning." She'd said it so calmly that Arthur felt obliged to follow her into their bedroom.

She whispered softly, "Arthur, you know she was very old. Nobody is going to think she was murdered."

But Arthur knew better. He had told Steve and Graham what she'd said about wanting to get rid of her mother, and now it appeared that she had just done so—except it wasn't her, it was him. Of course, tongues would wag. Maybe he *should* pin it on her, as from the look on her face, she seemed quite smug about what he'd done.

Was this something she had planned? Had she hypnotised him into doing it? After all, she had been climbing the ladder at her psychology job. She was always changing her career, wanting to try new things or learn something different. She could never settle for anything, and her most recent interest was hypnotherapy, which would require years of study and practice. Was he being paranoid?

He lay there with Amelia, who was comforting him and stroking his hair as he sobbed into her chest. She didn't seem bothered by him killing her mother—she seemed to be pleased. Maybe she did have something to do with what happened, but he didn't know what, and he didn't want to ask her, because if it was true, she was even more evil than he had originally thought.

Arthur eventually dozed off, and after tossing and turning all night, he opened his eyes to a cloudy cold morning, with Amelia scowling at him from the bedside. The events of the previous night rushed back to him, and he felt sick to his stomach. He dry-heaved over the bed, hoping to bring something up, but all he got was a painful stomach ache.

"Arthur, get your act together. We need to do something before the boys wake up." She clenched her fists on her hips and stared at him.

He nodded, unable to speak because he was afraid of puking up on her.

"Now get up. We can talk about it over breakfast." She backed away, allowing him to get out of bed.

He couldn't believe Amelia could be so ridiculously calm and content with the situation. She was tottering up and down in a new pair of high heels, admiring herself in the mirror while Dotty lay dead in her room a few feet away.

"How come you're so calm?" he accused.

She smiled as she continued admiring herself in the mirror. "Because it's a lovely day," she said as she smoothed her hair down.

It was at that moment that Arthur was convinced Amelia had something to do with his mother-in-law's death. His gaze was drawn to the stack of books on her nightstand, and he scanned the titles. There were several books on hypnotism and how to use it. Amelia noticed Arthur's hesitation, as well as him suspiciously staring at her books.

"I've almost finished them all. They're fascinating. I'm learning about the human mind and how it can actually be hypnotised into doing something it doesn't want to do. Perhaps you should read it. You might learn something."

"Have you ever tried hypnosis on anyone?" he asked.

Her lips curved into a small smile. "Of course not. That's not something I'd do. I simply enjoy reading about it."

Amelia pursed her lips the way she always did when she was lying. It was all he needed. Now he knew she was responsible for last night's events. She'd forced him to kill Dotty, but how?

His fingers twitched as he stared at the books, desperate to find out how she could have hypnotised him. It takes years to perfect the art of hypnosis, and here Amelia was, using him as her guinea pig to do her dirty work after only reading a few books. Why would she do such a thing ... and to him of all people?

She stood next to the mirror, watching his facial expressions, and trying to read his thoughts.

"So, are you planning on going downstairs? I'll catch you up. I just need to apply some makeup." She pulled out a tube of mascara and pressed the small brush against her eyelashes. Arthur shuddered, and that was his signal to leave Amelia admiring herself in the mirror.

Once outside the bedroom he hesitated as he looked towards Dotty's room. He looked down at his hands, overcome with sadness.

"How could I have done something like this?" he wept to himself. He wanted to go into the room and make sure that he hadn't dreamt it, but the thought of seeing her ghostly face again was too much for him. They would have to act fast with a plan to not get into trouble before someone noticed.

He walked down the stairs slowly, sobbing quietly. He mindlessly stared at the cereals on the counter. He wasn't even hungry. He felt nauseated and the last thing he needed was food. Maybe he should call the police and turn himself in, but that would allow Amelia to get away with it, and he couldn't let that happen, not if it meant the boys would be left in her care. He straightened up and stretched his back. No, he wouldn't let her get away with it. He needed to fight for both himself and his boys. If Graham and Steve started asking questions, he would tell them that Amelia was responsible for Dotty's death.

"You look very serious. What are you thinking?" Amelia asked as she entered the kitchen.

"Nothing much, I was just thinking about when to call the ambulance for Dotty."

He sat down and watched Amelia pour herself a big bowl of cereal. She sat opposite him, ramming spoonful after spoonful into her mouth like a ravenous hyena. She wasn't acting herself at all, and her eyes were wild as she stared at him.

"What?" she asked through a mouthful of chewed food.

"You seem different."

"I'll take that as a compliment." She smiled and shoved another spoonful of cereal into her mouth. "So, plan is, we'll call the ambulance in a minute and tell them we went in there and found her dead. She must have died during the night. She had a weak heart anyway, and she was nearly ninety."

"What if they do a post-mortem on her?"

"They won't. She has a DNAR form on her records. No resuscitation, no need for a post-mortem," she replied happily. "Leave the call to me and just stay in here."

"What if there's evidence of foul play?"

Amelia sighed loudly. "Go and check if there is."

She stood up, left the empty bowl on the table, took out her phone and left the room, closing the door behind her. He heard the lounge door close, so he headed up to Dotty's room. It was still early in the morning, so it seemed reasonable that they had only just discovered her. The hall felt extra long and eerie, as he headed to her bedroom. It seemed to take an eternity to reach her bedroom door. He stood outside, hesitant to enter but knowing he needed to. It had to be realistic.

His hand hesitated over the doorknob before slowly opening it. He poked his head around the door. The bed was empty. There was an indent on the sheet where Dotty had been, but she was nowhere to be seen.

"Amelia!" he screeched. He could hear the terror in his voice as he yelled her name.

She came racing up the stairs, still clasping her phone. "What is it? I'm waiting in a queue."

Arthur couldn't speak. He just pointed into Dotty's room and waited for Amelia's reaction.

She quickly hung up before anyone could answer and yanked the covers off the bed.

"Where is she?!"

"You think this is funny, don't you? Playing cruel tricks on me. Where is she? She's still alive, isn't she?" he growled at her.

"This is not my fault! She's got to be here somewhere," Amelia yelled, pulling out the drawers from cupboards, as if she would find Dotty's body rammed inside one. "I can't believe this. I can't bloody believe this."

"You can stop playing these games now," Arthur shouted. "If she was dead, she wouldn't have gotten up and walked out of the room, would she?"

"Just shut up and help me find her!" Amelia wailed.

The phone ringing stopped them dead in their tracks. She held it up for Arthur to see who was calling. It was the emergency services operator. Amelia's hand began to tremble, and she dropped the phone to the floor. Arthur quickly grabbed it and answered. Amelia heard what he was saying, but none of it made any sense to her as she stood frozen to the spot watching his lips move.

"Yes, yes, that was me. I need to report my mother-in-law missing." Arthur's voice quivered. "Yes, she has dementia and can get very confused at times." He gave the operator a few more details about Dotty before he hung up and dropped the phone on the bed. "They're going to start a search. And, they're going to stop by to get some more details."

Amelia's heart raced as she tried to process what was happening. The room seemed to close in around her, the walls pressing closer with each passing second. She forced herself to take a deep breath, willing her mind to clear.

"Why would you say that? Now the police will get involved!"

"If I hadn't, and someone started asking questions about your mother's whereabouts, then wouldn't that look suspicious?" Arthur said.

Amelia bit her lip, her mind a whirlpool of worry and fear. She knew Arthur was right, but the thought of the police searching for Dotty felt overwhelming.

"I suppose you're right."

Arthur stared at her, his anger boiling over. "I suggest you start being honest with me. Where is your mother?"

"The last time I saw her, you were smothering her with her own fucking pillow!" she spat. "*You* tell *me* where she is!"

Her words were icy enough to make Arthur flinch. They cut through him like a knife, piercing his already shattered heart into tiny pieces.

His last ounce of affection for Amelia vanished at that moment, and was replaced with pure hatred.

"You think this is funny?" Arthur glared at her with his hands on his hips.

"Do you see me laughing?" She returned his hostile glare.

"No, but this doesn't make sense. She can't just up and leave," he said, joining her in the search.

"Perhaps you didn't kill her after all," she replied.

"Why are you disappointed?" Arthur stopped searching and looked at her suspiciously. "Were you behind this? Did you hypnotise me to do it?"

Amelia looked guilt-ridden. Her face said it all. "She should've just stayed dead."

Even though Arthur knew Amelia had something to do with her mother's death, it still hit him like a tonne of bricks when he saw her expression.

"I can't believe you. How could you do that to me?"

"It was pretty damn easy, actually, but we can argue about that later. We need to find my mother. She could be out wandering the streets," she stated matter-of-factly, without a hint of remorse.

Arthur didn't think that he could have an argument with her at that moment. He was far too shocked and disgusted by what she had done, and by how much she had used him. He could guess why; so that if her plan had worked, she would look innocent while he would be charged with murder. Oh, she was cunning, brilliant even. She had planned and executed the perfect murder without getting her own hands dirty.

A smile crept over her face. "So, you've finally figured it out?"

"How did you do it?" He trembled.

"I have complete control over you. I found a word in one of my books that I could use to put you into a hypnotic state. Do you remember when I was practising, and you let me try it out on you before we moved here?" He nodded. "Well, that's when I planted the seed in your mind, ready to use whenever I needed it, and this was the perfect example of what I can do to you if you don't do what I say. If I were you, I would tread very carefully from now on."

Arthur could tell by the look in her eyes that she was telling the truth and that she would go to any lengths to get her way. He needed to get away from her. She was insane and he knew it was only going to get worse for him. She could do anything to him if she wanted—or get him to do anything, and he'd never know. That terrified him greatly.

"Do you realise how sick you are? You're insane!" he yelled in her face.

"As I said," she returned with a grin, her eyes taunting him, "you should tread very carefully from now on."

He was like a puppet to her; do as he was told and he would be rewarded, misbehave and he would be punished. Was it this house that was making her go mad? She certainly wasn't the Amelia he had fallen in love with. She was something twisted and cruel. Even her face was different.

"Daddy? Mummy?" A voice said from behind him.

He turned around to see Charlie standing in the doorway, staring at them.

"Hello, buddy, should we get you changed?"

Arthur jumped at the chance to get away from Amelia. He took Charlie's hand and led him back to his bedroom, where Dylan was also awake and bouncing on his bed. He sat on one of their beds for a while, watching their sweet, innocent faces as they played. They had no idea how evil their mother was, poor little tykes. It was then that he suddenly remembered the cameras, surely they must have recorded everything from last night. Maybe he did have evidence after all.

He pulled out his phone and opened the app. The footage was on there. He had fallen asleep on the couch and Amelia had crept into the lounge and knelt beside him with a taunting smile on her face. She whispered something to him while he slept, and within a moment or two, his body moved on its own, heading up the stairs to Dotty's room. He could see that his eyes remained closed when he entered the room, and that Amelia was following close behind him. He could also see that her lips were still moving, which meant that she was speaking to him, even as he did the unthinkable and covered Dotty's face with a pillow. It wasn't until Dotty's arms stopped flailing, that Amelia flicked the light on and started screaming at him, which was when he awoke. It was all the proof he needed to keep Amelia away from him.

He skipped through the footage in Dotty's room, hoping to see when she went missing. He didn't have to wait long. A strange black figure appeared on the wall beside Dotty's bed a few moments after he and Amelia had left the room. Arthur leaned in for a better look at his phone. He couldn't believe what he was seeing. His stomach flipped, and he fought the urge to vomit.

CHAPTER 12
The Terrifying Truth

Arthur held his hand over his mouth, as if to hide his fear, as he watched Dotty's frail body being dragged from her bed like a ragdoll by something which he could only describe as an extremely tall, skeletally thin, old man with long, lank hair. But he knew it wasn't a man; it couldn't have been. The creature entwined his bony, elongated fingers around Dotty's legs, and dragged her over to the wall from which it had emerged, pulling her back through.

The creature wore a long black, pinstriped cloak, which had a tear right down the middle at the back, revealing its impossibly bony spine, which protruded like knuckles through the fabric—it reminded Arthur of something from a gothic horror. The impossibly tall hat perched on its head appeared to be from an eighteenth-century circus; it almost reached the ceiling, narrowing into a small oval at the top. This creature, whatever it was, had long wiry hair that reached its hips, and a lank fringe that draped across the top of its face, which was deathly pale and webbed with black veins. Arthur caught a glimpse of its mouth, not unlike that of the Cheshire cat, a too-wide grimace taking up the majority of its gaunt face and pushing its pointed cheeks up to its brow. Arthur was most terrified by the eyes, or lack of them—just two deep, hollowed-out craters, which seemed to suck in everything in their path, like black holes.

With a large chain tied around its back, it moved rigidly. He couldn't see what the chain was holding, but he noticed something moving in them as it walked. Dotty hadn't been mad; she had just tried to warn everyone about an evil presence in the house, but no one had believed her. She had called it the Taranock.

Arthur's hands trembled, and he nearly dropped the phone as he watched Dotty disappear through the wall with the creature. He sat for a while, motionlessly staring ahead at nothing, unable to move and trying to process what he had just seen.

Amelia was skulking around, banging doors and moving furniture in the hope of finding her mother, but Arthur knew better. Amelia was never going to find her mother, or rather, her mother's body. Who knows where it went? It could be anywhere, but it wasn't in the house. The Taranock had taken it. Arthur couldn't sit there any longer. He needed to get out and clear his mind.

He moved quickly, changing the boys into their day clothes and grabbing snacks from the kitchen on the way out of the door while dragging them along with him. They went eagerly, they would have been happy to explore their new garden, but Arthur had other ideas. He needed to get to Graham and Steve's. He needed to be with people that would understand his situation, and Graham and Steve were his best option. He headed straight for their house, not bothering to say goodbye to Amelia on the way out. Let her suffer, he thought. She deserved to worry.

Graham saw them from the bedroom window and quickly rushed to let them in. He could tell by the look on Arthur's face that something terrible had happened.

"Oh, my darlings, come in, come in," Graham said as he ushered them inside. "I'll put on a fresh pot of coffee."

Graham had collected several matchbox vintage toy cars over the years, and the twins had a great time playing with them. He didn't mind them playing with them; in fact, he thought it was cute that the boys were making good use of them.

It didn't take long for Steve and Graham to watch the video of the Taranock. Arthur left out the bit with him suffocating Dotty. They didn't need to know about that. The remaining video made it look as though the Taranock had killed Dotty. When they handed Arthur back his phone, their expressions had changed from shock, to fear, and then back to shock.

"I'm at a loss for words." Graham finally said, breaking the uncomfortable silence that was lingering between them.

"It's all so surreal. I can't seem to get that thing's grin out of my head." Steve said shakily, burying his face in his hands, and shaking his head, trying to remove the images from his mind. "You've been living with that thing this whole time?"

"Unfortunately, it seems we have." Arthur nodded weakly. "I don't know what to do. I'm half in shock, and half in complete fear for our lives. I really don't want to go back there."

"You don't have to! You can stay here. We can make the guest rooms up for you to stay in until we figure this out," Graham announced.

"Yes, that's a brilliant idea," Steve agreed. "Will Amelia be joining?"

Arthur looked out of the window, towards his house.

"I don't think she'll want to. She hasn't seen the footage, I just upped and left with the boys. We're not really on speaking terms at the moment."

"Fuck her, then," Graham stated.

"Graham! Behave yourself. We have children present." Steve slapped Graham's knee.

"Well, you know what I mean. If she wants to stay in a house full of demons, then she can. I don't want her here anyway. She's bad news, Arthur, and you know it."

"Oh, I do, trust me," Arthur muttered.

~

That evening, Arthur left the boys at Steve and Graham's place to go and fetch a few things from the house, while Amelia finally watched the footage. To Arthur's surprise, it didn't bother her. Instead, she smiled as she watched the Taranock drag her mother into the wall.

"That's one problem out of the way. She has gone for good."

"How can you be so heartless? She was your mother, and she's been taken by what looks to me like a devil or demon. The problem hasn't gone away either." Arthur kept his voice low in case the Taranock was listening. "I'm going to be staying at Steve and Graham's house with the boys. You are welcome to join us if you wish, but you must behave."

"I'm not going into that ridiculously colourful house," Amelia scoffed. "It irritates my eyes."

"Then you'll have to stay here on your own," Arthur said through gritted teeth. "It's too dangerous for our children to stay here."

Arthur was relieved that Amelia had declined his invitation to join him. He wanted to avoid her as much as possible. He might be able to arrange something with the boys' school and his work hours. That way he wouldn't need to see Amelia unless absolutely necessary.

She went over to the refrigerator and took out a bottle of wine. "I'm not going to let an ugly looking creature with no style push me out of my own house."

Arthur looked at the bottle, knowing that in an hour or so, it would be completely empty and she would be drunk, but as long as he and the boys were safe, he didn't care about her. Deep down, he wished the Taranock would take her, so he could be free of her claws and find a nice woman who would cater to his needs rather than the other way round. He was tired of having to follow her rules and having her spend his money on herself. It was unfair on him and the boys. They deserved a proper mother—a woman who would look after them instead of ignoring them while getting her nails or her hair done for the hundredth time that month.

Arthur couldn't figure out why she needed to go to the salon all the time—her hair rarely changed style—but as he looked at her now, slurping her glass of wine loudly, she appeared unkempt. Her hair was wild and unruly, and she was dressed in a plain white vest top and sweatpants, something she would never normally wear. Her skin was oily, and her usually perfect manicured nails were chipped and far from perfect now.

"Then stay here," he said, walking towards the door. "I'm leaving now, and I don't know when I'll be back."

"Do what you want." She shrugged. "I don't give a shit."

She poured herself another drink and turned away from him. He walked away without saying anything else. He had a week's worth of clothes and toiletries and hoped that would suffice. Graham was delighted to see him, but Steve remained sceptical, peering over Arthur's shoulder making sure Amelia hadn't joined them. He breathed a sigh of relief when he realised she wasn't there.

The guest room had been freshly made up for them, and the air held a hint of bleach. Arthur was grateful for their hospitality.

After dinner, Steve and Graham helped Arthur put the boys to bed before planning what to do with the house.

"I may know someone who could help. She's dealt with things like this in the past," Steve said as he handed Arthur a steaming mug of hot coffee. "She's an old college pal of mine. She's helped other families in similar situations, and she may be able to assist you as well. Should I contact her?"

"Please do." Arthur looked at him hopefully. "I want that thing out of my house as soon as possible."

"I'll be right back," Steve said, leaving Arthur and Graham alone.

Arthur looked out of the window at the dark and foreboding house. There was only one light on, in the lounge, the rest of the house was pitch black. Arthur imagined Amelia lounging on the sofa, while sobbing into a bottle of wine.

Graham noticed the worried look on Arthur's face. "Don't worry, she's probably just moping around the house. I'm sure she's safe."

"I'm not worried about her. She can rot in hell. I've just remembered that Trish is meant to be coming over this evening. She offered to help me with the renovations. I completely forgot, and now it's too late to ring her as she's probably already on her way."

"It'll be OK. She is perfectly welcome to stay as well." Graham offered.

Arthur shifted his gaze from the window to Graham. "But she doesn't know about the Taranock yet. I don't want her getting freaked out and causing a scene."

"Oh, Arthur, you need to tell her. Don't stress yourself out about it. Let me handle it. I'll explain everything to her. Just keep an eye out for her car and we'll bring her here instead."

Steve walked in with a big grin on his face. "It's all done. She'll be here tomorrow to check the place out."

"Oh, thank goodness, and thank you." Arthur relaxed back into the sofa, allowing the cushions to cocoon him.

Outside, a freshly valeted car pulled up in front of Arthur's house. No one had noticed Trish getting out of the car and heading through the gate. They were too busy conjuring up a plan for tomorrow.

The evening air was cool as Trish made her way along the path and up the steps. She wrapped her coat tightly around her. She could feel winter was drawing closer, and the promise of snow was soon to come. Damp leaves lined the steps, sticking to her boots as she headed for the front door. She knocked loudly, hoping that Arthur would answer the door instead of Amelia. Her smile dropped when she saw it was Amelia.

Trish noticed her pink lacy bra peeking through her almost transparent white vest. Amelia began slurring her words, and Trish turned away in embarrassment.

"Oh, it's you," Amelia said.

"Is Arthur around?" Trish asked eagerly.

"Come on in, come on in," Amelia slurred and drew her arm into the foyer.

Her unruly, curly hair cascaded down her shoulders, and her red lipstick was smeared across her pale, white cheeks. Silently, they walked to the lounge. Trish had instantly noticed that Amelia was not her usual self, normal Amelia would never ask Trish to come inside. She always left her on the doorstep, leaving Arthur to greet her.

"You can sit here." She motioned to the brown suede sofa, which was still crinkled from her lounging around drinking wine. "Would you like a glass of wine?"

"Sure." Trish nervously took a seat next to her and nodded.

Amelia grabbed a lipstick-smeared glass and poured it to the brim, handing it to Trish who observed the dirty rim carefully. She politely took a sip before setting it down.

"Where's Arthur?"

"Dunno." Amelia half-heartedly shrugged her shoulders and took another swig from her glass, her head swaying from side to side. "And I don't care."

Trish had only been there five minutes and was already annoyed by Amelia's drunken behaviour, so she quickly got up and left the room, leaving Amelia giggling to herself like a little girl.

"You won't find him here!" Amelia called after her.

Trish was terrified by something in the air—a feeling—something tense and unsettling.

A prickling sensation on the back of her neck sent goosebumps up and down her spine as she quickly checked the rooms upstairs. She stopped abruptly outside Dotty's room. She could hear movement on the other side of the door, a jangling, scratching sound, like metal scraping against metal. The noise jarred her for a moment, it was growing louder with each passing second. She cautiously pushed open the door. The noise stopped, and Trish could see nothing in there that could have been causing it. The room appeared normal, but Trish could sense that there was something off about the atmosphere. She felt that she was suffocating, and she steadied her breath trying to stay calm. The entire room felt oppressive, and she could feel an anxiety attack waiting to happen.

Small beads of sweat dribbled down her brow as her eyes scanned the room, eventually resting on a large human-shaped shadow on the wall, a grey smudge covering the majority of the space beside the bed. When she touched it, something sooty fell onto her fingers. It had the appearance of charcoal but was a different texture.

Trish was so focused on the shadow that she didn't notice Amelia approaching from behind her. She grinned as she watched Trish examine the shadow.

"Oh, that's where the Taranock took my mother through the wall. The stain from her body seems to have become embedded in the plaster. I can't get rid of it." She gulped down the last of her wine and licked the remnants from her lips. "Every time I scrub it off, it comes back."

"Where is Dotty?" Trish anxiously asked.

"I already told you. The Taranock took her. The evidence is right in front of you." She slurred her words again, her gaze darting nervously between Trish and the shadow on the wall.

"Where is my brother?" shouted Trish, grabbing Amelia by the shoulders. "What did you do with him?"

Amelia gave her a sly grin. "He isn't here."

"What's happened to him?" Trish shook Amelia's shoulders violently, causing her head to snap back. "What's happened to the kids?"

Amelia swiped Trish's arms away and retreated into the hallway, away from her grasp. "They're at Graham's house, if you must know."

"Then why didn't you just say that, instead of being a dick about it?"

Amelia's smirk returned as she looked Trish dead in the eye. "Because I like playing with you, that's why."

Trish threw her hands up in frustration and pushed Amelia aside so she could leave. She hurried down the stairs without looking back, yanking open the front door. A gust of cold air blew in, slamming the door against the wall.

"He's coming after you as well," Amelia yelled at her over the bannister.

Trish turned around and wished she hadn't. She could see Amelia's evil, twisted expression staring down at her. She couldn't tell if Amelia's eyes were black or if it was just a trick of the dim light. She grabbed the handle and slammed the door behind her, blocking out Amelia's sadistic smile. She could hear laughter coming from the foyer as she rushed down the steps towards Graham's house across the road. She wanted to get as far away from Amelia as possible. The girl had lost her mind. She completely understood why Arthur was at Graham's house with the kids. She didn't want Amelia anywhere near the twins, and she wanted Arthur to divorce her, even more now. It was bad enough that she and Amelia had never got along, but now her disturbing behaviour was driving everyone out of the house. She seriously needed to get some help. She hoped Arthur would see that this not only had an impact on him, but also on the children. Trish could not allow them to be subjected to their mother's creepy antics. Enough was enough, and Amelia would seek help, even if she had to force her to.

Trish pounded on the door and was met with Arthur's confused expression.

"Trish! How did you know we were here?"

"Amelia told me," Trish said, barging past him. "You really need to get her some help. She's lost her marbles over there—she's completely insane!"

Arthur's eyes widened with fear and surprise as Trish's words slowly sank in.

"I know," he eventually whispered. He averted his gaze, ashamed of what she had become. "What happened? What did she do to you?"

"She refused to tell me where you were, and when I went to look for you, she started rambling on about the Taranock dragging Dotty through the wall." Trish could see there was more to it from the look in Arthur's eyes. "It's not true, is it? This Taranock thing can't be real. Can it?"

Arthur nodded slowly, not wanting to admit it. "I have the footage from one of the cameras, it shows what happened to Dotty."

The door opened and Graham appeared. He smiled when he saw Trish. "There you are, darling! Come in and get warm by the fire." He took Trish's hand and led her into the lounge.

Steve was sitting on the sofa, with a glass of wine, ready for bed in his stripy blue pyjamas, flannel dressing gown, and grandad-style, blue slippers. Graham was still dressed in a pair of slightly wrinkled trousers with a small coffee stain on the leg. He practically pulled Trish to the small, antique armchair next to the roaring fire.

"Coffee or tea?" Graham asked, still beaming.

"Coffee, please."

He scurried off and Trish could hear him tinkering away in the kitchen. She returned her focus to Arthur, who was looking at her with a very worried expression on his face.

"How drunk was she?" he asked.

"Very, she looks a mess. The worst I've ever seen her," Trish replied.

"Trish, I'm at a loss." Arthur paused for a moment, his eyes filled with anguish. "I don't know what I can do. I can't stand being around her any longer, but I'm not sure if it's her, or if it's the house that's driving her insane."

"She's always been like this, just a bit more low key until now. She needs help. I can call my doctor and get her referred to a psychiatrist, if you like?" she asked, a little too eagerly for Arthur's liking.

His expression hardened. "Do you think that's wise? I mean, it might make her worse."

"It's the only choice we have. I'll call them in the morning and see what they say. They might be able to fit her in before the end of the week."

"This doesn't feel right. Perhaps we should wait."

Steve held up his hand, stopping the conversation before it turned into an argument.

"Arthur's right. Let's not be too hasty about this. Let my friend come round tomorrow morning and assess the situation before we jump to any conclusions. She's good with this sort of stuff."

Trish looked at him, confused. "Who's your friend, and what's she got to do with any of this?"

"I rang her earlier. Her name's Sandra. She has the gift of seeing things us normal people can't. She'll know what that thing is and how to get rid of it," Steve explained.

Trish looked sceptical, but after a few moments of thought, she finally agreed. "Okay, but if this doesn't work, then we'll do it my way and get her the help she needs."

Graham appeared with a mug of coffee for Trish. He plopped down next to Steve, almost knocking Steve's glass out of his hand in the process.

"Sorry, darling," he muttered.

They talked about other things for the rest of the evening, trying to divert their attention away from the Taranock and Amelia's strange behaviour.

Steve set up camp in Graham's room, so Trish could have his bed. She felt embarrassed, but nonetheless grateful that Steve had thought of her needs. She didn't want to leave her brother and the kids. She wanted to be there to support him in case things got ugly with Amelia. And she wouldn't want to miss that.

"I'm a gentleman," he teased as he led her into his room.

"I've changed the sheets, and there's an extra toothbrush in the en suite. Help yourself to my toiletries if you need them."

Trish muttered a thank you as she stood awkwardly in the doorway. He grinned a big boyish grin that made Trish's heart skip a beat. For the first time in a very long time, Trish found a man attractive. Since her divorce, she hadn't even looked at another man, trusting only her brother, yet she couldn't help but smile as she watched Steve smoothing down the bed covers. He was kind of cute, a bit short and stocky, but with a kind and loving face.

He caught her looking and grinned. "Like what you see?"

"Sorry," she mumbled. She turned away, her cheeks growing crimson.

"What have you got to be sorry for? I like it," he chuckled, straightening up and heading for the door. "I'll leave you to get settled."

He gave her one last look before leaving the room, humming happily to himself. Maybe he also sensed a connection, or was she overthinking things again? He only gave her a friendly smile. But Steve appealed to her. She liked the way he spoke, and his one cute little dimple that appeared whenever he laughed.

She sat on his bed, slightly ruffling the perfectly smoothed sheets, before clambering beneath them. Trish noticed that they were already warm, it would appear that he had switched on the electric blanket for her. Maybe he did like her, she reasoned, or perhaps he was just being a gentleman.

The house fell silent as Arthur, Trish and the twins settled in for the night, allowing their bodies to relax for the first time in ages.

CHAPTER 13
Fear

Graham woke with a start and glanced out of the window at the house across the street, desperately hoping that it wasn't a scream that had awoken him. He tiptoed over to Steve's makeshift bed and nudged him awake.

"Steve, Steve ... I think I just heard a scream." Steve groaned in his sleep, not wanting to be pried from his perfect dream, which involved making out with Trish. Graham shook him again. "Steve, wake up!"

"What is it?" Steve sat up suddenly, nearly knocking Graham off his feet.

"I think I've just heard a scream coming from Arthur's house," Graham hissed.

Steve kicked his legs out from his sleeping bag and peered out of the window. Graham followed him and they both stared out at the house. There were no lights on, and the house was bathed in complete darkness.

"Maybe we should check it out?"

"Why should we? She's a bitch," Steve replied wearily.

"I know, but what if she's in danger?" Graham insisted.

Steve would have none of it. He shook his head and climbed back into his sleeping bag.

"If you're worried about her, you go look for her. I'm staying here where it's nice and warm."

Graham huffed and stormed out of the room. Even though Amelia was a bitch, he still couldn't let her suffer in that house all alone. He had to make sure.

He stuffed his feet into his slippers, wrapped his dressing gown around him and quietly left, being careful not to wake anyone else. He strode over to Arthur's house, but with every step he took, his mind was urging him to turn back. An image of the Taranock entered his mind, stopping him in his tracks. It was an awful image, and he didn't really want to take another step.

He shivered as he looked up at the dark, sinister house. A pang of guilt washed over him as he remembered the family who had lived there before. If he had known there was something evil in the house, he would have told the family to leave, however insane he might have sounded. He couldn't bear the thought of that thing entangling its fingers around the twins and dragging them away. He retched violently, his puke splattering on the path, forcing him to manoeuvre around it. He was terrified of what he might discover in there, and the images of the family from before weren't helping. He approached the front door and hesitated. What if she was alright and it wasn't her who screamed? Could she accuse him of trespassing?

He couldn't think about it right now. He needed to make sure she was okay. He didn't knock, instead he tried turning the doorknob—it was open—he entered the dark foyer. He took another step inside, allowing his eyes to adjust.

Even though it was freezing outside, the house, now quiet, was warm and musty. He could smell the embers of a burnt out fire lingering in the air, and there was something else, something else that he couldn't quite place. As he crept up the stairs to Amelia's room, his legs began to shake.

Every nerve in his body screamed with primal instinct, urging him to flee, to turn back and escape the impending horror lurking in the depths. But he pressed on, driven by morbid curiosity and a gnawing sense of inevitability. With each creak of the wooden boards beneath his feet, his heart pounded louder, a rhythmic drumbeat of dread echoing through the empty hallway. A slither of light shone out from beneath the gap in the door, spilling out into the hallway, and alerting him to the presence of someone inside. Graham could hear a low sobbing from within the room.

"Are you okay, Amelia?" he called out, hoping she wouldn't be alarmed by his presence. "It's Graham. I heard a scream, so I'm just checking on you."

The sobbing stopped, but there was no response. Graham's heart pounded loudly in his chest, and he wouldn't have been surprised if Amelia could hear it from inside her room.

"Amelia?" he called out again, but this time there was silence.

Something didn't feel right, and he knew he'd have to check on her. He forced his legs to move towards the door and opened it slowly. His breathing became more rapid when he realised that the room was empty. His body demanded that he run from the house as fast as he could and never return, but instead, he pressed on, hoping Amelia wasn't hurt. He looked at the clock on their bedside table and noticed that it was only one o'clock.

He had assumed it was later. Graham's eardrums vibrated as the clock downstairs chimed loudly, and he retreated from the bedroom, pressing his hands over his ears to drown out the noise.

He brushed up against something behind him, turned quickly around to see what it was, and gasped in horror.

"What are you doing here, Son? You were warned not to enter my room!"

Graham looked at his father's stern face staring down at him as if he were still a child.

"I apologise, Father," he spluttered, fearing for his life. It was an old fear; something he hadn't felt in years.

Despite his father having been dead for decades, he hadn't changed one bit since the last time Graham had seen him, back when he was a little boy. His eyes were dark and menacing, and his thin lips formed into a grim line as he reached for Graham's face. He wore the black suit and white tie he had been buried in. It was the most expensive outfit he had owned.

"You know what happens when I catch you doing something you shouldn't!" The man drew a sleek black belt from his trousers and prepared to pounce on Graham.

Graham took a step back from his father, his heart in his throat. "This can't be real. You're dead!"

"Dead, am I? Then this shouldn't hurt a bit," he snarled, and brought the belt down hard against his son's cheek.

Graham stumbled backwards, howling in agony and clutching his swollen cheek.

"Did that hurt, Son?"

Graham moved out of his father's reach and crawled across the hallway to safety before he could do it again.

"Amelia! Amelia, help me!" he screeched as he ducked away from another blow.

"Amelia? You got a girl with you, boy? You know that's not allowed under my roof!" his father shouted, aggressively whipping Graham over and over again.

Graham struggled and was able to grab his father's wrist and throw him backwards into the vase of flowers on the table.

"I'm no longer a little boy! You cannot treat me this way."

All the pent-up anger Graham had been carrying for so many years erupted, and he lunged at his father, but before he could reach him, his father disappeared, leaving Graham terrified and confused. How could he just vanish like that? It didn't make sense.

Graham touched his cheek and winced from the pain. He'd had enough. He didn't want to be there any longer.

—*Screw Amelia. She can sort herself out.*

He staggered down the stairs and was just about to leave when he noticed the lounge light was on. He didn't want to go in, but selflessness got the better of him, and he kicked open the door. Amelia was face down on the floor, holding a glass of spilled wine.

As she slept, she snored peacefully, her nose softly whistling.

"I can't leave you like this," he muttered.

He grabbed her arms and hoisted her over his shoulder. She didn't wake up but grumbled quietly under her breath. He noticed something dark in the corner of his eye that brought him to a halt; a shadow, which grew as it sped across the back wall. Graham's blood ran cold as he realised what it was; the Taranock. He had no wish to see its hideous face again.

He needed to move, but he couldn't, his feet were rooted to the spot. The Taranock, now fully formed, slowly came towards Graham, its arms and legs moving jerkily in time with the ticking grandfather clock behind him, its fingers clicking as it lifted them toward Graham.

Graham's stomach heaved, as through its lanky hair, he saw the black holes where its eyes should have been. Its pasty white skin, speckled with blue and black veins, glowed in the light, and it appeared to be translucent. It was dragging a large chain behind it, which slid out of the wall and landed in a heap on the floor. Graham noticed arms and legs wriggling in the pile of chain. Screams echoed around the room as bodies were revealed, trapped in the links. He immediately recognised Dotty in amongst them, her face filled with torment. Her pale blue eyes were despondent as she looked at Graham, and the chain was tightly coiled around her neck, lacerating the skin. Graham recognised the previous family, their faces tinged purple from the strain of holding the heavy chain, their eyes hollow and empty. The Taranock smiled, revealing its sharp, pointed teeth. Graham gulped, the blood draining from his face, making him dizzy. The Taranock let out a bloodcurdling scream and lunged towards Graham. Graham leapt into action, dashing for the front door, with Amelia flailing around on his shoulder.

He yanked open the door to find Steve standing there, somewhat surprised by Graham's grip on Amelia.

"Run!" Graham yelled.

Steve looked over Graham's shoulder to see the Taranock clenching its teeth and hurling its chain at them. Amelia began to slip from Graham's shoulder as the chain caught her arm. Graham grabbed her legs tighter and yanked her back, jolting her rapidly out of her drunken haze. The Taranock was now up close to Amelia, trying to grasp her arm. She let out a high-pitched scream, oblivious to the fact that Graham and Steve were trying to save her life. She kicked and fought against all of them, trying to break free. And all the while staring into the hollowed-out eyes of the Taranock. Terror stabbed at her heart as she attempted to unravel the chain from her arm.

"Let go of her!" Graham shouted at the Taranock.

"Graham?" Amelia looked up and could see Steve and Graham trying to help her. She allowed them to pull her out of the front door and onto the porch. The chain snapped and disappeared into a cloud of dust, and they all fell into a heap on the floor. The Taranock shrieked with rage and attempted to thrust its long hand toward them, but it was as though there were an invisible barrier preventing it going past the front door.

The three of them sat on the steps, stunned and staring at the Taranock, which was furiously screeching at them, with spittle dribbling down its chin. Graham was the first to move, dragging Amelia further away. The Taranock's hollowed-out eyes stared into Amelia's and she couldn't take her eyes off it. Steve and Graham watched as the Taranock leaned forward and gazed at Amelia's terrified face. Something moved in the bushes beside them, bringing Amelia out of her trance. They didn't wait to see what it was, instead they scrambled to their feet and sprinted down the icy, crumbling steps, leaving the Taranock wailing in the distance. No one looked over their shoulder, and no one stopped until they reached Steve and Graham's front door, where they knew they were safe. Steve ran to the kitchen window and looked out to see if he could see anything, but the Taranock was nowhere in sight, and the front door of 'Le Diable Rouge' was shut.

"What in the name of God happened out there?" Steve whispered, trying not to wake the twins.

Graham threw himself onto the sofa and, like a terrified child, pulled the cushions over him, sinking into the soft fabric.

"I saw something ... something from my past. Then I discovered Amelia passed out on the lounge floor. That's when that thing appeared and tried to grab her."

Amelia rubbed her aching arm, recalling the cold metal chains squeezing her skin.

"I have no idea what happened. I must have dozed off."

Steve rubbed his temples, trying to make sense of it all. Graham was still shaking on the sofa. He approached Graham and placed his hand on his shoulder.

"It's alright, mate. Everyone is safe now."

"But I will never unsee that thing's face," Graham sobbed. "Honestly, I was scared shitless. I've never been more terrified in my life." He stifled a few sobs and continued. "I saw ... my father."

"But, he's dead," Steve said, looking at him, puzzled.

Graham nodded. "I know. I knew it wasn't real, but he beat me with his belt and I felt every inch of it." He touched his cheek.

"Is that where you got that cut from? It looks quite deep; you might need stitches," Steve said, eyeing the red raw cut on his cheek.

"I don't think it needs stitches, but I should probably clean it up. I don't want an infection from some invisible force that just tried to take my life." Graham sighed, his eyes red from crying. "The Taranock must know our fears—it seems able to become them."

"You fear your dad? That's hardly something to be scared about." Amelia muttered, loudly enough for Graham to hear.

"You have no right to say that," snapped Graham, glaring at her. "You know nothing about me."

Amelia's lips curved into a smirk as she poured herself a glass of wine from the table in front of her. "All I'm saying is that if your fear is as simple as that, you shouldn't be helping me and Arthur with the house. The Taranock sniffs out the weakest ones, and now he knows you're one of them. He'll come after you, putting everyone else in danger."

Steve snatched Amelia's glass of wine and slid it away from her grasp. She appeared surprised, but masked it with a scowl.

"Give it back."

"If you're going to act like a bitch, you can go buddy-up with that thing back at your place." Steve lowered his voice and knelt beside her, looking into her eyes. "Graham didn't have to come to your rescue. He could have left you there, but he has a golden heart and did it out of love. You should be a little nicer and stop acting like an entitled cow for a change."

Graham could see Amelia clenching her jaw and digging her nails into the sofa.

"I'll be gone as soon as morning comes."

"Where would you go?" Steve laughed. "You have nowhere to run. We've welcomed Arthur, the kids, and Trish into our home, but you aren't welcome unless you change your tune."

"Trish is here?" she asked, sounding surprised.

Steve nodded. "You spoke to her earlier. She came to yours first before coming here."

"No, I did not." She paused for a moment, her brow furrowed. "If she had been at my house, I would have remembered."

"Yes, she was." Steve rubbed his chin, tired of Amelia's games. "You were so drunk that she left you and came here, after you finally told her where Arthur and the kids were."

"I wasn't that drunk." Amelia pursed her lips and crossed her arms over her chest.

"You were drunk enough not to remember," Steve retorted.

Amelia's eyes glazed over, and she sagged to one side.

"Amelia?" Steve asked, shaking her shoulders in an attempt to bring her out of it. Amelia's body began to vibrate, and her arms and legs twitched uncontrollably.

Graham leapt from his pillow fort to Amelia's aid. "She's having a fit!"

"Oh shit. We need to put her in the recovery position." Steve looked around him and his eyes rested on the coffee table in front of them.

"Graham, move the table out of the way. We'll lie her down there."

Graham grabbed the table, pushed it up against the other sofa, and made room for Amelia. Steve grabbed Amelia's shaking body and placed her onto her side on the floor.

"This doesn't look like a normal fit to me. Look at her eyes."

Graham knelt at Steve's side, and stared at Amelia's eyes, which were now ghostly-white with no pupils, as if she were blind. She twitched and flailed around as Steve and Graham looked on. There was nothing they could do to help her. They just had to wait until she stopped.

"What's happening to her?"

Steve could see the fear in Graham's eyes when he looked at him. "For the first time in my life, I don't have an answer. Perhaps we should get Arthur?"

"Allow the poor man to sleep," said Graham, shaking his head. "He's had enough of Amelia's misbehaviour. We'll just have to wait until she stops."

"But what if she doesn't stop? What happens then?"

"We'll give it a few minutes and then call an ambulance," Graham replied.

Amelia didn't stop. Her body convulsed, and her arms and legs bent in an unnatural way. Graham's hands trembled as he grabbed his phone and called for an ambulance. Steve remained constantly by her side until help arrived. The veins in her face had begun to burst, leaving her skin red and blotchy. The paramedics took one look at her and whisked her away to the hospital.

Both men slumped against the wall as the door closed.

"What do you think will happen now?" asked Graham, his palms sweaty, and his hair stuck to his forehead.

"They'll look after her. She's in good hands," Steve replied, rubbing his eyes in exhaustion.

It was only a few hours before dawn. Arthur and the kids would be up soon, and they'd had hardly any sleep. If they were going to help him with the house, then they needed to rest first. Steve grabbed Graham's arm and pulled him up.

"Come on, we need to get some sleep before they wake up."

Graham didn't argue.

CHAPTER 14
Sandra

Arthur sat there dumbfounded, afraid to even open his mouth as he watched Graham and Steve blabbering on about the events overnight, hardly stopping to breathe. He could tell from the way they were hunched that they were afraid and exhausted. Arthur felt bad for dragging them into the situation, but he had no one else nearby to turn to.

He watched Trish sitting there quietly, taking everything in. He noticed her smile when Graham mentioned Amelia was in hospital. He, too, felt relieved that Amelia couldn't bother him for a while, but he also felt something deep down in his gut, a yearning for her. He didn't really want her to be hurt, and wondered if he should have dragged her to Graham and Steve's, despite her resistance. He felt partly to blame for what happened last night and longed for the simple life he'd had before any of this happened.

"Arthur, please speak to us. We're sorry that we didn't wake you, but we wanted you to have a good night's rest," Graham urged.

"Sorry, I was just lost in my thoughts. It's alright, I'm sure she'll be fine. I'll give the hospital a call in a bit to find out what's going on."

"Good idea. You can use the office across the hall, it'll be quieter in there," Steve said as he motioned to the twins laughing and playing on the floor. The coffee table was full of empty breakfast bowls, and the floor was covered with crushed biscuits. Graham smiled lovingly at them and handed Charlie another biscuit.

"If you ever need a babysitter, I'm all yours."

"Hey, I'm the babysitter around here. Get off my patch," Trish joked.

"We can all chip in," Steve smiled.

Arthur noticed Steve's flirty smile directed at Trish. He also noticed the lustful look in Steve's eyes, and his body language; he wasn't doing a good job of concealing his emotions.

"Of course, we can," said Trish, averting her gaze from Steve, as her cheeks flushed bright red.

It was strange for Arthur to see his sister flirting with someone. He couldn't recall her having a boyfriend in years, not since her divorce. He stood up and straightened his clothing.

"I'll make that call."

He exited the room, clutching his phone, and made his way to the office, closing the door behind him, just in case it was bad news—he didn't want the kids to hear. Graham and Steve strained their necks trying to hear Arthur's conversation with the doctors, but all they heard was mumbling.

"I can't hear what he's saying. Hopefully, it's good news." Graham returned to his spot on the floor next to the kids. He picked up a toy car. "Vroooom"

"I hope so too, for Arthur and the kids' sake," Steve said.

"Only for their sake?" Trish asked.

A small knock at the door cut their conversation short.

"Saved by the knock." Steve chuckled and stood up with a smile.

He opened the door to reveal a spritely, short woman. Her face was long and narrow, with big bright blue eyes and slicked back blonde hair. She wore a thick, orange jumper with faded blue jeans, and trainers that had seen better days. However, she appeared neat in comparison to the man beside her, whose bulbous belly exploded out from below his stained vest top. His bomber jacket made him appear even bigger than he was, and a double chin took up most of his short, stumpy neck. His greasy mop of black hair stuck up in places. His brown eyes were the only thing small about him, contrasting with the swollen lips and a squashed nose. Every time he moved or spoke, his cheeks wobbled, and Steve stared at a pair of massive hands as the man reached out to him, pulling him in for a bone-crushing hug. He wore a ring on his wedding finger that matched Sandra's, yet his looked faded and dirty.

"Steve, my man! It's been a long time!"

"Hi," Steve said, staring at him, trying to remember who he was. The woman reached in for a hug as well.

"We haven't seen you since college! You still look the same." The woman gave him a lopsided smile.

"Welcome to our home, Sandra, and friend," Steve said politely. He wished he hadn't said anything because he could see the hurt look in the man's eyes.

"You don't remember me, do you?" he asked.

Steve wracked his brain, searching through memories of everyone he had met in college, but no one resembled the man standing before him now.

"I'm truly sorry, mate. College was more than ten years ago, and I was drunk for the majority of it."

The man pretended to throw a ball in the hopes of jogging Steve's memory, but Steve continued to stare at him blankly.

"It's me, Dave. I know I look different, but life has been difficult, you know?"

Steve's face was flushed with surprise as he looked the man up and down, unable to believe that the best sportsman from their college, whose popularity had outweighed even the sluttiest cheerleader, was now an overweight scruff. His college memories flooded back to him; those days of nearly drowning in the toilets, courtesy of Dave and his hooligan buddies, had been pushed to the back of his mind, only to resurface now.

Anger, embarrassment, and resentment rushed over him at once, but when he looked at Dave's sad puppy-dog eyes, he felt sorry for him. The man who had once been a college hero, with the world at his fingertips and numerous girls vying for his attention, had married the wackiest girl in college.

Sandra had been a geek, like Steve. She hadn't had any friends at the time, so had taken refuge in the college library, where she read every day, and if anyone came near her, she hissed at them like a snake. She had been a dark, gothic girl who always dressed in ripped clothes, which she had made herself.

Although, these days she had quite a good reputation for herself as a psychic; she even had her own TV show. Why had she gone for such a jerk when she could have had anyone she desired? Even though she looked scruffy, she had this aura and charm surrounding her, which could turn any man weak at the knees.

"Please come in, Dave," Steve said through clenched teeth and a fake smile.

As Dave passed Steve, he patted him on the shoulder, and Steve imagined himself grabbing his hand and breaking it. Graham could tell something was up when Steve followed them into the lounge, still wearing his fake smile.

"This is Sandra and her friend Dave." He emphasised the 'her', giving Graham a 'help me' look before discreetly pointing to his bad shoulder from where Dave had floored him in college to impress his mates. Graham understood immediately, as Steve had spoken about his college days before. He also wasn't too happy that Dave was in their house.

"What a lovely home you have," Dave said, turning around in circles and taking everything in. He looked like a child who had just entered their favourite toy store. "I love it!"

"Make yourself at home," Steve grumbled as he eyed Dave suspiciously, expecting him to tackle him to the floor again. Dave took a seat next to Trish, nearly crushing her. She moved up a few inches, allowing him more room.

"Dave, Sandra, this is Trish. She's Arthur's sister, and she's helping Arthur with the renovations for the house," Graham announced.

"Glad you're here," Trish said, nodding their way and smiling.

"I'm guessing this isn't the house, because I can only feel love and warmth in here," Sandra said as she took a look around. She then spotted the twins and smiled. "You have kids?" she asked Steve and Graham.

Graham blushed, but Steve looked angry.

"No, we're just house mates. The children belong to Arthur and Amelia."

Graham was somewhat taken aback by Steve's aggressive tone, but looked away, hiding his emotions before anyone noticed.

Arthur returned with a blank expression on his face, giving no indication of how the conversation with the doctor had gone.

"Oh, you have guests?" he questioned, looking them up and down.

"This is Sandra. She will be taking a look at your house to see if anything can be done about it," Steve explained, deliberately leaving Dave out.

"I'm Dave, her husband." Dave huffed and held out his hand for Arthur to shake.

"Welcome, welcome," Arthur muttered, his thoughts elsewhere.

Graham could see Arthur was struggling with his emotions and took him back into the office before he burst into tears.

"What happened with the phone call?" Graham asked. He was right, Arthur's eyes moistened as he fought back the tears.

"They can't find anything wrong with her, but she keeps having fits. They are mystified. Plus, she's gone blind, and they have no idea why. She's blind, Graham! How did this happen?" he wailed, grabbing Graham's shirt and howling loudly into it.

"They will find out what's wrong with her. They will do test after test until they find something. She's in safe hands." Graham stroked Arthur's hair, soothingly.

"I bet you it's that bloody house that's done this to her!" he sobbed.

"It's not the house, but what's inside it, which hopefully Sandra can get rid of." Graham gave him a sympathetic look, wiped a falling tear from Arthur's cheek and smiled reassuringly. "Let's get her to check out the house, and later on, we can go and visit Amelia."

Arthur nodded, wondering whether he should go to the hospital, yet something inside him told him to remain with the others.

"Thanks, mate."

Arthur wiped the tears from his eyes and followed Graham back into the lounge. Steve stared at Graham, waiting for an answer, but he simply mouthed 'later'.

"Trish and Dave, can you wait here and keep an eye on the kids while we take Sandra to the house?" Graham asked.

Dave huffed, looking annoyed, but finally agreed. Trish on the other hand was eager to stay with the kids, and looked relieved when Graham asked her.

"I'll stay here too and keep Trish company." Steve winked at Trish. She blushed again, but this time held his gaze, her breath becoming hot as she took in some of Steve's more alluring features.

"That's settled then. Come on Sandra, we'll show you the way," Graham said, leading Sandra and Arthur out of the front door.

It was another chilly morning, with a bitter frost covering the bushes as they walked past. The clouds in the sky looked dark, casting a gloomy shadow over the house. The gate creaked open, and they carefully made their way up the icy steps. Sandra stopped outside before they entered the house.

"I need to know more about this place. What you've seen, how the spirit appears. I need everything."

Graham was the first to speak, telling her everything that had happened there, and showing her the footage of the Taranock on Arthur's phone.

Arthur kept quiet, relieved that Graham had taken the lead. Sandra stood silently watching the footage, taking in every detail of the Taranock. Her eyes filled with fear, and as she returned the phone to Arthur, her hands began to shake uncontrollably.

"I've never seen anything like it before," she said, finally.

"This is what we've been up against. It took the family who lived here before Arthur and Amelia moved in," Graham explained.

"This may be beyond my area of expertise, but I'll give it a shot," she stated. "First, I'll take a look around to get a sense of the place. After that, I'll decide what to do, and what I might need to get to banish this thing."

Arthur nodded. "Thank you for helping us. I really appreciate it."

"This is my job," Sandra said, taking his hand and squeezing it gently. "I help families that come face-to-face with evil spirits."

She pushed open the front door and took a step inside, inhaling sharply when she noticed a large claw mark etched into the wall to the left of her. She stroked it with her finger, inspecting the deep grooves, before pulling something out and holding it up to the light. It was a long black and grey fingernail. Her heart pounded as she held it up for Arthur and Graham to see.

"This is no spirit ... this ... this is ... well ... this is something entirely different." She could already feel the Taranock lurking in the shadows, but she couldn't pinpoint where it was. The hairs on the back of her neck bristled as she moved around the house, sensing its eyes upon her.

She stood outside Dotty's room and pressed her hand against the door, feeling a strange pulse vibrating through the wood.

"Whose room is this?"

Arthur paused, wondering whether he should tell her the entire story, but then decided against it. He didn't want anyone to look at him as if he were a murderer.

"It was Dotty's room, Amelia's mother. She passed away in this room recently." He opened the door and stepped inside, trying not to panic. Sandra was immediately drawn to the large black smudge on the wall. She went straight for it, raising her eyebrows at Arthur in anticipation of an explanation.

"Um ... yeah, that appeared the day after Dotty died," he said.

She closed her eyes and pressed her palm against it. Her breathing changed abruptly, and her head jerked to the side, as if she were being possessed. Arthur approached her, but Graham grabbed his wrist and tugged him back.

"She's trying to find Dotty," he whispered.

Sandra's face screwed up in concentration. Graham and Arthur watched, somewhat in awe of her, despite their apprehension. Sweat began to form on her brow, and her jaw clenched tightly as though she were in pain. She finally opened her eyes and returned her attention back to the two men.

"I've found her. She didn't die of natural causes, she was murdered. By what though, I don't know, but she's trapped here."

Arthur's heart lurched forwards. Would she figure out that he had something to do with Dotty's murder? She was staring at him pretty intensely, but her face showed no emotion. He breathed a sigh of relief as she smiled at him. He had to tread carefully so that he didn't make a mistake and let his secret out.

Bringing Sandra here might have been a mistake. She could learn what he had done, but then what? It wasn't his fault, after all. Amelia was the mastermind behind the murder, and he was merely a pawn. He wouldn't fare well in jail. He didn't appear scary or have any tattoos.

His thoughts drifted off to prison, and images of him becoming someone's bitch flooded in.

The police had already visited them, bombarding him and Amelia with countless questions about Dotty's disappearance before conducting a thorough search. Posters were plastered around town, pleading for any information on her whereabouts, but no leads emerged.

In the end, the police concluded that Dotty had likely wandered onto the moors, where she may have met with some unfortunate accident.

But Arthur still worried that Dotty's body might turn up unexpectedly. He felt awful about what had happened and couldn't shake the feeling that it was his fault, even though it was Amelia who had masterminded the plan to get rid of her, using him as her pawn.

Every creak of the floorboards and every unexpected knock at the door sent Arthur's heart racing.

The guilt gnawed at him day and night, his conscience a relentless tormentor. He often found himself staring at Dotty's old photos, memories of her flooding back, only intensifying his remorse.

Amelia, on the other hand, remained cold and unrepentant.

"We did what we had to do," she had said, her voice devoid of emotion. "My mother was becoming a danger to herself. It was the only way."

He despised her for it, and he lived in constant fear that the police would uncover evidence and come to arrest him.

—No, no, no, I can't think about that right now. It won't happen. There's no evidence of a body, only a strange black smudge on the wall.

"Earth to Arthur. Are you listening?" Sandra's voice interrupted his thoughts, bringing him back to the present.

"Sorry," he muttered. "It's just really hard for me to be back in this house."

She rubbed his arm reassuringly. "Do you need to step outside?"

He shook his head. "Let's just get this over with."

"Of course. Show me your room."

Arthur led the way to his room and waited outside. Sandra took a quick tour of the remaining rooms, her eyes scanning each and every detail, before resting on a nervous-looking Arthur in the hallway.

"There isn't much energy in here, nor is there much in the kids' room, but Dotty's room and the downstairs lounge has *a lot* of negative energy."

"But, you haven't been in the lounge yet." Arthur said, confused.

She smiled and there was a twinkle in her eye. "I don't have to go into a room if the energy is strong. I can feel it from here. It's suffocating."

"Do you know where the Taranock is coming from?" Graham asked eagerly.

"It's blocking me from seeing that part. I know it's here, but I cannot seem to find the source of its resting place." She noticed Arthur's concerned expression. "Don't worry; I can still cleanse the area to remove it. It might take a few tries, but I'm confident I'm strong enough." She looked around nervously, wanting to ask something but unsure if the time was right.

"What is it?" Arthur asked.

"Err ... well, it's just that I was wondering if I could bring my film crew here, and we can film the process for my TV show?" Her eyes were pleading.

Arthur must have looked surprised and concerned, because Sandra began rambling on about the show and how it would help her gain more viewers, as this was something entirely new to her.

"I don't think that's a wise idea. It's too dangerous to have so many people in the house at once," Arthur said.

"I'll cut you in on the deal, if you'd like. It will help you with the money side of things." Then, she whispered in Arthur's ear how much she was willing to pay him. His eyes widened with surprise.

"I like the sound of that, but I think it's too risky," Arthur stated hesitantly.

She appeared dissatisfied at first, but then changed her tune. "What if I only have one camera person?"

Arthur could tell she wasn't going to drop the subject, so he sought advice from Graham.

"What are your thoughts, mate?"

Graham looked unsure. "If there is only one cameraman, I don't think it would be a problem, but if this does happen, it's probably best if you sign a contract with Sandra that states that you will not be held liable if anything goes wrong. Agreed?"

Sandra nodded; her face lit up with a smile. "That's perfectly feasible. I'll call my studio. But before I do anything else, I'd like to check out the lounge."

She motioned for them to follow her downstairs and into the lounge, where she was struck by an invisible force of energy. It caught her off guard, and she collapsed to the floor, fighting it. Graham and Arthur rushed to her aid, shouting something at her, but all she could hear was the rattling of chains, and a loud ticking clock.

She felt sick to her stomach, and her head was spinning. Her heart started to race as she lay, frozen to the spot. She couldn't move, she began to hyperventilate, unable to concentrate on anything other than her fear.

"Wait a minute." She struggled to find the words, unable to hear their voices. Eventually she took a few quick breaths and got up, Graham supported her as she looked around the lounge. "It's really strong in here."

"What can you feel?" Arthur asked.

Her mind whirled, and the voices of people moaning for help entered her head and clouded her perception.

"I can hear them screaming for help. It's here; I can feel its energy." She gazed around the room, and settled on the grandfather clock in the corner. "Who does that belong to?" she asked, pointing to it, her hand trembling with fear.

"It came with the house; apparently it's been here since the house was built." Arthur explained.

She moved towards it, her legs struggling to keep her upright. The polished surface of the clock shone brightly in the sunlight, and Sandra could hear ringing in her ears, which coincided with the rhythmic ticking as she pressed her palm against it. The vibration was so powerful that it sent an electric shock shooting up her arm and knocking her off balance again. She crumpled to the ground, taking deep breaths as she tried to process everything. Images of the Taranock flooded her mind, its menacing presence sucking the life force from her. She could see it all clearly in her mind, the grandfather clock was the portal to its resting place. She could see the souls of those the Taranock had taken, trapped forever in its chains, in a dark, menacing place full of evil and despair, and little Dotty's face full of fear and sadness.

"Get it out of my head! Get it out of my head!" she screamed.

Arthur and Graham dragged her rigid body out the front door and sat her on the porch. She appeared stunned by what she had just witnessed; this was unlike anything she had ever seen before. She'd dealt with evil spirits, spirits who either couldn't or hadn't moved on but none of it compared to this. She could still feel the evil wrapping itself around her like a thick blanket, suffocating her, and she took a few deep breaths trying to relax.

"Can you tell me what you saw?" Graham knelt beside her, rubbing her arm, trying to warm her icy body. "What did the Taranock do to you?"

"I discovered its lair," she said, still quaking with fear. She curled into the warmth of his body, trying to rid her mind of the images.

"The Taranock lives inside the clock, which is a portal."

"So, we get rid of the clock?" Arthur asked.

She shook her head. "It's not as easy as that. If we just get rid of the clock, the Taranock will find somewhere else to hide. It's made this house its home, and it will put up a fight. We need to thoroughly cleanse this place."

She tried to stand, but her legs were still very weak and even with Graham's assistance, she couldn't quite manage it.

"Grab her legs," Graham said, while seizing Sandra's arms. "We need to take her back to the house."

Arthur followed orders and grabbed Sandra's legs. Her body felt limp as they carefully carried her down the steps and rushed to Graham's front door, where Steve greeted them with a concerned expression.

"What happened?"

"It's far more powerful than I expected," Sandra said, as they laid her down on an empty sofa.

"What happened, darling?" Dave rushed to her aid and sat next to her, almost crushing her legs. He stroked Sandra's sweat-soaked hair and whispered sweet words in her ear.

"She needs rest," Graham stated, turning to Steve and adding. "Make us a cup of coffee and we'll explain everything."

CHAPTER 15
The Ridding of the Taranock

The house was bustling, with the TV crew running up and down the stairs positioning equipment and leaving wire trails covering nearly every surface of the floor.

Amelia was still in hospital, undergoing test after test. There had been no change in her condition and the doctors didn't seem to know what was causing it or what they could do. She had been there a week and Arthur had no idea when she would be allowed home.

A man emerged from the lounge, barking orders at the TV crew, dragging Arthur's attention away from his thoughts. The man's light brown skin was silky-smooth, and he had sleek, shiny, jet-black hair that would make any girl jealous. He was wearing a tight-fitting, crisp, business suit, with a headset, into which he growled his orders. He had a silver badge on his shirt that said 'Director: Ardy'.

Arthur thought he looked stern, yet there was a kindness in Ardy's eyes when he looked at Sandra. Arthur watched how his face lit up whenever she entered the room; he was fascinated by how Ardy changed his posture to face her whenever she spoke. He could tell straight away that Ardy had feelings for Sandra, and he wondered if Dave had noticed it too. Dave didn't seem very interested in his wife's work and spent most of the time sitting in the corner, playing video games on a small console he kept in his pocket.

"Right, I'd like a static camera in the room's left corner and another in the foyer," Ardy yelled, for what seemed like the hundredth time that morning. "I want to get as much footage of the beast as I can!"

Sandra had requested that Arthur be interviewed by one of the crew members, but he had refused to participate. He didn't mind sitting in the shadows and watching them, but that was the extent of his involvement. He had a lump in his throat that wouldn't budge. It had been there ever since the crew arrived with their filming equipment.

He felt restless; his heart was racing, his palms were sweating, and he'd already had to change his shirt several times. There were too many people in the house, he thought, it would be easy for the Taranock to choose its next victim. Some members of the crew were already reporting mysterious scratches appearing on themselves.

Of course, everyone, including himself, had to sign a waiver; Ardy had no wish to deal with a lawsuit. He was playing a very dangerous game, and Arthur wasn't sure that this was a game anyone could win.

He looked across the room at the crew, as they weaved their way around his home. He spotted Graham in the corner of the lounge; he also looked nervous, biting his nails and staring at the cameramen. Arthur pushed his way through the group, almost tripping on one of the wires, before reaching Graham's side.

"I have a horrible feeling about this," Arthur said.

"We probably shouldn't have agreed to the TV crew being here," Graham agreed, and looked as if he was about to cry. "It's too dangerous. There's a horrible dense atmosphere in the air, can you feel it too?"

"I thought it was just me, but if you can feel it too, then maybe we should call this off, and find another way to get rid of the Taranock?"

"No, trust me on this. This will work. We just have to be patient." Sandra said, appearing beside Arthur. She looked stressed. "I need this. If anything goes wrong, then we will have video footage, as evidence for the police."

Arthur gave her a sideways glance. "I suppose you're right."

"I always am," she stated with a smile. Ardy gave her the thumbs up. She nodded at him before turning back to Arthur. "We're ready to roll. If you don't want to be in camera shot, then have a seat in the kitchen, or stand against the wall in the foyer."

Arthur didn't need to be told twice, he left the lounge and took his position against the foyer wall so he could still see what was going on from a distance. Graham followed him, dragging his feet.

Ardy took his place behind the cameraman, pointing at Sandra.

"Positions ready! Cameras rolling in five ... four ... three ... two ... and action!"

Sandra plastered on a fake smile and turned to face the camera.

"Good day, and welcome to another episode of Spirits Beyond the Grave. Today's episode is extra special because I'm standing in a house that is currently haunted by a terrible demon. I've never encountered a demon before, so it's quite exciting to be able to show you something that has never been filmed on live television!"

She stepped back and stood next to the grandfather clock, which was ticking loudly.

"Many spirits cling to household objects, haunting the owner of the object. This clock has been here since the house was built, but no one, until now, knew it was a portal to the demon's realm. Let me show you what I mean."

She took out a small glass bottle with a cross engraved on it, opened it and splashed some of the contents on the clock. There was a loud hissing, and a small trail of steam rose from the clock face.

Arthur watched transfixed as Sandra smiled and held up the bottle to the camera.

"This is holy water, and as you can see, the clock is not fond of it." She returned the bottle to her pocket. "There is only one reason the clock disliked it, and that is because there is something evil lurking inside. After the break, I'll attempt to entice the demon from its lair and show you what the owners of this house have had to cope with. I assure you, it's not pretty."

"And cut!" Ardy yelled, triumphantly clapping his hands. "As usual, Sandra, you were brilliant."

"Thanks." Sandra smiled and bowed.

Despite her polished performance and bravado, Arthur noticed that Sandra appeared to be in pain. She hid it well behind a fake smile, but every now and again, he could see a pained look.

Arthur went into the lounge and pulled her to the side, "Something is wrong. I can tell," he said in hushed tones.

"I'm alright," she replied, wiping the sweat from her brow and shaking her head. "The Taranock has a strong presence, and it's very hard to concentrate when all I can hear in my head is screaming."

"I understand, but if this is too much for you, then I want you to call the whole thing off. I can't have another attack in this house," he warned.

"Everything will be fine," she reassured.

The door to the clock creaked and slowly swung open, the room fell silent, and everyone stopped what they were doing. A blood-curdling scream echoed around the room accompanied by a strong gust of wind.

Ardy stared at the clock in disbelief, "Roll camera," he said into his headset. "This needs to be recorded."

Inside the clock, a series of scraping noises—metal clashing against metal—could be heard, becoming louder the closer it came. Sandra's blood ran cold. She clutched Arthur's hand, terrified and shaking, but Arthur remained calm, patiently waiting for the Taranock to appear so he could put an end to this horrific intimidation.

"Can you tell us what's going on, Sandra?" Ardy demanded, gesturing toward the clock.

Dave approached Sandra, his face ashen with fear. "Please, Babe, let's just go. This is far too risky."

Ardy shot him a look. "Dave, get off set!"

"I'm protecting my wife." Dave's cheeks flushed, but he kept his cool.

The strange noises from the clock persisted, and there was chaos, as everyone panicked and ran out of the room, except Ardy, Arthur, Sandra, and Dave, the latter pulling Sandra by the arm towards the door. The cameraman also raced for the door, leaving the camera unattended but still filming.

"You're fired," Ardy muttered beneath his breath.

The cameraman wasn't hanging around. He didn't care what Ardy thought as he opened the front door, and ran down the steps, not noticing the cold wind or the ice covered steps. Graham heard the inevitable fall and shuddered at the sound of the cameraman's skull smacking against the concrete.

Everyone fell silent. No one went to the cameraman's aid. They were too scared of what they might find. Ardy shrugged and waved his hand at Sandra to carry on, assuming that this had been staged by her and the cameraman to attract more viewers. He was oblivious to the petrified faces surrounding him. His only concern was money.

The sounds continued to echo from the clock, and a pair of skeletal, white hands, with elongated fingers, appeared from the inside, and wrapped themselves around the sides of the doorframe as an entity slowly hoisted itself out.

Ardy grabbed the abandoned camera and whipped it around to capture the Taranock's face, which was mostly obscured by its lanky hair.

"This is incredible. This will be broadcast on every news channel!"

Sandra couldn't believe it. Ardy was usually so sceptical of anything paranormal, it was why he did this, hoping to be proved wrong. When a gust of wind blew in, revealing the Taranock's face with its hollowed-out eyes, Ardy's expression changed from excitement to terror. He stepped back from the camera, ran out into the foyer, and fixed his gaze on the Taranock from a safer distance.

"This cannot be real."

The front door smashed against the wall as most of those who had remained in the foyer ran outside. Someone picked up the cameraman, who was lying at the bottom of the steps in a heap. The lounge doorway was now filled with the enormous frame of the Taranock, and there was nowhere that Arthur, Sandra or Dave could escape to. Ardy and Graham stood in the foyer shouting hollow words of encouragement to them, urging them to get out.

The lights flickered in time with the ticking clock as the Taranock arched its spine, its vertebrae clicking into place, before turning its head towards Dave, who was currently cowering behind Sandra.

The Taranock opened its mouth to speak. "Daaaavvviiid," it screamed. Its voice was high and piercing, penetrating everyone's eardrums.

Dave hid behind his wife and attempted to make himself as small as possible, all the while sobbing uncontrollably. Sandra appeared to be confused and she shifted her gaze from Dave to the Taranock, and back to Dave.

Arthur watched the Taranock carefully as it approached them.

"I don't think that it will go for us. It seems to want Dave."

"But, why does it want me?" Dave wailed as he pressed himself up against the wall. "Someone do something!"

"Arthur, what do we do?" Ardy called from the foyer.

Arthur tried to think, but all he could hear was Dave wailing. He sounded like a spoilt child wanting sweets, having a full-blown tantrum in front of everyone, shouting incoherent words at the Taranock. It reached its thin, spider-like fingers towards Dave, snarling and dribbling.

"Sandra, start blessing the place quickly. We need to distract it," Arthur said. He reached for the lamp beside him and held it above his head for protection. "Dave, come here—get behind me."

Dave was crouched on the floor with his hands over his head and face. He scuttled over and hid behind Arthur's legs, clutching them so tightly that Arthur struggled to remain upright himself.

The Taranock changed course and moved towards Dave, ignoring the lamp in Arthur's hands. Sandra moved in front of Arthur, the expression on her face was one of determination. She pulled out her bottle of holy water.

"Get back!" she hissed, clutching it like a grenade.

The Taranock hesitated, before, revealing its razor-sharp needle-like teeth.

"Daaavvid." Another screech escaped its lips, and it lunged towards Sandra. She side-stepped around the room, trying to distract the Taranock, so Arthur could get Dave out of there. Her light footsteps startled the Taranock, who watched her for a moment.

"You know what to do, Arthur. Get moving!" Sandra shouted as she splashed the Taranock in the face with her holy water. It let out a loud high-pitched scream, forcing everyone to cover their ears. Chains slithered like snakes across the floor towards Dave, who squealed in pain as one of them wrapped itself tightly around his leg, cutting into his flesh.

"Get it off me!"

"Graham, Ardy, do something!" Arthur growled.

They both looked at each other, trying to think how they could help the others.

Ardy entered the lounge without mentioning his plan to Graham. He felt sick and his stomach churned as he grasped one of the chains that were bound around little Dotty's flailing body. He pulled it towards him, hoping to distract the Taranock, but instead he angered it. The Taranock grabbed Ardy by the neck and lifted him into the air with one swift movement. Ardy tried to fight back, scratching at its pale wrist, but he was no match for the Taranock. It sneered at him before slamming him into the wall, where he crumpled into a heap next to Dave.

"Sandra, you need to banish it! Why are you waiting? It's going to get Dave." Graham shouted.

"There's a bowl of sage in the kitchen. Go and get it!" Sandra yelled over the Taranock's screams.

Despite the chaos, Sandra's hesitation in helping Dave became more obvious. Arthur found it odd that she had waited until now to begin the process of banishing the Taranock.

—*Surely she didn't want it to snatch Dave, did she?*

While Arthur was watching Sandra, Graham had returned with the bowl of sage. Sandra once again, pushed the Taranock back, but Graham could see she was getting tired.

"Now, light the end of the sage stick and blow it out once it's alight," Sandra said. Graham did as he was instructed. It took several attempts before the sage caught fire, but eventually smoke began to erupt from the sage stick. "Now, waft it around the room while praying."

"I don't know any prayers." Graham was terrified.

"Then create one," she snapped.

Graham began to whisper an old Latin prayer he vaguely remembered from school assemblies, he hoped that would suffice. The Taranock's neck clicked as he turned to face Graham. It looked afraid and let out a high-pitched wail. The words Graham was speaking seemed to be hurting it in some way. It writhed in agony as Sandra continued to splash holy water on its face.

"Go back to where you came from, and don't return," Sandra spat, hesitating a little.

She took a step towards the Taranock, causing it retreat back into the clock. Sandra pushed it further into the clock, and it screamed and wailed, causing the ears of those nearby to bleed. She slammed the clock's door shut, spraying it with more holy water and praying quietly to seal the clock. From her pocket she drew a long set of rosary beads, which had an ornate gold cross at one end. She tied them around the clock and motioned to Graham to pass her the sage.

He handed it over and stepped back. She walked around the room, wafting smoke into every corner to purify it and remove any negative energy.

Her whispering became louder and more intense as she grew nearer to the clock. The clock itself, she smothered with sage. Her hands were trembling almost uncontrollably but she remained resolute. She was more than a little embarrassed by Dave's infantile behaviour, quivering with fear in front of everyone. Her plan had failed. Maybe she had been too quick to banish the Taranock. It should have taken Dave—that's what she had intended—but now that the Taranock has been banished empty-handed, would it come after her instead to replace her husband?

She knew it was dangerous to make a pact with a demon, but she was desperate to get rid of Dave. She should never have married him in the first place. He was a misogynist—a nobody with a shattered reputation.

She'd made a name for herself, and she was making a lot of money, for what? So he could sit on his fat arse all day drinking beer, paying for it with her money. She'd been miserable for far too long.

For years she had spent the majority of her time on the road, filming for her TV show. That was, until he decided to tag along with her. He was constantly demanding her attention; he was like a child, and she had never wanted children, and certainly didn't want to be married to one.

Making a pact with the Taranock had been an act of desperation. Dave would take half of her hard-earned money if she divorced him and she couldn't kill him, she wasn't like that, but if enough people witnessed him being taken by a demon— well, then she would be in the clear. She needed to come up with another plan, one that would permanently get rid of him.

She took a deep breath and turned to the others, wearing her best fake presenter expression.

"I've kept it in there for now, but I'll need to stay here tonight to make sure it doesn't come back."

"Sandra, I don't think I can stay here. I think I should see a doctor. My head is spinning." Ardy sighed, rubbing the back of his neck.

Sandra noticed Arthur eyeing her suspiciously.

"No one needs to stay. I can do this alone. All you need to do is set up the cameras, so there's footage." She looked at Dave with pleading eyes, hoping that he would also stay, but he avoided her gaze and stared at the ground.

"Dave, will you stay? Just so I have *someone* with me."

He finally looked up. "Sandra, I'm not sure about that. I'm way out of my depth. I never want to see that thing again."

"Well, you won't have to ... see it I mean." She forced another smile. "You are welcome to remain in the other room, but I really need you to be here, just in case I need help."

Dave looked around at everyone else, hoping that someone else would step in, but judging by the expressions on their faces, they too, wanted to get as far away as possible. He didn't hold it against them. How could he? After all, the thought of facing that thing again sent shivers down his spine, but if he said no, he knew they'd all label him a coward.

"OK, fine, I'll stay, but only because it's you."

His voice was trembling, and he instantly regretted his decision. His gut was telling him that something was very wrong and that he needed to get out of there as soon as possible. He took a deep breath and pushed it to the back of his mind, for now, as he would do nearly anything to see that twinkle in Sandra's eyes.

"Thanks," she purred.

Graham helped Ardy back to his feet. "I'll take Ardy to the hospital while the rest of you clean up. One of you should check in with the rest of the film crew to make sure they're all right."

"I'll take care of it," Sandra said before turning to look at Arthur. "Go back to Graham's for one more night. By the morning you will have a lovely home, free from monsters and demons. I promise."

There was something in Arthur's eyes that Sandra didn't like. He had been staring at her for a while, and it was starting to make her feel uncomfortable. Had he guessed her plan? Had she slipped up somewhere? She felt as though he could read her mind, by the way his eyes focused on hers. She had to be cautious, she couldn't have anyone suspecting her. She had worked so hard for what she had achieved, and nothing was going to get in her way. She'd throw him to the Taranock too, if she had to.

"All right, I'll do it," he eventually replied and sighed as he looked around the room. It was carnage. "First, I'll help clean up, and then I'll leave."

Sandra knew she couldn't refuse him, and risk rousing suspicion so she nodded and began returning the furniture to its proper place, still carefully planning her next move.

CHAPTER 16
Double-Crossed

By the time everyone had cleaned up, it was dark. Arthur had given Sandra one last look before leaving for Graham's. She was already a nervous wreck and Arthur's look just made it worse. Graham had whisked Ardy off to the hospital, and Sandra had sent Dave home to get her another set of clothes. This, she hoped, would give her time to figure out how best to get rid of her husband, and ideally the Taranock, once he had taken Dave. After careful meditation and using her psychic skills to communicate with the Taranock, she was able to form an alliance with it.

As she meticulously rearranged the furniture, her mind raced with thoughts of the impending arrival of her husband. The events of the evening had left her shaken, but she was determined to finish this once and for all.

With a sense of urgency, she made her way to the foyer, where the static camera stood as a silent witness to the unsettling occurrences. Quickly, she reached out and turned it off, ensuring that no further evidence of the night's events would be recorded. Placing it back in its original position, she took care to make it appear as though it was still operational, a subtle deception to maintain the façade of normality.

Turning her attention back to the clock, she carefully removed the rosary beads, handling them with reverence as she wiped away the traces of holy water. With a shaky hand, she cleaned the surface of the clock, erasing any lingering signs of the supernatural encounter.

She hummed to herself nervously, hiding in the shadows of the lounge waiting for Dave to return. She could sense the Taranock's hunger. It craved another soul, and Dave was ideal. However, it wasn't aware that once it had Dave firmly in its clutches, she planned to banish it for good. She desperately needed her plan to work, otherwise her life would be like this forever. She would be constantly burdened with this child of a husband.

"It's show time," she muttered to herself, as she pressed the record button on the camera.

Dave walked in, nervously peering into the lounge, searching in the darkness for her.

"Sandra?"

"In here," she called to him.

He followed the sound of her voice, trying to adjust his eyesight to the darkness. His feet felt heavy, and he had to force them to move. He didn't like this; he didn't like it one bit. He caught the scent of a strange musky odour emanating from a corner of the lounge.

"Are you in here?"

"Yes, I'm just getting prepped. Come in." She tried to keep her voice steady, but she was also afraid.

"Why is this place so dark? Can I switch on a light?" he asked, fumbling on the wall for a switch.

"Go ahead. The switch is in the left-hand corner, nearest to you."

Dave moved forward, the musty odour intensifying with each step, and he could hear the faint sound of breathing. His hand brushed against something coarse, making him flinch and snatch his hand back. Eventually he found the light switch and turned it on. The light instantly blinded him, forcing him to close his eyes for a few seconds.

A low snarl forced him to open them again; he was face-to-face with the Taranock, whose hollowed-out eyes were staring back at him. In an instant, it grabbed Dave's throat and lifted him into the air.

Sandra was too stunned to do anything, and remained rooted to the spot, as Dave yelled for help. Her eyes followed the Taranock as it wrapped a chain around her husband's neck, then dragged him to the entrance of the clock, knocking over the camera. Sandra heard the crack of the lens, and hoped that this wouldn't be caught on camera.

Dave screeched, and his eyes bulged with fear. She watched, motionless as his face turned various shades of purple; the chain slowly cutting of his air supply. Other souls attached to the chains groped at his legs and arms, crying and wailing for help. She knew Dave would soon be another one of the Taranock's tortured souls.

Just then, the front door flew open, and Ardy appeared with a bandage round his head, looking dishevelled and confused. Sandra looked at him. She had not anticipated this.

—*Ardy should still be in the hospital. Stupid guy. Stupid, stupid guy.*

Ardy stood frozen, his mind reeling with shock as the Taranock dragged Dave inexorably in the gaping maw of the clock. Dave's anguished screams pierced the air, a desperate cacophony of terror and agony which echoed off the walls, reverberating through Ardy's very soul.

They both watched, helpless and paralysed, as the creature's twisted chains ensnared Dave's flailing form, pulling him closer and closer to his doom. Each agonised cry tore at Sandra's heart, a dagger of guilt piercing her conscience as she realised the dire consequences of her actions.

In the dim light, she could see Dave's face contorted in sheer terror, his eyes wide with disbelief and fear as he fought desperately against the Taranock's relentless grip. But it was a futile struggle, a futile resistance against the force of the creature's power.

As Dave disappeared into the yawning darkness of the clock, his cries fading into the abyss, Sandra felt a profound sense of guilt wash over her. She had condemned her husband to a fate worse than death, a fate from which there was no escape, and Ardy had witnessed all of it.

Trembling with a mixture of dread and despair, Sandra could only watch in silent horror as the clock chimed the hour, its mournful toll a grim reminder of the irreversible tragedy that had unfolded before her eyes.

After Dave disappeared into the clock, she sprang into action and slammed the door shut, holding it there while Ardy staggered over to the cross and bible. With each step, a wave of throbbing pain pulsed through his skull, a relentless reminder of his vulnerability. He knew he was too weak to have helped Dave, and although he felt guilty for just standing there watching him being dragged into the clock, he was happy that it was Dave that was taken, not Sandra.

As he handed the cross and bible to Sandra, a profound sense of relief washed over him like a tidal wave. Dave had always been there, a constant annoying presence by Sandra's side, always getting in the way. He couldn't count the number of times Dave pestered Sandra with questions or offered unsolicited advice about her work.

Ardy's instincts kicked into overdrive.

Adrenaline surged through his veins, sharpening his focus and drowning out the throbbing ache in his skull. With grim determination, he pushed through the pain, every fibre of his being screaming for him to run.

"We need to keep it in there and make sure it never comes back out," he said, taking over Sandra's position to hold the door shut on the clock.

She lit the sage, circling the clock and said a prayer.

"Hear my words, O Lord. Suck out this demon from within. Banish its soul to the Devil. I pray thee. Conjure up strength within me, and surround us with your purifying light."

She moved quickly, repeating her prayer and going through her routine like clockwork. She began breathing deeply before sprinkling more holy water across the clock, signing the cross over her chest and shouting, "In nominee Patris et Filii et Spiritus Sancti. I command the Taranock to return to the depths of Hell!"

A massive bang sounded from inside the clock, stopping her in her tracks. She quickly grabbed her rosary beads as another bang resonated through the room, making her heart beat twice as fast. A terrifying scream, along with scratching sounds penetrated her ears, forcing her to back away. She repeated the prayer, shouting over the sound of the Taranock screaming.

With the Taranock straining against the weight of the clock's door, Ardy's muscles bulged beneath his skin, the raw power of his determination evident in the cords of his neck and the flex of his arms. Beads of sweat trickled down his brow, mingling with the blood that seeped from the wound beneath the bandage wrapped tightly around his head.

Despite the searing pain that pulsed through his skull with every beat of his heart, Ardy refused to yield, his grip on the door unwavering in the face of the malevolent force that threatened to break free from within.

The Taranock screamed louder, its voice reverberating throughout the room, sending shivers down both their spines. With trembling hands, Sandra clutched the rosary beads tighter, seeking solace and protection in her faith. Each bang from inside the clock seemed to intensify the terror gripping her heart. Desperation fuelled her prayers as she repeated the sacred words, her voice rising above the cacophony of noise. But the scratching persisted, echoing ominously around the room. Fear threatened to overwhelm her, but she fought to maintain her composure.

With each passing moment, the sense of dread deepened, as if an unseen presence lurked just beyond her sight. She could feel the weight of malevolence in the air, pressing down on her with suffocating force.

Summoning every ounce of courage, she continued to chant the prayer, refusing to yield to the terror consuming her. The Taranock's screams grew more frenzied, its unearthly wails filling the room with an oppressive aura of darkness. But she refused to surrender to despair. With unwavering resolve, she confronted the darkness head-on, her faith acting as a shield against the encroaching evil. And as she stood her ground, her prayers filled with renewed fervour.

By the time Sandra had finished, they were both hot, sweaty and exhausted. She stood in the middle of the room for a while, gathering her thoughts—and her excuses—for when she would be questioned. She had Ardy as a witness, which boded well for her.

Ardy slumped against the wall, his face flustered and red. "How did this happen?"

"The Taranock tried taking me and Dave saved my life." Sandra had to get her story straight, there should be no cracks in it. "He pulled me away from the demon but it got him instead."

Ardy clutched his head, his face screwed up in pain. He spoke slowly, unsure of his words.

"The police are going to want to know everything that has happened here. Check the camera. We can use that as evidence to show them we had no part in it."

Sandra made herself busy cleaning up the room, before picking up the camera from the floor and checking it over. The lens had cracked when it was knocked over, and the sound was the only thing that had been working throughout the ordeal.

She handed it to Ardy. "The sound works but the camera is buggered."

He nodded, placing it down beside him. "It should be enough for the police. Help me up and let's get out of here. I want to be as far away from that clock as possible."

With trembling hands and a heart heavy with guilt, Sandra reached out to Ardy, offering him her support as he struggled to his feet. His movements were clumsy, his footing unsteady as he rose from the floor, the weight of his injured head dragging him down like an anchor.

With Ardy leaning on her for support, Sandra guided him slowly but steadily out of the house, their footsteps echoing hollowly in the stillness of the night. Each step was a laborious effort, Ardy's weight bearing heavily on Sandra's shoulders as they made their way down the stone steps.

The cool night air enveloped them like a comforting embrace as they emerged into the open, the darkness broken only by the soft glow of moonlight filtering through the trees. Sandra cast a fleeting glance back at the house they were leaving behind, a shiver coursing down her spine at the memory of the horrors that lurked within its walls.

But there was no time for fear now, no time to dwell on the past. With Ardy's well-being foremost in her mind, Sandra focused all her energy on guiding him safely down the stone steps, each movement deliberate and measured to prevent any missteps or accidents.

As they reached the bottom of the steps, Sandra felt a surge of relief wash over her. They were almost there, almost to safety. With renewed determination, she urged Ardy forward, his footsteps faltering but resolute as they made their way to Graham and Steve's house, a beacon of hope in the darkness.

"Could the demon return?" Ardy asked through the stillness of the night.

Sandra shook her head. "No, although it may try. It could find some other way to get through, and hopefully, by that time, we'll be on a different continent filming something else."

A small smile grew across his lips. "We could go to Las Vegas. That's something you always wanted to do."

Sandra's voice trembled with emotion as she spoke. "Yes, but Dave wouldn't let me."

"You can now. Dave's gone and it wasn't your fault."

Sandra knew if the Taranock tried to come through again, it would know what she had done, and she prayed that it would never step foot back into this realm—she knew if it did, it would come for her. She had blood on her hands; she was a murderer.

They reached Graham and Steve's house and the door flew open to a startled Steve. He looked them up and down. Their hair was soaked with sweat, their faces ashen white, and they were both still shaking with fear. He could see that something dreadful had happened, and he ushered them inside and slammed the door.

"Where's Dave?"

"The Taranock took him." She sat on the sofa and started to sob.

Steve ushered Ardy to sit down before sitting next to Sandra.

"How?" he asked. Steve placed his hand on hers, her skin felt icy cold.

Graham and Arthur appeared upon hearing the commotion; both wearing their pyjamas, Graham carrying a hot water bottle.

"Oh, my darling, what's happened?"

Graham sat down next to her on the opposite side and wrapped his arm around her shoulders; she was shivering. Arthur remained in the doorway, staring at her, his eyes cold and empty.

"The Taranock took Dave," she wailed.

"How did it do that? I thought Dave was meant to stay out of the way," Graham said passing her a tissue.

She shook her head and blew her nose loudly.

"No, the demon tried to attack me and Dave came running to my rescue, only for it to take him instead. Then Ardy came in but it was too strong for us. We only just managed to escape."

"Is the Taranock still there?" Arthur asked. His face remained stoic and his cold expression unnerved her, but she tried to remain calm and not let anything slip.

"The Taranock has been banished. It can't return. I'm just so upset that I couldn't save my husband."

"That is an inconvenience," Arthur said flatly. "I'll make you both a coffee to calm your nerves so you can get your story straight for the police."

He didn't bother waiting for a reply before leaving the room. Even Steve and Graham were confused by his somewhat harsh comment.

Sandra's attitude had convinced Arthur that something wasn't right, even though she was crying, she appeared evasive. Ardy looked like hell, but he seemed just as confused as everyone else. Arthur wondered, had he stayed, would Dave still be alive? He couldn't trust her. He didn't know Sandra very well, and the way she kept glancing at him suggested something was wrong. He wouldn't have been surprised if she had used the Taranock as a convenient way to murder her husband. However, he was relieved that she had banished it, so he could now live in peace.

He stirred the coffee and thought about Amelia. She was due to return in a week or so. Hopefully, she wouldn't be too hard on him. Hopefully her hospital stay would remind her that she wasn't invincible.

He carried the coffee into the lounge, spilling a bit onto the carpet, which slowed him down, as he attempted to keep the remaining liquid in the mug. Sandra could still be heard sobbing, pleading with Graham and Steve not to call the police, at least not while she was still in shock.

Arthur came through the door and placed the mug in her trembling hands. "Sip this, and then we'll call the police."

"I need some space to grieve, Arthur." Her lower lip wobbled as she looked desperately at Steve and Graham.

"I think we should contact them now," Ardy chimed in. "I'm going to go and sort my head out. It's still bleeding."

"You may need to go back to the hospital. I can take you if you'd like?" Steve offered.

Ardy nodded. "Yes, please. It's throbbing, and I can't seem to think straight."

Steve got up and gestured for Ardy to follow him. "I'll get my coat. Come with me and I'll find a towel for you."

They left, leaving the others to talk. Arthur turned his attention back to Sandra, who had now stopped crying.

"There will be more of an investigation if we don't contact them now. Did you document everything?" Arthur questioned.

She nodded. "I did, but the camera was knocked over, so I don't know how much it captured, but it does still have the sound working."

Arthur cast her another suspicious glance. "Really? That's a pity. Still, I guess at the very least, the police will believe us about the Taranock." He turned to Graham. "Where's your phone? I'll call them."

"It's next to the front door on the table."

Within an hour, the neighbourhood was surrounded by police vehicles. They flooded both houses, inspecting the crime scene and asking questions. Sandra eagerly handed them the cameras, and Arthur thought for a moment that she appeared to be trying not to smile. Everyone present was on edge as the detective watched the earlier footage of the Taranock emerging from the clock and the terrified crew fleeing the house. He also tried to watch the footage of the Taranock taking Dave, but only the sound could be heard.

The wails and screams from the Taranock, and Dave, blasted through the camera, with Sandra screaming for the Taranock to drop Dave. To Arthur, it sounded as if Sandra was forcing her screams, but to the detective, there wasn't any indication of foul play from anyone apart from the demon, which he had trouble believing was real.

The detective also checked the camera from the foyer and watched the events which had taken place before Sandra had concocted her plan to get rid of her husband. He didn't say anything for a while, and his face changed from fear to confusion and back again as he watched it through twice more, before he finally spoke.

"I'm taking this to be analysed."

The interrogations continued for several days, but they all stuck to their stories, and as the days passed, the house itself became a celebrity. People from around the country came to see it, and Arthur began to get fed up with it. Whitely Bay had become overrun. He was followed to work by reporters, horror fans and ghosthunters. He was followed around the grocery store. Reporters pursued him wherever he went. He despised it.

The police hadn't left them alone since the incident, as they also tried to come to terms with the apparently supernatural murder of Dave. A funeral service was held for him, although his body had not been recovered. Sandra was adamant that the police were not to remove the rosary beads or open the clock in order to find her husband. She explained that if they reopened it, all of her hard work in banishing the demon would be for nothing.

The police had no idea what they were up against. This was the first time in history that there was actual video evidence of a supernatural murder, and naturally, it was widely publicised.

Arthur had reviewed the footage from his secret cameras, confirming that Sandra had indeed coaxed her husband toward the demon. He knew he was right.

Unsure whether to show the police the footage, he decided against it. Revealing the existence of the cameras might lead them to request footage from the time Dotty disappeared, which would implicate him in her murder.

Sandra and Ardy appeared to have already moved on and were having a good time in Vegas, lapping up their newfound celebrity status. Before Sandra had left, she had told Arthur that she would never set foot inside that house again.

CHAPTER 17
Arthur's Confession

Five days had passed since Dave's funeral, and the Taranock had not been seen. Arthur, in all honesty, was surprised that Sandra had succeeded in banishing it. The house had felt different since then, the atmosphere was much lighter, and far more amicable. He had grown quite fond of his new home, and worked tirelessly to renovate it with the help of Trish.

Following the banishing, his boss had granted him additional paid holiday. Trish hadn't left his side since the horrific event. He owed his life to her; she had got him out of trouble more times than he cared to admit. Even now, she was helping him out, buying the materials he needed for the house.

Arthur had become good friends with Graham and Steve, and they would come over most nights to keep him company. Arthur suspected that Steve mostly came over to see Trish, but he didn't mind. He hadn't seen his sister this happy in a long time, and it was nice watching their relationship blossom.

Christmas was approaching, and everywhere Arthur went, shops had begun to spread festive cheer. There were twinkling lights, and decorated Christmas trees in every colour imaginable. Christmas music blared out from the speakers in every store, adding to the festive atmosphere. Arthur adored this time of year. He had already overspent on the twins, but he felt they deserved it, especially after the year they'd had. He'd even brought Graham along to help pick out the toys for them; Graham had been overjoyed and had dragged Arthur into every toy store he could find. This was the first time in ages that Arthur had felt hopeful about the future, although Amelia's strange behaviour was still weighing heavily on his mind.

⮌

Graham and Arthur had just returned from another Christmas shopping trip, their arms filled with bags. It had snowed again, and small snowflakes were still melting on their hats when they entered the lounge. Steve and Trish were happily snuggled up watching a Christmas movie, with the twins sitting next to them, their lips smeared with bits of chocolate; their hands dipping in and out of the tub of chocolates which Arthur had left on the table for them before he left.

"What did you buy this time?" asked Steve, counting the number of bags on Graham's arm.

"You know you're not supposed to know until Christmas," Graham scoffed.

"But that's still three weeks away. I want to know now," Steve said in a high-pitched child-like voice.

Graham chuckled as he sat down. "I'll be hiding these away from your prying eyes, young man."

Trish giggled and Arthur noticed Steve's hand moving around beneath the blanket.

"There are children in the room," Arthur scolded. He sat down next to Graham, and the twins ran up to him, squealing at the top of their lungs. He took them and sat them on his knees.

"What did you do with Auntie Trish today?"

They both started talking over each other, and Arthur couldn't understand a word they were saying. He laughed as their little faces lit up and a spark of fire twinkled in their eyes. He sat back on the sofa, snuggled up with the kids, and watched the roaring log fire.

The grandfather clock chimed loudly behind him, briefly jarring his senses, but he reminded himself that it was just a regular clock now and nothing evil was going to jump out of it. It wasn't only him who jumped sometimes when it chimed either. He often noticed Trish and Steve's worried expressions. He knew he should get rid of it, and he really wanted to, but Sandra had warned him that moving the clock in any way could undo all of her hard work, and he didn't want anyone else to suffer at the hands of the Taranock. It was best left where it had always been. Sandra had done a good job of banishing the Taranock, yet he still couldn't help but wonder whether it could, or would, ever return.

He pushed the thought to the back of his mind and focused on the kids, who were still babbling about their day. Arthur could tell they'd overindulged in the chocolate, but he didn't mind, after all, Christmas was fast approaching. He relished the moment, savouring every word they said, knowing that he'd be back at work all too soon. Even though he had taken two weeks off over the holidays, it was never enough for him. He longed for the opportunity to watch his children grow up, he didn't want to miss one more second of their development; he had missed every milestone they had reached since their birth. He sat there for a while, taking it all in, watching his children squeal with delight about Christmas, knowing that this was a moment he should cherish for the rest of his life.

Graham sat up in his chair and reached into the tub for a chocolate.

"I think we should make snowmen tomorrow." He unwrapped the candy and popped it into his mouth, trying to communicate as the soft caramel oozed out from the chocolate. "The snow has settled outside, so I think we're in for a chilly night."

Arthur sat the kids on Graham's lap and drew the curtain behind him. As his eyes adjusted to the darkness, he could make out thick white snowflakes falling from the sky.

"I think you're right. I don't think anyone's going anywhere tomorrow. There's already a thick layer on the ground."

"Ah, bugger, I have work tomorrow," Steve announced. He tossed the blanket aside and joined Arthur at the window. He, too, peered into the darkness, but he could see something out of the corner of his eye, something dark in the window's reflection. He spun around to check the back wall, but there was nothing there. He felt a familiar sensation creeping over him, a primal instinct warning him of imminent danger. His heart quickened its pace, a steady drumbeat of apprehension echoing in his chest, while his palms grew slick with nervous sweat.

Graham noticed Steve's fearful expression and turned to face him. "What? What did you see?"

Steve shakily pointed at the wall. "I thought I saw something." His voice cracked as if he was about to cry, and he slumped down on the windowsill to regain his balance.

"You can't have done. Sandra got rid of it," Arthur said, instantly assuming Steve was implying that he had just seen the Taranock. "There hasn't been anything for weeks. Why would it come back now?"

"I'm not sure," said Steve, burying his face in his hands, attempting to calm his thoughts. "I still have this uneasy feeling. I know it's gone, I really do, but I have this horrible feeling it might return."

"I know, mate. I have the same feeling, but Sandra assured me it won't return," Arthur said.

"I believe we're all still shaken by what happened," said Trish. "Sometimes I feel like I'm being watched. I hope it's just our minds playing tricks on us. What we went through was terrifying and horrific, and I doubt we will ever be the same again, but we must try to move on. It can't hurt us anymore." She smiled reassuringly at each of them, hoping that her words would soothe the tense atmosphere.

Steve sighed. "Yeah, it was probably just a shadow that my mind turned into something else, but I can't help remembering that we are actually sitting in a room where people died, and sometimes it seriously creeps me out."

Arthur turned away from Steve, irritated by his remark. They were all just about getting back into the normal swing of life and Steve was bringing it up again.

Graham tried to lighten the mood by chuckling and slapping his thigh.

"If we think about it that way, then death has occurred everywhere on Earth. The high street is basically made up of 15th century buildings and we have an abbey which is over a thousand years old.

Whitely Bay is a very old place, and is bound to have had many deaths. You can't think like that or you'll never go anywhere."

"I suppose you're right," said Steve. He tilted his head and pressed his lips together in thought. "Things will calm down soon enough. As Trish said, what we went through was absolutely awful, and I wouldn't wish it on my worst enemy, but it's all done and dusted now."

Arthur closed the curtains, trapping Steve behind them. Steve pulled himself out and punched Arthur playfully on the arm, causing Arthur to stumble into the clock beside the window. He stopped the clock from falling and winked at Steve.

"You're very lucky I caught that. It could have set the Taranock free." He stroked the varnished wood tenderly before sitting down next to Graham. "If I could afford to move, I would, but then I wouldn't have you amazing neighbours, so you'll just have to put up with me and my torture house." He leaned in and took a chocolate from the tub. "Besides, I've put too much time and money into this place. The Taranock won't return."

"Have the reporters given up on this place now? I haven't heard anything more in the news lately," Graham asked.

Arthur nodded, chewing on a chocolate.

"There are still a few hanging around, but they're probably bored now because nothing else has happened."

"Hopefully they'll find someone else to annoy. This place was swarming."

"What about the detective?" Trish asked.

"He's still poking around, looking for evidence that it might have been one of us, but as much as he'd like a murder case, even he can't deny the camera footage. They examined it and decided the footage was genuine."

He still couldn't shake the feeling that Sandra was responsible for Dave's death, but pointing the finger at Sandra after he had murdered poor, innocent Dotty, didn't give him much room to talk. He knew it wasn't his fault and that he'd been used as a pawn in Amelia's evil games, but the guilt still hadn't left him, and perhaps never would.

If his mother was still alive, he knew she'd say, *'I told you I was right'*, and Arthur would have to agree with her. He should not have married a neurotic, spiteful woman who used her intellect to manipulate others. It was her intelligence which Arthur had initially liked about Amelia; she was knowledgeable in a variety of subjects, but her preference was the study of the human mind and body. He used to enjoy staying up late with her discussing how the human body worked, hearing her enthuse over the latest scientific experiment or discovery she was following.

He used to love the way her face lit up when she talked, but now, everything had changed; what she had done to him was unforgiveable, how she had manipulated his mind into doing something abhorrent. He despised that side of her, and he loathed her intelligence and how she used it to belittle him. He was not looking forward to her coming back, and if he could have afforded private healthcare, he would have sent her away to have her mental health evaluated without hesitation.

He nervously looked at the clock, mentally counting down the minutes until her return. It had been so peaceful without her, and he knew once she was back he would be walking on eggshells again. He desperately wanted to divorce her, but she had threatened to take everything he had, including his children, and he, more than anyone, knew just how spiteful she could be.

"You've gone quiet, Arthur. What are you thinking about?" Graham asked, bringing Arthur's thoughts back to the here and now.

Arthur paused for a moment, then blurted out, "I don't really want Amelia to come back. It's been so nice here without her. I just wish that she'd stay away."

"I'll put the kids to bed, and then we can talk about it. They've already had their tea." Trish interjected.

Arthur nodded, hoping he had made the right decision in expressing his thoughts.

～

Trish's voice was warm and comforting as she tucked the twins into their beds, their excitement palpable in the air. They giggled and wriggled under the covers, already imagining the fun they would have in the freshly fallen snow.

"We'll make the biggest snowmen you've ever seen," Trish promised with a grin, her eyes sparkling with anticipation, mirroring theirs. She leaned in to kiss each of them goodnight, their cheeks flushed with excitement.

As she moved to turn off the light, Charlie rolled over in his bed to face her, "Where's Theo gone?"

She stopped, her hand hovering on the light switch. "Who's Theo?"

Charlie grinned. "He's our other twin."

Dylan nodded eagerly. "He plays with us."

"Other twin?" she asked, confused.

"He's the same as us, but he said don't tell anyone about him. Only Mummy," Charlie said.

Trish's heart skipped a beat, a shiver of unease creeping up her spine. She glanced around the room, half-expecting to see another figure lurking in the shadows.

"Boys, there's no one else in this house, apart from you two," she said gently, trying to keep her tone reassuring despite the sudden knot of worry tightening in her chest.

Charlie's grin widened, his eyes twinkling mischievously in the dim light.

"But Theo's our special friend," he insisted, his voice filled with innocent conviction.

Trish exchanged a puzzled look with Dylan, who nodded along with his brother's words. She tried to brush it off as their active imaginations running wild before bedtime.

"Well, it's time to sleep now, sweethearts. Theo can join us in making snowmen tomorrow," she said with a forced smile, hoping to ease their minds.

As she finally turned off the light and left the room, a nagging feeling lingered in the back of her mind, leaving her wondering about the mysterious Theo and the implications of the twins' vivid imaginations.

Graham had made coffee while they'd waited for Trish to return. Arthur slumped down in a seat next to the fire. As soon as Trish joined them, all eyes were upon Arthur.

"Talk to us," Graham said, as if he were a therapist.

"You all know how spiteful and vindictive she can be," Arthur began, his palms sweating. He felt as if he had been put on the spot.

They all nodded.

"You know full well that I've never liked her," said Trish, taking advantage of the opportunity to express her own feelings regarding Amelia. "It's about time you realised what a bitch she is. Personally, I think you should divorce her."

"It's not quite that simple. If I divorce her, she'll bleed me dry. I guarantee she will take everything I own, and no doubt take the kids away."

Steve gave Graham a sidelong glance before speaking. They had often discussed Amelia at home. "The money—the house, definitely—but I seriously doubt she'll take the kids away from you. You can see she doesn't want them, I mean, she barely acknowledges their presence. I think she'd settle for most of your money."

"She's already done that," Trish spat as she angrily poked the fire with a stick. "I've seen how she spends my brother's money on herself, all those manicures, the countless number of hair appointments each month, not to mention the designer clothes she buys and that bloody Louis Vuitton purse that cost an arm and a leg."

"It's true, she does spend my money on those things, but it's more than that." Arthur stared despairingly into the fire. "It's as if I'm walking on eggshells around her. If she doesn't get her way, she has these silly outbursts and acts like a child."

"What you are describing is an abusive relationship." Graham lightly patted him on the arm. "You must see that this relationship is toxic."

Arthur stood up, enraged, and glared over Graham with his hands on his hips.

"I know this relationship is toxic. I despise the bitch!"

Graham held his arms up in defence. "Woah, calm down. I didn't mean to upset you."

Arthur backed away, realising that the pent-up anger and resentment he had harboured for so long was finally erupting, and he was taking it out on his friends.

"I'm sorry. I didn't mean to yell at you. I just can't think of a way out without her taking everything I love. You don't know what she's like. She is pure evil. She takes advantage of others. She ... she ..." Arthur couldn't finish his sentence without mentioning Dotty. If he admitted to what had happened to her, then he wouldn't be able to go back on it. It was eating away at him, and he knew he needed to change the subject very quickly.

Graham's ears perked up, and he could tell Arthur was struggling to say something.

"You can tell us, mate. Whatever it is, we won't judge you for it."

Arthur fiddled with his hands, becoming increasingly nervous. He began to stutter, unable to form the correct words without sounding like he was a murderer.

Trish sat in her chair, quietly trying to figure out what was bothering Arthur. He had always told her everything, and she felt certain that whatever he was trying to say now was important. She leaned toward Arthur; the anticipation was unbearable. "Tell us, Arthur."

"I'm trying." Arthur looked up at Trish, his eyes watery. "I can't seem to find the right words."

"Is it something Amelia did to you?" Steve asked.

"Yes," Arthur replied, looking down at his sweaty hands.

The heat from the fire was too much for Arthur, he needed to get some fresh air.

"I'm sorry," he mumbled, leaving the room.

They stared at him confused as he walked away. Graham drew back the curtain and peered out of the window, to see Arthur standing still, just staring out into the night.

"Should we go after him?" Graham asked.

Trish shook her head. "Leave him be. He'll tell us in his own time. Whatever it is, it must be quite bad because he usually tells me everything."

Steve stood up and joined Graham at the window, curious about what Arthur was up to. He felt sorry for the man.

"We need to help him, but what can we do about Amelia? She's only small, Trish could always take her down," he said as he watched Arthur, who was now sobbing.

Trish rolled her eyes at Steve's remark. "This is not the time to joke about it. He's just scared that she will take everything from him if he divorces her, which she will definitely try to do. So, we need to come up with a plan to help him."

Graham remained quiet in his chair, his brow furrowed, as he thought long and hard about what to do for his friend. He couldn't stand Amelia, she was a stuck-up bitch, who took advantage of everyone, especially her husband, who obeyed her every command just to keep the peace. As far as Graham was concerned, it had all gone too far. Arthur's relationship with Amelia was gut-wrenching and dismal. He could tell something extremely bad must have happened to Arthur. Then he remembered what Arthur had said about

Sandra and her husband. It would have been a good plan, had the Taranock still been around.

"Maybe ... just maybe, there could be a way to get rid of her without her ... without her taking everything," Graham mused, choosing his words carefully.

Steve and Trish both looked at him, intrigued.

"Go on," they said in unison.

"This is just a thought, so try not to look at me like a serial killer, but maybe Arthur was on to something earlier. What he said about Sandra planning to get rid of her husband might not have been such a bad idea. It's a long shot, but what if Amelia was to be taken by the Taranock? That way everyone would be happy."

For a brief moment, there was silence, as they took in Graham's heinous plan. It was Steve who was the first to speak.

"That is a bloody terrible plan. Arthur already has enough to deal with without bringing back that dreadful demon."

"I don't know, maybe Graham is right." Until now, nobody had noticed Arthur standing quietly in the doorway.

"I'm sorry, mate. I had no idea you were there. It was just a stupid idea," Graham mumbled, embarrassed. "I was just trying to think of ideas to be rid of her without her taking you to the cleaners."

Arthur stared intently, the atmosphere in the room was growing thicker by the minute.

"I think it's a good idea."

"Arthur!" Trish shrieked. There was a trembling in her voice as she continued. "You're not thinking clearly, for a start the Taranock has gone.

We can't just get it back. Surely, there must be another way?"

"I'm thinking clearly for the first time in my life. Amelia will not stop until she has taken every last penny from me. You know what she's like, and you know she will use the children against me. If I don't stop her now, she'll ruin my life."

There was venom in Arthur's voice and his face contorted, showing his rage and hatred for Amelia.

"I agree with Trish. This is a terrible idea. We spent so much time and effort trying to get rid of the Taranock, and now you want to bring it back? No way!" Steve reassuringly put an arm around Trish.

The atmosphere was becoming increasingly tense, and Trish was uneasy with the direction the conversation was taking.

"This cannot happen. This is murder."

Arthur threw up his hands in despair, his face contorted into an ugly scowl as he spat out the words. "What she did—getting me to smother Dotty—that was murder, and she got away with it!"

Silence enveloped them. They stared at Arthur, who continued ranting about Amelia and how manipulative she could be.

Arthur told them about her fascination with hypnosis, how she had practiced on him and how she had eventually used it to bring about Dotty's untimely demise. They couldn't believe what they were hearing. They had definitely underestimated Amelia's intelligence.

"Let me clarify something," Steve began "Amelia hypnotised you into killing her mother?"

Trish hugged her brother, who allowed himself to collapse in her arms, sobbing loudly.

"It's no wonder you couldn't tell us earlier. How did she do it?"

"I honestly don't know how she did it, but she did. This has been weighing heavily on me the whole time, and I just can't get rid of this horrible guilty feeling," he sobbed.

"It wasn't your fault at all. Remember that." Trish wiped the tears from Arthur's face.

"Perhaps my idea isn't so bad after all." Graham laughed.

Trish gave Graham a look to shut him up and sat Arthur down.

"Look, there are other ways to get rid of her. Even if you divorce her, I won't let you fall. I have money, and I'll spend every last penny on you and the kids if I have to. You're my little brother, Arthur, and I'm here to look after you."

Arthur nodded, his eyes wet with tears. "I can't expect that from you. It isn't fair. I'm the man of the house, and I should be able to care for my family without relying on my sister."

Trish gave him a warm smile. "I've been where you are. I went through all this with my ex-husband. Things will improve, I promise. In the meantime, allow me to make it easier for you."

"You are the best sister on the planet."

"You idiot, I'm your only sister."

Graham clapped his hands together suddenly. "Well, at least we've got that sorted, and we don't need an ancient demon to kill her."

"Shut up, Graham," Trish scowled, taking Arthur's hands in hers, she rubbed them together to soothe him. "When she returns, you will give her the divorce papers so she can sign them. I can help you and usher things along, but we need this done as soon as possible. I'll see to it that you keep the house. Is her name on the deed?"

"Yes it is." Arthur looked up at everyone, and for the first time in ages, he felt hopeful. He patted Trish on the hand and smiled. "Thank you, sis. This means a lot to me."

"Hey, what are big sisters for, eh?"

Steve cleared his throat, interrupting their conversation. "What if she gets angry and doesn't want to sign the papers?"

"Then we switch to plan B and get the Taranock to kill her off." Graham laughed.

"You are the least funny person in this room, Graham," Steve said, mocking Graham's voice.

Graham scowled at him. "I'm only trying to lighten the mood."

"Thanks, mate, I know you mean well." Arthur smiled.

Arthur felt as if a huge weight had been lifted from his shoulders and by the end of the night, he was relieved that he had talked to them about everything, including Dotty.

Alone in bed he allowed himself to wonder. He wondered how Amelia would react. She probably wouldn't know what had hit her when she got home from the hospital. He despised her and would go to any lengths to be rid of her, even if it meant bringing back the Taranock. He thought it would be worth it just to see her terrified expression as it dragged her into the clock. That would be his last resort if things didn't go according to plan with the divorce.

As he lay in his bed watching the shadows make shapes on the wall, he couldn't shake the feeling that the Taranock hadn't finished with them just yet.

CHAPTER 18
Amelia's Return

The hospital building was dark and foreboding. An imposing structure built with old, brown bricks that were riddled with time-worn holes and crumbling edges. The windows of the building reflected the dull grey sky and enhanced its gloomy appearance. The car park nearest the main entrance was full, making it difficult for Arthur to find a space. He eventually found one tucked away in the corner after a full ten minutes of driving round and round. He reversed in.

"Damn," he muttered as he tried to open the door.

There was hardly enough room for him to get out as the car next to him had parked at an angle, taking up almost two spaces. The car was a sleek and shiny BMW, and he had to fight the urge to bang his door into the side of it. Instead, he shimmied his way out of his car and slammed the door shut, grumbling to himself.

As he pushed open the large double doors at the hospital entrance, a swarm of people rushed past him. He hated old hospitals, with their dimly lit corridors; they reeked of death and disease. There was barely enough room to move, but he made his way to the ward and could see Amelia, ashen-faced, sitting on one of those awful hard plastic seats, waiting to leave. She looked sad, but once she saw Arthur bee-lining towards her, her face twisted into a scowl.

"And just why didn't you come to visit me?" she demanded with such venom that it caught Arthur off guard.

He stood there awkwardly, trying to think of an explanation she would accept. He noticed that she had gained some weight while in the hospital, and she appeared dull and drab in comparison to the Amelia he was used to. She was holding her discharge papers scrunched up in her fist like she was about to ram them down his throat.

He preferred not to see her glaring at him and opted for reading her discharge papers instead.

He could see Amelia sneering at him out of the corner of his eye, and he desperately wanted to slap the smile off her face. He could tell she was enjoying his discomfort as she stood there all smug with her arms crossed.

"Just pick up my bag, will you? I need to get home to have a shower. I haven't had one in days," she demanded.

Arthur looked back at the large bag which had been brought to her by one of her work colleagues when they had visited.

"You had it brought here; you bring it back."

Her eyes widened. Why wasn't he obeying her like he should? Like he always had. Suddenly she realised that she was losing control of him, but she had no idea how or why. She put on a false grin and smiled sweetly at him.

"Arthur, could you please? After all of the tests they've given me, I still feel very weak."

"Which was a waste of time because they found nothing wrong with you."

He began to walk away from her toward the hospital exit, shouting over his shoulder, "That's not my bag, you carry it."

She looked sad, like a lost child. Her eyes were brimming with tears as she slowly picked up the luggage, trying to juggle it under her arm.

She eventually got to the front of the hospital. Arthur watched from the car as she struggled with the bag and high heels, nearly tripping over several times in the process. He saw a man approach her, and offer to help. His huge muscular arm easily picked up her luggage.

Arthur rolled his eyes and muttered to himself, while she fluttered her eyelashes at the man, flirting and giggling with him.

He started the engine and approached them slowly from the parking space, desperately wanting to run over the tall, muscular man, crushing his stupid, manly biceps. He looked in the rear-view mirror and noticed how thin and grey his hair was in comparison to Mr Muscle, with his thick mop of hair. He couldn't understand why Amelia had stayed with him for so long when she could have had any man she fluttered her eyelashes at. He'd seen men fall to their knees for her, and he had to admit he used to be one of them, but not any longer. He'd had enough of her stupid mind games.

He pulled up beside her as she walked through the car park with Mr Muscle, and got out of the car.

"Thanks for helping mate, I can take it from here."

The man looked down at his short frame and smirked, eyeing his wedding ring.

"I'm sure I can handle it better than you. You just sit in that warm car of yours and I'll help your little lady out."

Arthur wanted to punch him, but he knew he'd be pummelled to the ground in seconds. Instead, he nodded and walked back to the car, trying to avoid Amelia's smirk. She enjoyed things like this—men fighting over her, but she was disappointed by Arthur's retreat. She wanted him to fight for her like he used to, but when she looked at him now, he appeared old and withered. Life had taken its toll on his body, and it was beginning to show.

"You're so thoughtful," she said to the man, putting her hand on his bicep and lightly squeezing it. "Thank you so much for your help."

"Any time, love." He winked as he slid her luggage into the boot. He took her hand in his and assisted her into the passenger side of the car, before walking over to the BMW that was parked next to the spot that Arthur had come out of. Mr Muscle gave Arthur a last menacing look, before speeding away, leaving tyre tracks behind.

Arthur laughed to himself. "Bloody typical."

Amelia raised her brow at Arthur. "What? He was nice enough to help me, as you couldn't be bothered."

"You have the entire male population at your fingertips, Amelia. I'm sure that you can get help wherever you go." Arthur shrugged and drove out of the car park.

He drove in silence for the next few miles, ignoring Amelia's pout as she stared out of the window. Buildings whizzed by, merging into a blur of depressing grey. The only things that made Arthur happy were the brightly lit Christmas displays in the shop windows. A variety of reds, greens, and whites, which gave him a warm fuzzy feeling inside. He wasn't sure whether to give Amelia the divorce papers once they got home, or to wait and see if she had changed since her illness. He knew that being hospitalised could change a person, especially after a life-altering experience.

However, based on how Amelia had acted towards him and with the other man outside the hospital, there seemed little chance that she had become less narcissistic. The wife and mother he had once known was a distant memory.

The air between them felt dense and suffocating, and Arthur had to work extra hard not to yell at her about the divorce. He despised every fibre, every cell, every aspect of her. He pitied the microorganisms that had to live on her body. Even her shifting gaze from him to the window irritated him. He couldn't go on living with her. He wanted her to leave. He was ashamed of himself and embarrassed by how much money he had wasted on her, and for what? So that she could look good, while he looked like a tired old man with little to his name? No. She needed to leave.

But there was something unusual about her, something he had noticed out of the corner of his eye whilst driving. Her eyes were darker than usual, almost black, and her skin was whiter than it had ever been. The energy around her was horrifying and gut-wrenching. Even the way she sat made him feel uncomfortable. He wasn't sure if it was just his hatred towards her or if she really had changed since she had been in the hospital.

"Stop staring at me," she snapped, gazing out of the window.

He drove along the narrow lanes that led to their neighbourhood. It was cold and it had begun to snow again, causing Arthur to skid. He slowed gently, straightening the car, and fighting back the urge to throw Amelia out of the window, he repositioned the car so it would carefully slide over any icy patches.

She smirked as she watched him grip the steering wheel tightly.

"Are you having trouble controlling the car?"

He didn't bother answering her, he was clenching his jaw so tightly it ached. He was determined not to argue with her because he knew that was exactly what she wanted. She looked out of the window once more and spoke quietly.

"Have you got the boys anything for Christmas yet?"

He nodded, his gaze fixed on the road. "Graham helped me select a few presents for them."

She rolled her eyes and spat out callous words about Graham. He slammed on the brakes, causing her to hurtle forward, and narrowly miss colliding with the dashboard.

"If you're going to talk about my friend like that, you can get out and walk!" he screamed.

She looked at him with wide eyes and pursed lips. "Don't speak to me like that!"

"Then don't insult my friend."

He accelerated, and the car choked and Arthur struggled to get it moving. Amelia rolled her eyes at him, as they both listened to the engine splutter before it finally stalled. This made him even angrier.

"Get out and push."

"No way, I'm not going to do that. You get out and start pushing." She locked her door and leaned back in her seat, her feet resting on the dashboard.

He shot her a hostile look, and she froze like a deer caught in the headlights.

"If you want to get home, Amelia, I highly suggest you get out and push."

She pressed her lips into a thin line, a bitter expression forming on her face.

"Please don't force me to do this. I'm going to freeze out there."

"Get. Out. And. Push."

His words cut through her like a knife, and she knew he wasn't going to budge on this. Something had changed in him since she'd been gone, and she didn't like the way he looked at her with disgust. She could feel herself losing her grip on him, which she also didn't like. If she wanted to keep him, she'd have to step up and be extra nice. She needed him to pander to her every whim. That's what she had found appealing about him, right from the beginning of their relationship; he would do anything for her. Now he was staring at her with hatred in his eyes, and she wasn't sure if she would ever be able to persuade him to do anything for her ever again.

She remained silent as she opened the door, fully aware that this time she had lost the battle. The blast of cold air hit her hard, nearly knocking her to the ground. The snow was falling heavily, and she had to push her way to the back of the car through the icy slush in completely unsuitable footwear. For the first time in her life, she regretted wearing heels.

She gripped the car tightly; and braced herself, ready for whatever Arthur was about to do.

As Arthur started the car, she could hear the engine sputtering and whining. She pushed. She didn't feel strong enough for this. Her arms still ached where the cannula had been inserted to take numerous blood samples. So many she felt faint at the thought. The wheels started to slide across the sludge, splattering her sleek black pants and cream cashmere sweater.

"Great," she muttered as she pushed again.

The car jerked forward, causing her to fall forwards into the snow. She looked down at her ruined sweater and heard Arthur laughing inside the car. Her blood began to boil, and her heart rate increased with every chuckle that came from Arthur's mouth. She yanked the door open, her blue eyes turning a menacing black.

It caught Arthur off guard. Amelia's face became twisted and distorted as she climbed in and grabbed him by the throat. She yanked him towards her, making his neck click. With her face just inches away from his, he could smell garlic on her breath as she spat out the words.

"Don't you fucking dare make me do that again, you little viper."

Her voice had lowered to a level he had never heard before. It was almost like a man's voice was talking through her, and she dug her nails into his skin, as if to drive the point home.

Her words cut through him like glass, and he felt a surge of pain in his neck. He couldn't breathe properly and although he tried to push her hand away, she was surprisingly strong—stronger than he had ever known her to be. Her pupils dilated until they took up most of the whites of her eyes; it was as if she was on drugs.

She eventually loosened her grip and sat back into her seat, breathing calmly as though nothing had ever happened. Her eyes returned to their normal blue, she repositioned her feet on the dashboard, and settled back down in her seat.

"Do you want to go, or do you want to be snowed in?" The sarcasm in her tone was obvious. She had, it seemed, returned to her normal self.

Arthur flinched as he touched his neck and noticed the small nail marks that were now oozing trickles of blood down onto his shirt. She smiled sweetly at him, like a little girl eager to go on a ride. He couldn't say anything because his throat hurt too much to speak, and even if he had wanted to talk, he wouldn't have known what to say to her. He was terrified by what had just occurred. He had a feeling that Amelia wasn't the one who squeezed his neck; he couldn't explain what had, but he knew that there was something evil and unnatural about it. He'd seen something lethal in her eyes, and it terrified him to his core. It wasn't her doing that to him, it was the Taranock. Somehow, it was inside her.

CHAPTER 19
The Truth Comes Out

Trish opened the front door and immediately knew something was wrong. Arthur's face was ashen, and she could see small scratch marks on his neck. He was shaking as he entered the foyer with Amelia's bag, but Amelia was oblivious to Arthur's strange behaviour. She smiled at Trish as though she were an old friend, an unnaturally wide smile that almost reached her cheek bones.

"Hello there, Trish. It's so wonderful to see you again." Amelia hummed seductively.

Trish looked at Arthur, attempting to piece together what might have happened, but he remained poker-faced.

Trish returned her attention to Amelia. "Are you feeling any better?"

Amelia bounced into the lounge and headed straight for the grandfather clock, nodding excitedly. "I'm so glad we didn't get rid of this. It's such a beautiful work of art. Don't you think?"

Trish began to panic, unnerved by Amelia's unusual behaviour. "I would have thought after all that has happened with that thing, you would want to get rid of it," she said.

"Gosh, no! This belongs to the house. This belongs to me." She smiled at Trish while stroking the ornate wooden case.

Arthur sat down, trying to avoid Trish's questioning looks by staring into the fire, the image from earlier still weighing heavily on his mind. He had seen something ancient and evil in Amelia's eyes, something which frightened him, and he couldn't get the image out of his head. He wasn't sure if it was the Taranock somehow living inside her mind. He felt it was, but how could it have happened? He did, however, know one thing; bringing Amelia back to the house was a mistake. The atmosphere inside had changed dramatically from the moment she stepped inside, and she was now acting even stranger than she had on the drive home.

Amelia was guilty of many things, but she had never used physical violence before, she wouldn't have dared. Besides, she didn't need to, she was very good at playing mind games; it was as if something was inside her manipulating her body. She stood beside the clock, admiring it, as though it were her most treasured possession.

"Would you like to know why this clock is so special to me?" She turned her attention to the others, unable to hide her cruel smile.

Trish glanced at Arthur, who shrugged his shoulders and frowned.

"I suppose so," she replied.

"Because it goes all the way to the thirteenth hour. Would you like to know why it goes to that hour?" Her cruel grin broadened, revealing her pearly-white teeth, and her eyes gleamed with cunning. She appeared to be devising a plan, Arthur could see her mind working like the clock, cogs winding and whirring as she formulated her evil scheme.

"Once again, I suppose so." Trish spat, before Arthur could answer. She was clearly irritated by Amelia's disturbing behaviour.

Amelia laughed as she tapped the side of the clock. "That's when he's at his most powerful."

"Who?" Arthur asked, for the first time appearing interested in the conversation.

"You know who I mean." Amelia extended her arms, as if she were inviting in an unseen guest. "I can still feel him here."

"It's a he?" Trish inquired, looking over at the children who had, until now, been playing quietly in the corner of the room. Now, however, they were looking up at their mother, with smiles on their faces.

"It's Theo! He lives in the clock but comes out to play with us." Charlie chirped happily.

Arthur's stomach dropped at the very mention of the name. He had only just realised that the boys hadn't welcomed their mother back, when usually, they ran to her as soon as she walked through the front door. They hadn't said anything to her or paid any attention to her until now. Amelia, likewise, had yet to acknowledge their presence. Her focus had been on the clock the entire time.

"Why did you say that name, Charlie?" Arthur's hands began to tremble as he spoke. He felt a chill run down his spine as he met the manic gaze of the twins. Their synchronised smiles sent shivers through his entire being, and the way their eyes darted between him and the clock added an eerie intensity to the moment. He couldn't shake off the feeling that something ominous was about to unfold.

"Theo is our friend. He told us that you like that name, so he chose it." Dylan and Charlie said in unison.

"What do you mean, boys? What are you both talking about?" Trish demanded.

Trish felt a knot form in the pit of her stomach as the twins' unblinking gaze shifted to her. The intensity of their stare made her skin crawl, and she couldn't shake off the feeling of being under scrutiny by something otherworldly.

"What ... what's going on?" Arthur stammered, his voice barely above a whisper.

The twins remained silent, their smiles unnervingly fixed, their eyes gleaming with an intensity that seemed to pierce through him. Time seemed to stand still in that room, with only the ticking of the clock echoing in the tense atmosphere.

Arthur's heart raced as he struggled to make sense of the situation. Were they playing some kind of twisted game with him? Or was there something more sinister at play?

Before Trish and Arthur could gather their thoughts, the twins suddenly broke into identical manic grins, their lips curling up in a way that sent a shiver down the spines of their father and aunt. They turned back to their game, playing as if nothing had happened.

Trish and Arthur's eyes met, a silent exchange of shared bewilderment and fear passing between them. Amelia grinned at them as she stood beside the clock, her eyes showing them that she knew what was going on.

"What do we do now?" Trish whispered, her voice barely audible above the pounding of her own heart.

Arthur shook his head, his mind racing with possibilities but finding no explanation.

"I don't know," he admitted, his voice tinged with uncertainty. "But we need to figure it out fast before ... before something else happens."

Trish turned her attention to Amelia, her determination overriding the unease swirling in her stomach. She needed answers, and she knew that Amelia might hold some clue to the bizarre behaviour of the twins.

"Amelia, do you have any idea what's going on?" Trish asked, her voice steady despite the turmoil within her.

Amelia nodded eagerly. "Yes, I do. But why should I tell you?"

Trish couldn't contain her frustration any longer. She threw her hands up in exasperation, the weight of uncertainty and confusion bearing down on her.

"Just tell us!" Arthur shouted.

"This is insane!" Trish exclaimed. "You need to tell us what you know. You said it is a male, yes? What does he want with us?"

Amelia nodded, grinning from ear to ear. "Of course, couldn't you tell?"

Trish sighed and rolled her eyes. "Actually Amelia, I was too preoccupied with its disgusting face to notice it's gender. Anyway, how do you know all of this? You've not even been here, you were in the hospital, so you didn't see the Taranock get banished from the house."

Amelia's devious smile faded and was replaced by a scowl. "Do you really believe Sandra could exorcise such a malicious demon?"

"Err … Well, we haven't had any problems since, so, yes, I think she did," Trish replied, becoming increasingly nervous about the direction of the conversation.

"Can't you feel him? Can't you feel his powerful energy?"

"No, I cannot, and I think you need to have a lie down or something. You're acting weird. I need to know what the twins are seeing. Who is Theo?"

"I see you enjoy mothering my children, don't you Trish? Perhaps you wish they were yours, rather than mine." She grinned again, her arms folded across her chest. She stared at her as though she were an insect that needed to be stamped on. "I'm willing to bet you even wish Arthur was yours, despite the fact that he's your brother. Maybe that's why you keep giving him money to keep him sweet."

Trish's cheeks flushed with embarrassment, and her face became twisted in rage. She stood up, and Arthur knew exactly what she was about to do. He grabbed her and pulled her back before her fist could make contact with Amelia's face.

"No, Trish. Don't do it. She's not worth it."

"She's a bitch! She's a complete and utter bitch! Give her the divorce papers already!" Trish screamed as she attempted another lunge for Amelia.

"Divorce?" Amelia stared in surprise at Arthur.

Arthur couldn't deny it any longer, besides, Amelia would know if he was telling the truth or not. He sighed and moved away from Trish.

"I do want a divorce, Amelia, and I have the documents all ready for you to sign."

Amelia was taken aback. How dare Arthur divorce her. She was the best thing that he had ever had. No other woman would ever get to lay eyes on him, she'd make sure of it.

"I'm not signing them," she stated bluntly.

"Yes, you bloody are," Trish hissed, getting ready to pounce on her again.

"So, let me get this straight. I've been in the hospital, on the verge of death, while you have been encouraging, and no doubt paying for, my husband to divorce me. I'm guessing Graham and Steve are in on this as well."

At that moment, Graham and Steve came in through the front door and kicked off their shoes, which Graham neatly lined up against the wall. They both stopped dead in their tracks when they saw Amelia there. She glared at them, her eyes blazing with fury.

She pointed her finger at them and growled. "Get in here, both of you."

Steve sat down on the sofa casually, ignoring Amelia's menacing stares. Graham trailed behind, his head bowed like a disgraced child. Amelia focused on Graham; she knew he was weaker than the others and would be first to snap if she applied enough pressure.

"Graham, can you tell me who suggested Arthur divorce me? He doesn't have enough brain cells to carry out such a large plan," she asked, pseudo sweetly.

Graham shifted in his seat uncomfortably. "All I know is that Arthur wants a divorce."

She leaned over him with her hands on her hips, and softly, but menacingly, repeated the question. "Whose idea was it?"

He shrugged and turned away from her. "I'm not sure."

"Amelia, leave him alone. Just face the facts: Arthur wants a divorce. I don't know why you're worried, I'm sure everything will work out fine. You can get that dream city apartment you've always wanted." Trish hoped reminding her of this would lighten the mood.

Instead, Amelia's face contorted into such an ugly expression that Arthur couldn't be sure if it was actually her standing there before them. He cast a glance at the twins as they stared at Amelia. He stood up and gathered them into his arms.

"I'm going upstairs with the kids. They shouldn't have to hear about our problems." He led them out of the room, leaving Trish, Graham, and Steve to deal with Amelia's rage. She didn't even bother looking at the kids; her attention was fixed solely on Graham, who was becoming increasingly anxious. He sunk into the sofa, wishing it would swallow him safely away from Amelia's irate gaze.

"One of you is going to tell me the truth. So, whose idea was it for Arthur to divorce me?"

"It was mine," Trish said, getting up and facing Amelia. She wasn't scared of her. She despised the bitch Amelia had become; she had turned her brother into nothing more than a shell.

Amelia stalked across the room, stopping only a few inches from Trish's face. "It had to be you. You simply cannot allow your brother to be happy. You even have to get involved in our marriage."

Trish grinned. "It's a very rare occasion I see him happy. He's told us everything, all about your manipulative ways, including the murder of your poor, innocent mother."

Amelia froze, her gaze fixed firmly on Trish. Trish could see that she had struck a nerve with her when her breathing dramatically changed. Amelia's left eye twitched as she contorted her face into a scowl. Her eyes darkened to almost black, and the air around her seemed to become dense and heavy. Trish instinctively backed away from Amelia in case she swung for her. Amelia could feel everyone's attention on her as she stood in the middle of the room. For the first time she was lost for words. They all knew. They all knew what she had done to her mother, and how she had manipulated Arthur.

"As I said, it's best to get a divorce and that way no one will ever speak about what you have done. How does that sound?"

Something snapped inside Amelia, and she snarled at Trish. The intensity of Amelia's stare put Trish on edge, she couldn't believe what she was seeing. They all watched as Amelia's face began to twist and morph into something evil. Her skin grew pale, almost transparent, revealing the veins beneath. Her hair darkened, becoming lank and greasy and her lungs erupted in a high-pitched howl; the furniture vibrated around them. Her eyes were the most terrifying, they were jet black; deep obsidian pools of hatred, identical to the Taranock's.

Trish recoiled in horror as she witnessed the sudden transformation. The once-familiar face contorted into something grotesque and malevolent. She stumbled backward, her heart pounding in her chest as she struggled to comprehend the nightmarish scene unfolding before her.

The intensity of Amelia's stare bore into Trish, filling her with a primal fear. The air around them seemed to crackle with dark energy, and Trish could feel the hairs on the back of her neck stand on end.

"What ... what's happening?" Trish asked, her voice trembling.

But there was no answer, only the unearthly screech that emanated from Amelia's twisted form.

Trish watched in horror as the room vibrated with the sound, the furniture rattling as if in response to some unseen force. Her mind raced with fear and confusion, her instincts screaming at her to run, to flee from whatever unholy entity had possessed Amelia's body. But she was rooted to the spot, unable to tear her gaze away from Amelia's black eyes.

In that moment, Trish realised that they were facing something far beyond their understanding; something ancient and malevolent that sought to consume them all.

Graham and Steve stared, frozen in disbelief, their eyes wide with shock as they witnessed the horrifying transformation. They exchanged a glance, their expressions mirroring each other's.

Amelia clenched her fists and lunged at Trish, who backed away into a corner, terrified of the change in Amelia's appearance.

CHAPTER 20
Possession

Arthur suddenly appeared and grabbed Amelia from behind, throwing her to the ground.

"Steve, Graham, help me!" he shouted.

Before Amelia could kick herself free, Steve and Graham lunged forward and grabbed her arms and legs. The scream coming from Amelia petrified Trish. It didn't sound female. It didn't even sound human. Arthur's suspicions about Amelia were right. The Taranock hadn't gone at all; it was lying in wait, hidden inside Amelia, just waiting to return to the house.

"We'll take her ... the Taranock ... it ... upstairs and lock it in her bedroom." Arthur puffed as he restrained the possessed Amelia.

It screamed and kicked violently, yelling incoherent words at them as they dragged it up the stairs to the bedroom. It was stronger than the three men combined, and they struggled to detain it, the veins on its face bursting from the strain of screaming.

"Trish, get the bedroom key from inside the door!" Arthur shouted over his shoulder.

Trish retrieved the old-fashioned key and thrust it into the outside lock. The others made their way out of the room, and Arthur slammed the door shut.

"Keep the handle in place so she can't escape!"

Graham and Steve held the handle tightly in place, while Arthur turned the key until he heard a click. Amelia, or the thing which possessed her, banged on the door and kicked it, and her voice grew deeper and more aggressive. They paused, trying to catch their breath as they listened to the wailing coming from the other side of the door.

"Dad?" a small voice called from behind them.

They turned to see the twins standing in the hallway, staring fearfully at the bedroom door.

"Shit," Arthur hissed loudly. "We must get the children out of here. They cannot see their mother like this."

Trish nodded. "I'll take them out for a bit."

She took their hands in hers and led them down the stairs. She began singing loudly to distract them from the terrible noise their mother was making.

"What should we do now?" Graham asked, his voice trembling.

Arthur was at a loss for words. What could they possibly do? Amelia obviously needed help and support, but it wasn't a doctor she needed. She needed someone spiritual who understood how to deal with situations like this. What she needed was an exorcist.

"I think two of us should stay here and keep an eye on Amelia, while the others bring the twins to our house to keep them safe," Steve expressed his thoughts aloud.

"Trish can take the kids out shopping or something to take their mind off things and then they can stay over at yours. I want them as far away from here as possible until their mother calms down," said Arthur, nodding in agreement. "Graham and I will stay here and try to work something out. We need Sandra and Ardy here."

"I'll call Sandra when I get home," Steve said over his shoulder as he dashed down the stairs, leaving a glum-looking Graham and Arthur to deal with the banging and screaming.

"I hope this door holds," Graham mumbled.

The front door opened and closed, and then there was silence downstairs.

Arthur grabbed Graham's arm and pulled him away from the deafening noise. "Would you like a cup of coffee?" he asked, calmly.

He could tell Graham was struggling to keep it together. He was sweating profusely and nervously picking at his fingers. Arthur needed Graham to remain calm as well, otherwise he feared they would both lose their minds.

The two men sat at the kitchen table, trying desperately to ignore the noise coming from upstairs. Graham frowned before taking a sip, his mind was clearly elsewhere. He was nervous of anything supernatural at the best of times, and now he seemed to be in the middle of a particularly terrifying haunting. Goosebumps began to appear on his arms as he thought back to his encounter with his father, even though he knew that it wasn't actually his real father. He was petrified of what had happened, and he couldn't go through something like that again. Things like this shouldn't happen in real life. It was as if they were both in a horror film, but unlike the real actors, they didn't know how it ended.

"What are you thinking?" Arthur asked, his voice soft.

Graham sighed, unsure what to say. He didn't want to admit to Arthur that he was scared. His mind was racing, and it didn't help that Amelia, or whatever she had become, was still screaming at the top of her lungs upstairs. He took another sip before setting the cup down.

"This doesn't seem real to me. I can't get my head around it. What do we do? I mean, we can't leave her upstairs like that forever."

Arthur stared at the indents on the kitchen table, deep in thought. He wished that he could go back to a simpler time, before all this happened.

"First, we'll see if Steve can reach Sandra and Ardy, and then we'll make a plan. We must keep the kids away from the house. It's too dangerous for them to be here, and they're acting strange."

"What if she can't help us? I believe she went into hiding after what happened before."

Arthur could see the desperation in Graham's eyes, the deep frown lines on his brow, and the way he kept picking at one of the indents on the table. Arthur knew that if anything else happened, it may well push Graham over the edge, and he couldn't let that happen to his friend.

"Even if she can't, she might know someone who can help us."

Then a thought occurred to Arthur. The library that had come with the house—nearly every book dealt with the supernatural.

He grabbed Graham's arm and pulled him to his feet. "Come with me."

Graham followed him, wondering what Arthur was up to. Arthur stopped outside the library, and threw open the door, amused by Graham's reaction to the room. His eyes lit up, just like Arthur's had when he had first found it.

"Oh my, I've never been in this room before. This looks amazing." Graham said, spinning around in circles, trying to take it all in.

"This is my safe haven," Arthur said, as he smiled and sat down on the old suede sofa. "I come here to read and, of course, to escape Amelia."

"I'm not surprised at all. I'd love to have a room like this in my house." Graham stroked the leather-bound books, admiring their fine craftsmanship.

"Right, well, I brought you in here for a reason." Arthur gestured toward the books on the shelves. "Take a look at their titles. This library's books all have one thing in common."

"What's that?" Graham asked, scanning the titles.

"Demons, hauntings, and exorcisms," Arthur replied bluntly.

Graham whipped round to face Arthur to see if he was lying. "Why?"

Arthur shrugged. "They were all here before we bought the place, but it's starting to make sense. The previous family may have attempted but failed to get rid of the Taranock."

Graham read the titles of each book as he went through them. "Do you believe they were trying to get rid of him?"

"Well, what do you think? The whole of this library screams of an obsession with the supernatural—" He stopped mid-sentence and looked up at the ceiling. "It's stopped."

For the first time in a while, Graham could only hear Arthur's breathing as he sat there staring upward. "Maybe she's asleep?"

From upstairs, a soft rapping sound could be heard. There was no obvious reason for it. It was muffled and very peculiar. Both of their senses were heightened, focused on the sound, attempting to decipher what it was and what might be causing it. Arthur turned to Graham and motioned for him to follow.

As Graham followed Arthur up the stairs, an odd sensation crept up his spine. With his heart pounding and his legs trembling, he began to fear that any more jump scares and he may well have a heart attack.

Arthur pressed his finger to his lips and pulled out the bedroom key from his pocket. He paused for a moment, hoping that he was making the right decision, and that she wouldn't pounce on them the moment he opened the door.

The door clicked unlocked, louder than Arthur would have liked, and he froze, listening to see if Amelia had also heard it. There was nothing, only silence. As quietly as he could, he opened the door slowly.

An icy cold draught curled around them, and they couldn't see anything at first. Arthur moved into the centre of the room, and saw Amelia standing in the corner, tapping her head lightly against the wall.

Amelia hadn't noticed Arthur behind her, nor could she hear him talking to her. Her mind, it seemed, was no longer her own. A tremendous pressure had taken over, clouding her feelings and thoughts. Anger was starting to build up inside her, but it wasn't her rage, it was the Taranock's. She could feel his presence inside her, he was taking over everything, manipulating her mind and body. She wanted to scream and shout, but all she could manage was a faint wail.

With bated breath, Arthur touched Amelia's trembling form, his heart pounding in his chest as he braced himself for whatever horrors awaited him. And as his hand made contact with her skin, he felt a surge of dark energy pass between them.

"Amelia?" he asked, trying to keep his voice steady. Arthur's fear gripped him tightly, like a vice constricting around his chest.

"Is she alright?" Graham asked, peering into the room to see what was going on.

Amelia looked up at Arthur, her eyes pleading. "You should stay away from me." Her voice was coarse and uncharacteristic. Arthur could feel her shoulders tense and her face was contorted and unnatural. "I can't stop it. It's too strong."

"You need to fight this. You have to," Arthur whispered, while stroking her hair.

"I can't. I can't," she cried. She smacked her head against the wall once more, this time harder. The force would normally have knocked a person out, but it only aggravated her. "You need to leave!"

Graham grabbed Arthur from her and yanked him away. "Let's go. Leave her alone. We'll figure something out downstairs."

When Amelia saw Graham, she lunged at him, her fingers outstretched, intent on clawing his face, but before she could reach him, Arthur shoved him out of the way.

"Amelia, stop!" Arthur shouted grabbing her round the waist.

She struggled against Arthur's grip, letting out an ear-splitting scream. The pain was unbearable, and Graham fled the room, terrified for his life, leaving Arthur to deal with Amelia. She tried to wriggle free while clawing at his arms, and he retaliated by launching her across the room onto the bed. He quickly shut and locked the bedroom door before she got a chance to attack him again.

She didn't bother trying to escape this time. There was no banging or kicking on the door, just a quiet sobbing.

Arthur knew that Amelia was in danger. This thing was taking her over, and she wasn't strong enough to prevent it from doing so. He may have despised her, but he couldn't leave her like that. He had to think of a plan, something that would help her be rid of the Taranock for good.

The sobbing stopped and a deafening silence took over. Arthur sighed with relief, but remained outside the door for a minute to make sure she wouldn't start again.

As he returned downstairs, he saw Trish standing on the front doorstep with the twins and a bag full of toys, hesitant to take a step in.

"Is it safe to return?"

Arthur nodded. "For the time being. Take them upstairs. They can play in their room for a bit while we figure out what to do."

Trish agreed and took the boys to their room with a bag of new toys to play with before returning to Arthur in the foyer.

"There are a few things that I need to do at the office. I won't be long, I promise. I'll be back as soon as I can," She placed her hand on Arthur's shoulder and gave him a reassuring smile. "My phone is on loud if you need me."

"Thanks," Arthur said as he opened the front door for her. "Please don't be long."

"I won't," she shouted over her shoulder as she left.

He returned to the library to find Graham rocking back and forth on the sofa, muttering to himself. He was pale and obviously terrified.

"I don't think I can take it much longer," Graham muttered, running his fingers through his hair.

Arthur took a seat beside him and put an arm around his shoulders. "I know, mate, but we have to keep our cool, for Amelia's sake."

"I would never have believed it, if someone had told me that one day I would be fighting a demon."

Arthur sighed. "In many ways, we're all fighting our own demons."

"But not like this. This is ridiculous. It's like being in a horror movie, where no one knows who's who."

Arthur chuckled. "I suppose. I mean, it's quite comical when you think about it."

"How can you be so calm about this?"

"Because if I flake now, who is going to help Amelia?"

Graham shrugged. "Maybe it's her own fault. She's always been a bitch to you. Perhaps she deserves this."

"No one deserves this. I wouldn't wish this on my worst enemy."

"However, your worst enemy is experiencing it right now," Graham whispered.

Graham was right, Amelia was his worst enemy. It hadn't always been like that, but he had grown to despise her, especially in the last few years. Arthur remained silent. Graham bit his tongue, realising he might have touched a nerve in Arthur, and decided to return to scanning the titles of the books in the library.

"Have you found anything useful?" Arthur asked.

Graham picked up a book and tossed it to Arthur. "She needs an exorcism."

Arthur flipped through the pages, coming across words he didn't recognise, mostly Latin words that were difficult to pronounce.

"I don't understand any of this," he said as he put it down it beside him.

"We need someone who can perform exorcisms. It would appear that is the only way to rid Amelia of the Taranock possessing her."

A knock at the door interrupted their conversation. Graham went to answer it. He was only gone for a few seconds before reappearing with Steve behind him.

"I'm hoping you have some good news, Steve," Arthur muttered.

"Um, yes and no, mate. The bad news is that Sandra will not return to the house, but the good news is that she knows someone who can help us, and they're only a few miles away."

"Why won't she return?" Arthur asked, but he already knew the answer. Sandra was too scared to come back and help. She had killed her husband and had got away with it.

"She didn't give a reason," Steve replied. He looked at Arthur, knowing exactly what he was thinking.

"Thought so." Arthur grimaced.

"Don't go there. Right now, we need to stay focused on helping Amelia," Steve warned, sitting down beside Arthur and picking up the book of exorcisms.

"Sandra said she knows a priest who performs exorcisms, but he would need evidence first."

"Why does he need evidence?" Graham asked.

"Because, he needs permission from the local bishop before performing an exorcism. Sandra gave me the priest's phone number, and I've already called him."

Arthur gave Steve a puzzled look. "Permission from the local bishop?"

"Yes."

"What did the priest say when you rang him?" Graham asked.

"He wants to meet in person, so he'll be coming here. He's the priest at St Ben's, the Catholic church on the other side of town. It's a few miles away."

Arthur's trembling hands betrayed the depth of his anxiety as he grappled with the looming prospect of the priest's arrival. The fear of the Taranock's potential aggression weighed heavily on his mind, threatening to engulf him in a whirlwind of uncertainty and dread.

"What if the Taranock attacks him?"

"I told him that Arthur, but he said he needs to see evidence of the possession, and the best way to do that is to come here. We just need to keep Amelia calm when he arrives."

Arthur pulled down his top to reveal claw marks on his neck. "This happened when I picked her up from the hospital. What makes you think she'll be calm if she sees a priest in the house? She'll totally flip out!"

Arthur felt a surge of frustration and helplessness. The marks served as a stark reminder of the dangers they faced, not only from Amelia, but also from the Taranock.

"She may or may not, but he was adamant about coming here."

"OK, fine, when does he want to come?" Arthur muttered.

"As quickly as possible. I've asked my mother to watch your children. We need as many adults as possible in case Amelia attacks one of us."

"Oh, your mother's coming? I haven't seen her in a long time." Graham grinned.

"She's already on her way. I just told her there was an emergency and asked if she could watch a friend's kids while we dealt with it. She enjoys working with children, so jumped at the opportunity." He looked at his watch, and quickly glanced out of the window.

"She'll be at ours soon. I'll take the boys over now and call you in a minute. You'd better get yourselves ready."

Steve rushed up the stairs. He knocked on the twins' door quietly before opening it, finding a bizarre sight in the middle of the bedroom.

His heart skipped a beat as he stepped into the room, his senses on high alert at the sight before him. The strange arrangement of sticks in the shape of a star filled him with a sense of unease, their presence casting a pall over the room. The bag of new toys had been left untouched in the corner of the room.

"Charlie, Dylan, what are you doing?" Steve's voice was tinged with a mixture of curiosity and apprehension as he addressed the boys.

The twins turned to face him, their expressions unreadable as they regarded him with an air of solemnity.

"We're making a spell," Charlie explained, his voice surprisingly shrill with excitement.

Dylan nodded in agreement, his eyes shining with a sense of determination.

"Theo told us to do it," he added, his words sending a chill down Steve's spine.

As Steve's gaze swept over the scene before him, his eyes fell upon the knife lying beside the twins, its presence sending a jolt of fear through his veins. His mind raced with a flurry of questions, each more urgent than the last.

With cautious steps, Steve approached the knife, his senses screaming danger at him as he examined it closely. Its blade gleamed in the dim light of the room, its edges sharp and menacing.

Beside the knife lay an empty bowl; its significance shrouded in mystery. What had the twins intended to place in it?

But it was the inscription in chalk at the centre of the makeshift star that captured Steve's attention, its meaning eluding him like a riddle waiting to be solved. He squinted, trying to decipher the cryptic symbols but the message remained stubbornly unintelligible.

"Who wrote this?" he asked, his voice tinged with fear.

Charlie and Dylan exchanged glances, their smiles turning to sneers. For a moment, neither of them spoke, the silence stretching taut between them like a tightly wound spring.

Finally, Charlie cleared his throat, his voice barely above a whisper. "Theo told us what to draw," he confessed. "We aren't meant to tell you."

Steve stared at them, trying to work out if they were playing around or if what they were saying was true.

"Who is Theo?"

"He's our friend. He plays with us. He said that this will help him stay here with us, so he can play with us forever and won't have to leave. He told us to do this." Charlie explained.

Steve's heart sank at Charlie's words, a cold knot of dread settling in the pit of his stomach. The realisation that Theo was not merely a figment of the boys' imaginations, but a malevolent presence with a sinister agenda, sent a quiver through his body. The thought of the Taranock acting as an innocent child and manipulating the twins for his own twisted purposes filled him with a mix of anger and fear.

Struggling to maintain his composure, Steve reached out to the twins, his voice gentle but firm. "Charlie, Dylan, listen to me carefully," he began, his words weighted with his own terror and fear for the boys' safety. "Theo is not your friend. Whatever he's told you, he's not here to play with you. He's dangerous, and you need to come with me."

"But if we don't do this, Theo will be upset with us," Dylan said angrily.

Steve kicked the sticks out of place, destroying the formation of the star. For a moment, there was silence in the room, broken only by the sound of splintering wood and the shuffling of feet. The twins watched in wide-eyed astonishment as Steve dismantled the spell they had worked so hard to create.

"Collect your things. You're both coming with me," Steve demanded, his voice grim at the thought of the Taranock getting to the twins without any of them realising. "I want no more talk about this 'Theo'."

Steve shuddered at the implications of what could have happened if he hadn't got to their room in time. What did the Taranock want with the twins? He watched as the boys silently picked up a pile of their clothes and teddy from each of their beds to take with them. They glanced at each other, their eyes staring. There was a solemnity to their movements, a sense of shared understanding that transcended words. It was as if they were communicating on a level beyond the ordinary, their connection forged by a telepathic wave which only they possessed.

They moved quickly past Steve, their silence deafening. He followed them down the stairs, observing their movements as they passed Graham and Arthur. As Steve followed the twins through the foyer, he couldn't shake the feeling of unease that settled over him like a heavy cloak. Their hurried movements and stony silence spoke volumes.

Graham's eyes met Arthur's, a silent exchange of understanding passing between them. They both knew that something was amiss, that the twins' sudden silence was a clear sign that something had happened upstairs.

"Are you okay, boys?" Arthur asked as he glanced at Steve.

Steve shook his head, his face full of worry. "I'll tell you later," he mouthed.

The twins stopped at the front door and turned to face Arthur and Graham. "We're fine," they said in unison.

Their synchronised voices sent a shiver down Arthur's spine. "Are you sure?"

"Yeah," Dylan said, a small smile playing at the corners of his lips.

"I'll take them to mine ... away from this place," Steve said, his voice full of dread. "I'll be back soon."

The twins opened the front door without waiting for Steve and began walking down the steps.

Steve turned his attention to Arthur. "I'll tell you what happened when I come back."

"What do you think Steve was on about?" Arthur asked.

"He will tell us when he's back. From the look on his face, he seemed pretty disturbed."

CHAPTER 21
Father Abraham

The front door slammed behind Steve as he returned to talk to Arthur and Graham. He paused for a moment, breathing in the last of the crisp winter air before the warmth of the house hit him.

Arthur stood at the window in the lounge, gazing out at the last of the sun's rays illuminating the frosty, overgrown garden, which appeared sad and abandoned. The neglected rose bushes just outside the window were a brief distraction before he turned his attention to Steve standing in the doorway.

"Don't worry, mate, this will soon be over," Steve said as he entered the lounge.

"I hope you're right," he replied, his expression strained with weariness. "We've been through so much already. I just want this nightmare to end."

Graham nodded in agreement from the sofa, his eyes reflecting the weariness etched into Arthur's features.

"We'll get through this together," he said, his voice filled with quiet resolve. "We won't let the Taranock win."

As the last of the sun's rays faded from view, casting the room into shadow, Arthur felt a glimmer of hope stir within him.

"What time will the priest get here?"

"After dark. He said evil stirs more at night than during the day ... or something like that. I can't quite remember, but he'll be here once the sun goes down," Steve said, taking a seat next to Graham. He looked anxiously at Arthur with his hands tightly clasped together resting on his legs. "I need to talk to you about the twins."

Arthur nodded gravely, his attention fully focused on his friend as he took a seat opposite Graham. "Of course," he replied, his voice calm despite the undercurrent of concern that pulsed through him. "What happened with the twins?"

Steve hesitated for a moment, his gaze flickering between Arthur and Graham before he spoke.

"I'm worried about them," he admitted, his face filled with genuine concern. "They've been acting strangely lately, especially since ... well, you know."

Arthur's heart clenched at the mention of recent events, the memory of their harrowing ordeal still fresh in his mind.

"What do you mean?" Graham asked, his tone mirroring Arthur's concern. "What happened upstairs?"

Steve sighed, running a hand through his hair in frustration. "It's hard to explain," he began, his words hesitant. "They've been distant, secretive almost. And the way they talk about this Theo ... it's like he's some sort of imaginary friend to them. I caught them doing something ... strange in their room."

Arthur's stomach churned at the mention of Theo, the mysterious figure who seemed to hold a malevolent sway over their lives. The triplet that should have been called Theo. He exchanged a worried glance with Graham.

"Tell us what happened," Graham said gently. He placed his hand on Steve's shoulder, watching as his friend struggled to get his words out.

"Well, as I entered the twins' bedroom, I saw that they were trying to conjure up a type of spell." He breathed heavily, trying to find an explanation for what he'd seen. "They'd brought in sticks from outside and made a star shape in the middle of their room. They had a knife."

As Steve recounted his unsettling discovery, a heavy silence settled over the room, punctuated only by the sound of his laboured breathing. Arthur's eyes widened in shock at the mention of the knife, his mind reeling with the implications of his sons' actions.

"A knife?" Arthur echoed, his voice thick with disbelief. "What were they planning to do with it?"

Steve shook his head. "I'm not sure," he admitted. "But whatever it was, it didn't feel right. The whole thing gave me chills. The twins are acting weird. How can they possibly know about spells, or whatever they were trying to achieve?"

Graham's grip tightened on Steve's shoulder, a silent gesture of support and understanding.

"Did they say anything to you?" he asked.

Steve nodded, his gaze fixed on the floor as he struggled to find the right words. "They mentioned Theo," he explained, his voice barely above a whisper. "They said he told them to do it, that it would help him stay with them."

"Who is Theo?" Graham asked, his attention turning to Arthur.

Arthur sat there quietly, taking it all in before speaking, his voice grave. "Theo was the name that I had chosen for my third child. The twins were meant to be triplets, but Theo was stillborn. Amelia doesn't know that I called the third triplet Theo. She hadn't wanted to give him a name.

It was her way of grieving. She didn't want anything to do with Theo's funeral. To her, Theo never existed."

As Arthur's revelation hung heavy in the air, a palpable sense of sorrow settled over the room, casting a shadow over the men's already heavy hearts. Graham's expression softened with empathy.

"I had no idea, Arthur," Graham said softly. "I can't imagine what you must have gone through."

Arthur nodded. His gaze remained fixed on the floor as memories of his lost child flooded his mind.

"Losing Theo was the hardest thing I've ever had to endure," he admitted, his voice wavering slightly. "And watching Amelia unable to grieve properly and become this stone-hearted person ... it was unbearable."

Steve remained silent, his own sadness mirrored in the lines etched into his weary face. He couldn't imagine the pain of losing a child, let alone the burden of carrying that loss in secret for so long.

"This thing that the kids are playing with isn't Theo." Arthur said, glancing up from the floor at Steve. "It must be the Taranock. Tell me more about what the twins were up to in their room."

Steve shifted uncomfortably in his seat, grappling with Arthur's assertion and the weight of the truth behind it. He took a deep breath, gathering his thoughts before speaking.

"I wish I could give you a clear answer but what I saw in the twins' room ... it didn't feel like anything I've ever encountered before." He paused, searching for the right words to convey the unsettling nature of his discovery. "The sticks arranged in that star shape with a strange inscription in the middle, the knife, the empty bowl ... it all seemed ritualistic," he explained, his voice heavy with unease. "And the way they talked about Theo, as if he were guiding them from beyond the grave ... it just doesn't sit right with me. It must have something to do with the Taranock. I've an awful feeling that it's using the twins to get to this side."

Graham's brow furrowed in concern as he processed Steve's words. "Do you think they're in danger?"

Steve hesitated, his expression troubled. "I think they are," he admitted. "Whatever's happening, it's clear that the twins are caught in the middle of something dark and dangerous. We need to keep them away from this house until the Taranock is gone. They can stay at ours for however long this takes."

Arthur nodded in agreement. "Thank you. I don't want them coming back here until I know that this place is free from the Taranock."

A loud knock at the door interrupted them. The sudden interruption sent a jolt of apprehension through the room, the tension thickening with each passing moment. Arthur's heart pounded in his chest as he exchanged worried glances with Graham and Steve.

"Who could that be?" Graham whispered, his voice barely audible over the pounding of their hearts.

Steve rose from his seat, his steps slow and cautious as he made his way towards the door.

"I'll go check. It's probably the priest," he said quietly, his hand hovering over the doorknob.

With a deep breath, Steve swung the door open, revealing the figure standing on the doorstep.

"Father Abraham," Steve said. "Thank you for coming."

As Father Abraham stepped into the light of the foyer, his presence seemed to cast a chill over the room, his dark coat billowing around him like a cloak of solemnity. Steve's gaze lingered on the priest's weathered face, his features etched with determination and a hint of weariness, his greying hair plastered against his forehead. From under the priest's coat Steve caught a glimpse of the white collar around his neck.

Father Abraham brushed the flakes of fresh snow from his shoes on the doormat, a stark reminder of the bitter cold that lingered outside.

"Thank you for coming, Father," Arthur said as Father Abraham entered the lounge. "We're grateful for your help."

Father Abraham nodded solemnly as he stepped into the lounge, his gaze sweeping over the faces of the three men as Steve bypassed him to sit down.

Despite the weariness etched into his features, there was a sense of determination in his eyes, a steely resolve that spoke of his unwavering commitment to his duty.

"It's my duty to help those in need," Father Abraham replied, his voice calm but resolute. "And I've been told that you are in need of assistance."

Arthur nodded, a sense of gratitude washing over him at the priest's words.

"We've been through a lot," he said. "But with your guidance, I believe we can put an end to this darkness once and for all."

Father Abraham nodded, offering Arthur a reassuring smile. "Of course. If there is evil here, I will coax it out." He looked around the lounge, his eyes resting on the grandfather clock in the corner.

As Father Abraham's gaze settled on the grandfather clock, Arthur shivered violently, even though he was sitting by the fireplace. The clock had long been a source of unease for him, its ominous ticking a constant reminder of the malevolent presence that lingered within its depths.

"Do you sense anything, Father?" Arthur asked, watching the priest nervously.

Father Abraham's brow furrowed in concentration as he studied the clock, his eyes narrowed in deep thought. After a moment of silence, he turned back to Arthur with a grave expression.

"Nothing," he said quietly, his voice certain. "But it could be hiding from me. Where's the young woman who's possessed? I need to see her."

Steve pointed toward the ceiling. "She's in her room."

"Take me to her," Father Abraham said.

Arthur felt a flicker of disappointment at Father Abraham's initial assessment, but he knew better than to let it diminish their resolve. If the Taranock was indeed hiding, they would find a way to coax it out into the light.

"Follow me," Steve said as he led the way towards Amelia's room.

As they ascended the stairs, Arthur's heart pounded in his chest, his thoughts consumed by the impending confrontation. He couldn't shake the feeling of unease that gnawed at him; a sense of foreboding that seemed to grow stronger with each step.

When they reached Amelia's door, Arthur hesitated for a moment before unlocking it and pushing it open, revealing the dimly lit room beyond. Arthur's gaze swept over the scene before him, his heart sinking at the sight of his wife lying motionless on the bed, her eyes vacant and unseeing as she stared out of the window.

Father Abraham stepped into the room, his presence commanding as he approached the bed. He studied Amelia's form with a critical eye, concentrating hard as he assessed the extent of her possession.

Amelia turned her head to look at Father Abraham. "What's going on?"

Father Abraham approached the bed, his expression filled with concern as he met Amelia's gaze. "My dear," he said gently, his voice calm and reassuring, "your family believes that you may be under the influence of a malevolent force. But fear not, I am here to help you."

Amelia's brow furrowed in confusion, her eyes clouded with uncertainty. "I don't understand," she said.

"Something dark may have taken hold of you," Father Abraham explained, his tone solemn but resolute. "But with your cooperation, we can work together to cast it out and restore you to your true self."

Amelia's gaze flickered between Father Abraham and the others in the room, her expression a mixture of anger and disbelief.

"What are you talking about?" she snapped. "What darkness? I was locked in here by my *loving* husband because we were arguing."

Arthur was taken aback by Amelia's sudden wellness. "No … we were not arguing. You're possessed by the Taranock, Amelia."

Amelia sat up in bed, glaring straight at Arthur. "No, I'm not. That woman got rid of it, remember?"

Father Abraham glanced over his shoulder at Arthur. "What's going on here?"

Father Abraham's wide-eyed glance at Arthur mirrored the confusion and concern that pulsed through the room. Arthur's heart sank as he struggled to find the right words to explain the situation, his mind racing with the implications of Amelia's outburst.

"Father, please, you must understand," Arthur began, his voice filled with urgency. "We believe that Amelia may be under the influence of something dark and malevolent. The Taranock."

Father Abraham frowned, his expression troubled as he turned back to face Amelia. "My dear, we only want to help you," he said gently, his tone pleading. "We believe that you may be in danger, and we are here to protect you."

Amelia's gaze softened slightly at Father Abraham's words, but the anger in her eyes remained.

"I don't need your help," she said defiantly. "I need to get out of this room and away from all of you. I want to eat something. I haven't eaten all day because I've been stuck in here!"

Father Abraham's mind raced as he tried to make sense of the perplexing situation before him. The uncertainty weighed heavily on his shoulders as he grappled with the possibility that Amelia's predicament was not as straightforward as it seemed.

Could she truly be a victim of demonic possession, or was there a more mundane explanation for all of this?

As he backed away from Amelia, Father Abraham's gaze remained fixed on her, searching for any sign or clue that might shed light on the truth. But try as he might, he found no evidence of the tell-tale signs of possession that he had encountered in the past. Instead, Amelia appeared to be a perfectly ordinary woman, frustrated and confused by the circumstances surrounding her confinement.

Father Abraham sighed in frustration as he considered his next course of action. He knew that he could not jump to conclusions without further investigation. He turned to Arthur, Graham, and Steve, his expression demanding an explanation for the confusing situation they found themselves in. His eyes held a mixture of concern and determination, his resolve unwavering despite the uncertainty about Amelia's apparent possession.

"Something isn't adding up here," Father Abraham said firmly, his voice cutting through the tension that hung heavy in the air. "I need to know the truth. What exactly is going on?"

Arthur exchanged a worried glance with Graham and Steve before speaking, "She's lying, Father. She is possessed. The Taranock is hiding from you. Please believe us."

"He's telling you the truth, Father," Steve said, coming to Arthur's aid.

Father Abraham turned his gaze to Steve and Graham, studying them intently for a moment before nodding in acknowledgment.

"Thank you for your honesty," he said, eyeing them all suspiciously. "It's imperative that we approach this situation with transparency and unity if we hope to succeed."

Father Abraham's attention shifted back to Amelia, his expression softening. "Amelia," he said gently, his voice calm and reassuring, "why don't you go and make yourself some food? You must be hungry after being cooped up in your room all day."

Amelia hesitated for a moment, her gaze switching between Father Abraham and the others in the room. Though uncertainty still lingered in her eyes, there was also a glimmer of relief at the prospect of being able to leave her confinement, even if only for a short while.

"Thank you," she said quietly, her voice filled with fake gratitude as she got out of bed. With a nod of acknowledgment, she turned and made her way out of the room, her steps hesitant but determined.

Father Abraham descended the stairs quietly, his footsteps barely making a sound as he followed Amelia. He noticed the confusion in her gaze as she glanced over her shoulder, her expression questioning his presence behind her.

"Amelia," Father Abraham said gently, his voice reassuring, "I just wanted to make sure you are all right. Is there anything I can do to help?"

"No, I'm fine," she snapped.

Arthur, Steve, and Graham appeared behind Father Abraham, watching her closely as she began making herself a sandwich in the kitchen.

As Father Abraham quietly pulled out a small bottle of holy water from his pocket, the others watched in anticipation, their eyes fixed on Amelia.

The tension in the air was palpable as they waited for Father Abraham to take action.

With a silent nod to the others, Father Abraham stepped forward, his gaze never leaving Amelia as he approached her. He held the bottle of holy water tightly in his hand, its sacred contents a potent weapon against the Taranock.

Amelia glanced up from her task, her eyes widening in surprise as she noticed Father Abraham's approach.

"What are you doing?" she asked, staring at the small bottle gripped tightly in his hand.

Father Abraham's expression remained calm and composed as he answered, his voice steady. "I just want to make sure of something," he said gently, his tone filled with sincerity. "This may seem strange, but just trust me."

Amelia's brow furrowed in uncertainty as she regarded Father Abraham, her confusion evident in her eyes.

With a silent prayer, Father Abraham sprinkled a few drops of holy water onto Amelia, watching as they glistened on her skin like tiny beads of light. As the last drop of holy water fell, Father Abraham stepped back, his gaze never leaving Amelia's face.

She flinched at the touch, but remained standing, her eyes boring angrily into his.

"Really? Now I'm all wet." She grabbed a tea towel from nearby and wiped off the holy water. "What are you trying to achieve here? You think I'm possessed? Maybe you should look at my husband and his friends. They're the ones who need help, not me."

The tension in the air grew denser as Father Abraham glared angrily at Arthur. "She's not possessed. The holy water did not have any effect."

"I ... I don't understand," Arthur stammered, his voice filled with disbelief. "She was possessed. I swear it!"

"I think this is a matter for a marriage counsellor, not for me. There is no evil in this house."

The tension in the room escalated as Father Abraham's words cut through Arthur like a knife. His heart sank at the realisation that his hopes of finding a quick solution to the Taranock had been dashed.

Amelia smirked at them over Father Abraham's shoulder as she held her sandwich up to take a bite.

"He's right, Arthur. We *do* need a marriage counsellor. It's not normal for a husband to lock his wife in the bedroom after a seemingly innocent argument. We should make an appointment first thing tomorrow morning."

"I was told that there was a possession here. I am a very busy man, gentlemen, and my time here has been wasted. There are no signs that this woman is possessed," he said, pointing to a very smug-looking Amelia.

"I apologise, Father," Arthur said, shaking with anger, trying to ignore Amelia's smirk. "We truly believed that Amelia was under the influence of the Taranock."

Father Abraham's expression softened slightly as he regarded Arthur, his gaze filled with understanding. "I know you acted out of concern for your wife," he said gently. "But it appears that your initial assessment may have been mistaken.

It looks to me that Sandra did banish the Taranock."

Steve's jaw clenched in frustration as he glanced at Amelia, who watched the exchange with a smug expression.

"I can't believe this," he spat, his voice full of venom. "Come with me. I want to show you what Arthur and Amelia's sons did after they listened to the Taranock."

Steve stomped out of the kitchen, gesturing for the priest to follow him. Father Abraham quickened his pace to catch up with Steve as they ascended the stairs, his expression filled with concern.

"Steve, wait," Father Abraham called out. "I know this isn't easy, and I know you all have been through a lot recently. But there is no evidence of evil here. This house is safe."

Steve paused in his tracks, his shoulders tense with frustration as he turned to face Father Abraham.

"It's not safe here, Father. You have to believe us. Amelia is manipulating the situation. The Taranock is here somewhere, probably hiding in plain sight." he said, looking at Father Abraham with desperation in his eyes. "The Taranock can appear in different ways. To Arthur's boys, the demon appears as a small boy called Theo. I'll show you what the demon tried to make them do."

Steve ushered the priest up the rest of the stairs to the twins' room and opened the door, allowing Father Abraham to enter. Steve turned on the light and gasped loudly.

"I don't believe this. This is not possible." Steve groaned as he took in the neat and tidy bedroom, lacking any sign of the ritual the twins had tried to achieve.

Arthur and Graham appeared beside Steve; their faces shocked at how tidy the room was.

"What am I meant to be looking at in here?" Father Abraham asked, his tone growing annoyed with the situation.

"The twins were trying to make a spell to bring the Taranock to them. They had sticks in the shape of a star, and the whole thing was so messed up. They're kids! They shouldn't know any of this stuff." Steve shouted, his voice ringing with frustration.

"And you saw this happen?" Father Abraham asked suspiciously, staring down at the spot where the ritual took place.

"Yes!" Steve cried, throwing his arms up in anger.

Father Abraham knelt and ran his finger across the floor. "This is very hard to believe, gentlemen, but I can assure you now, that there is no possession taking place in this house. My advice is to gather as much evidence as you can if something *is* going on and send it to me, so I can take a look at it." He stood up and faced them, brushing off the dirt from his finger. "The evidence could be photographs, video footage, anything that will help your case. Unfortunately, without that, I am unable to do anything for you."

"What should we do with her down there?" Steve muttered, his shoulders slumping in defeat.

"Leave her be. She is not possessed." Father Abraham replied as he followed Steve, Arthur, and Graham downstairs where Amelia was cheerfully humming to herself in the kitchen.

The tune rang in Graham's ears, making the hairs on the back of his neck stand on end. He peered into the kitchen and watched her hum the tune even louder. Fear gripped him, reminding him of his past. His father used to hum that very tune every night before going to bed.

Graham stared hard at Amelia as she took a bite from her sandwich. She winked at him and grinned maliciously, knowing full well that the tune was coming from the Taranock to taunt Graham.

Graham backed away, nearly colliding with Arthur.

"Watch it, Graham." Arthur muttered, moving out of Graham's way.

"What if she is possessed and you just can't see it?" Graham asked, his voice wavering as he stared at the priest fearfully.

"There would have been a reaction from the holy water if she was possessed," Father Abraham said.

Graham flinched as the priest placed his hand on his shoulder. "I'm scared, Father."

Father Abraham sighed, his shoulders slumping slightly with weariness. "I'm afraid there's not much more I can do," he admitted, his tone regretful. "I must return to my duties at the church but I will keep you all in my prayers, and if you ever need my assistance again, please don't hesitate to reach out. If what you're saying is true and the Taranock is hiding from me, then you should gather up evidence and send it to me. I will then make the necessary arrangements and return."

With a nod of acknowledgment, Father Abraham turned to leave, his footsteps echoing in the silence of the foyer. As the door closed behind him, Arthur, Steve, and Graham were left to grapple with the unsettling realisation that their troubles may be far from over.

CHAPTER 22
Death

The pavements on both sides of the street were bustling with Christmas shoppers, their arms laden with bags and packages as they hurried from store to store in search of the perfect gifts. Laughter and chatter filled the air, mingling with the sound of holiday music drifting from nearby shops. Twinkling lights adorned storefronts, casting a festive glow over the scene as people immersed themselves in the spirit of the season.

As Father Abraham navigated through the bustling streets of Whitely Bay, his mind couldn't shake the troubling thoughts of Arthur and Amelia. Despite the absence of any overt signs of evil in the house, a nagging feeling gnawed at him, whispering warnings of unseen dangers. His grip tightened on the steering wheel, his knuckles turning white with tension as he pondered the enigma.

The festive atmosphere surrounding him seemed at odds with the heaviness in his heart. Christmas decorations adorned the storefronts, and the merry sounds of shoppers filled the air, but for Father Abraham, the holiday cheer felt distant and muted.

As he drove, his gaze flickered from one passing scene to another, his thoughts consumed by the mystery unfolding in Arthur's household. With each passing moment, his determination to uncover the truth deepened, driving him forward through the maze of bustling streets, his mind filling with thoughts of the Taranock. What if they were right and the Taranock was cunning enough to hide from him?

Despite his nagging concerns and gut instincts, Father Abraham knew he had to approach the situation with a healthy dose of scepticism. Without concrete evidence of a possession or any clear signs of malevolent activity within the household, his hands were tied in terms of taking any direct action.

As he continued to drive through the streets of Whitely Bay, his mind raced with possible explanations for the strange occurrences surrounding Arthur and Amelia. Perhaps there were rational, albeit unconventional, explanations for their behaviour that didn't involve supernatural forces. Maybe there were underlying psychological or medical issues at play that required professional intervention.

Father Abraham reminded himself of the importance of not jumping to conclusions or making assumptions based solely on intuition. He knew that as a man of faith and reason, he had to approach the situation with a balanced perspective, seeking truth and understanding above all else.

With a sigh, Father Abraham resolved to keep a watchful eye on the situation, ready to offer support and guidance to Arthur and Amelia should they need it. While he couldn't intervene without evidence, he could still be a source of comfort and counsel in their time of need.

As Father Abraham continued his journey, the scenery began to blur around him, the familiar sights of the bustling town giving way to winding country roads and bare, snow-covered bushes. Trees with a dusting of snow lined the path, their branches stretching out like skeletal fingers against the dark, colourless sky. His headlights lit up the mounds of dirt-coloured snow lining the roads, glistening as his wheels skidded slightly over the ice.

The narrow, winding roads led him deeper into the vast, endless countryside, away from the noise and commotion of the town's Christmas decor. As he drove, the tension that had gripped him slowly began to ease, replaced by a sense of peace and serenity that often accompanied the quietude of nature.

Eventually, the large silhouette of his church came into view in the distance, its weathered stone walls standing as a beacon of solace amidst the rural, barren landscape. He couldn't yet see the track that led him to his church, but he knew he was close. The sight brought a familiar sense of comfort to him, a reminder of the sacred duty that awaited him within those hallowed walls.

As he rounded a tight corner, his eyes caught a fleeting glimpse of something extraordinary—a pair of black wings, large and ethereal, gliding gracefully past his window. His heart skipped a beat as he blinked in disbelief, questioning whether his eyes had deceived him.

As he pondered the mysterious sighting of the wings, he couldn't shake the feeling of curiosity that enveloped him. Despite the inability to discern the exact type of bird, its sheer size had captured his attention, leaving him in a state of awe.

He reached out to the radio, seeking solace in the soothing embrace of music. With a flick of his wrist, soft, gentle melodies filled the car, washing over him like a gentle breeze on a warm summer's day. He smiled to himself as he listened to the sound of a violin playing through the speakers.

He slowed the car to a halt on the side of the road, his senses heightening with anticipation coursing through his veins at the sight of another flicker of wings. With a focused gaze, he scanned the surrounding landscape, his eyes searching for any sign of the mysterious creature that had captured his attention.

The headlights of his car cast elongated shadows across the snow-covered bushes and blanketed fields. He strained his eyes, hoping to catch another glimpse of the being that had eluded him, but could only see the fields of snow.

As he marvelled at the sight of the untouched snow, his reverie was abruptly interrupted by the sudden spluttering and distortion emanating from the radio. The once-soft melody now twisted and warped, the tranquil notes morphing into an unsettling cacophony of static and discord.

Frowning, he reached out to adjust the radio dial, hoping to restore the soothing music that had accompanied his journey moments before. However, his efforts were in vain as the distortion only seemed to intensify, filling the car with an eerie sense of unease.

A chill ran down Father Abraham's spine as he realised the strangeness of the situation. Could this be mere coincidence, or was there something more sinister at play? His mind raced with possibilities, his instincts telling him that there was more to the disturbance than met the eye.

His breath caught in his throat as a sudden low growl erupted from the radio, accompanied by the sound of what he could only interpret as a bird's wings flapping. The hair on the back of his neck stood on end as fear coiled in the pit of his stomach.

The ominous sound seemed to reverberate through the car, drowning out any semblance of rational thought. It was as if a sinister presence had permeated the very fabric of the vehicle, filling the air with an overwhelming sense of dread.

Instinctively, Father Abraham's hand shot out to turn off the radio, desperate to silence the unsettling noise that filled the confined space. But even as the sound faded into silence, its echo lingered, haunting him like a ghostly whisper.

Heart pounding, he struggled to calm his racing thoughts, his mind reeling with the implications of what he had just experienced.

A tap on the windscreen made Father Abraham's heart leap into his throat as he tore his gaze away from the radio to the source of the sound, where he was met with a chilling sight. A pair of black, beady eyes stared back at him from the hood of his car, sending a jolt of fear through him.

Frozen in place, he could feel adrenaline course through his veins as he locked eyes with the mysterious, large bird outside his car. The darkness seemed to swirl around the black bird, shrouding it in an aura of menace and foreboding. It wasn't like any bird he had seen before. Its beak was as long as his fingers, the end sharp like a needle. Its black eyes looked bold and cunning, as if it could sense his fear. It spread its wings as far as they would go, reaching out as far as the width of his car bonnet. Its large talons dug deep into the paintwork, unnerving him to his core. From the look of the bird, it could easily rip apart its prey with one fell swoop of its claws.

With trembling hands, Father Abraham reached for the door handle, curious as to what type of bird it was, but his instincts urged him to flee from whatever sinister force lurked outside. Before he could act, the bird flew off, leaving behind nothing but an empty silence that hung heavy in the air.

For a moment, Father Abraham sat stunned, trying to make sense of what he had just witnessed. He had never seen a bird as large as that one before, and especially out at night. He was amazed, yet terrified.

With a shuddering breath, he grasped the steering wheel with trembling hands and continued his journey, speeding the car up from fear of coming across the bird again.

Father Abraham jumped in shock as a loud bang reverberated through the car, causing him to instinctively slam on the brakes and lose control. The vehicle veered off course, careening into a bush by the side of the road.

The impact jarred him, his body lurching forward as the car came to an abrupt stop amidst the tangled foliage.

Gathering his wits, Father Abraham slowly emerged from the car, his senses on high alert as he surveyed the scene before him. The bush loomed ominously in the darkness, its twisted branches casting eerie shadows across the deserted, icy road.

Despite the adrenaline coursing through his veins, he forced himself to remain calm, his mind racing with the urgency of the situation. With a steady breath, he began to assess the damage, determined to find what had caused the noise.

As he peered over the roof of the car, a sudden gust of wind roared through the night with ferocious intensity, catching him off guard. With a violent force, it slammed him against the open door of the car, causing him to lose his balance and stumble backward.

The impact was jarring, knocking the breath from his lungs as he landed amidst the soft cushion of snow. Pain radiated through his body as he lay there, dazed and disoriented, the bitter cold seeping through his clothes.

As he tried to catch his breath and regain his bearings, the wind ceased just as suddenly as it had appeared, leaving only the sound of his heart pulsing like a drumbeat.

The flapping sound of wings pierced through the sound of swaying trees, drawing his attention upward. With a sense of unease gnawing at his gut, he lifted his gaze to the night sky, squinting through the darkness to discern the source of the noise.

Father Abraham's eyes widened in astonishment as he beheld a cluster of dark objects circling above him. Though shrouded in shadows, he could make out the distinct shapes of birds— enormous in size and with wingspans that seemed to stretch across the sky.

A sense of foreboding settled over him as he watched the avian forms wheeling and diving, their movements synchronised with terrifying precision. The sheer number of them was difficult to gauge in the dim light, their dark silhouettes merging and overlapping in a mesmerising dance as they circled above him.

With each laboured breath, Father Abraham rose to his feet, steeling himself against the fear that grew quickly within him. Though battered and bruised, he refused to show his fear as he clutched the silver cross around his neck, his faith unwavering.

With each slow step he took towards his car, Father Abraham's senses remained on high alert, his gaze fixed unwaveringly on the swirling mass of birds overhead, the sound of their wings causing his heart to beat even quicker than before. Each movement was deliberate, every breath measured, as he edged closer to the safety of his vehicle.

With an unsteady hand, he reached for the car door, his muscles tensed with pure terror. The birds continued to circle above him.

He couldn't shake the feeling of being watched, the weight of the birds' gaze bearing down on him like a heavy cloak.

His whispered prayers echoed softly through the air, a solemn plea for guidance and protection in the face of uncertainty. With each word, he sought solace in the comforting embrace of faith, drawing strength from the belief that, even in the darkest of times, he was not alone.

"Lord, grant me strength," he murmured, his voice barely more than a whisper as he lifted his gaze heavenward, seeking reassurance in the silent expanse of the night sky. "Guide me through this darkness, and lead me to safety."

He cast a final glance toward the sky before slipping into the sanctuary of his car, the door closing with a reassuring thud behind him. Inside the confines of the vehicle, he felt a sense of relief wash over him, thinking he was safe from the birds' talons.

His hands trembled as he started the car, causing the birds to squawk loudly above him. He breathed an exasperated sigh and shifted into gear, the car lurching forward as he navigated the snowy terrain.

His hand found its way to the metal cross that hung around his neck, fingers tracing its familiar contours as he drew comfort from its presence. The cold chill of the metal against his skin served as a tangible reminder of his unwavering faith as his lips moved in silent prayer.

The radio suddenly blared to life, filling the car with a low growl that sent shivers down his spine, causing him to lose focus on the car's direction once more.

With each passing moment, the growling seemed to grow louder, its relentless assault on his senses leaving him feeling disorientated and vulnerable.

As his prayer continued, his voice rose in urgency, each word imbued with a fervent intensity that echoed like a clarion call. His normally steady tone quivered with emotion, a reflection of the gravity of the situation he was facing.

He could feel the pressure building in his ears, the unsettling sensation threatening to overwhelm him as his ears popped from the vibration of sound screeching from the car's speakers.

His fingers fumbled for the radio controls, trying desperately to turn it off as he shouted his prayer. Yet, as he repeatedly pushed the off button, the growling remained emanating from the speakers.

Before he could comprehend what was happening, a sudden onslaught of large, black birds swooped down from the night sky, their wings and talons crashing against the windshield of his car with a deafening cacophony. The impact sent shockwaves through the vehicle, causing the glass to crack and splinter under the force of the assault.

Father Abraham's heart raced as he stared wide-eyed at the swarm of birds, their beady eyes locking onto his with a predatory intensity. In that moment, he felt an overwhelming sense of terror grip him, his mind reeling with disbelief at the nightmare unfolding before his eyes.

With a surge of adrenaline, Father Abraham instinctively ducked down in his seat, shielding his head from the relentless onslaught. The sound of beating wings and shattering glass filled the air, mingling with his own panicked breaths as he braced himself for the worst.

The car lurched forward, skidding across the icy road, headfirst into a large Willow tree. Time seemed to slow as Father Abraham braced himself for impact, the sound of screeching metal and snapping branches filling the air. The car collided with the tree with bone-jarring force, the impact mangling and ripping through the vehicle's exterior like paper.

His body was violently thrown forward, his seatbelt straining against his chest as the world spun around him in a dizzying blur. Pain seared through his limbs as shards of glass and twisted metal rained down upon him, the smell of petrol hanging heavy in the air.

For a moment, everything was silent, the chaos of the night frozen in time as Father Abraham lay trapped amidst the wreckage. With trembling hands and aching limbs, he struggled to regain his senses, his mind reeling from the shock of the collision.

The sound of the growling had ceased from the speakers, yet the relentless assault of the birds continued unabated, their beady eyes gleaming with a primal hunger as they clawed and pecked at the mangled wreckage of his car, forcing their way through the smashed windscreen.

Desperation surged within Father Abraham as he frantically searched for a means of escape. With shards of glass littering the interior and the metal frame twisted beyond recognition, he knew that time was running out. The birds showed no signs of stopping, their relentless onslaught pushing him to the brink of despair.

His screams echoed through the night air as he cowered further down into his seat, shielding his face from the sharp talons. He could feel the skin and flesh of his arms shredding as the birds smothered him. With a final look through the smashed car window, he caught a glimpse of his church in the distance, calling to him, before darkness engulfed him.

CHAPTER 23
No News is Bad News

Over the next few days, Arthur, Graham, and Steve had filmed enough evidence of Amelia's possession to send to Father Abraham. Arthur had immediately emailed the footage, leaving no time for Amelia to deny that she was possessed by the Taranock. He wanted Amelia dealt with, and waiting for Father Abraham's response was beginning to irritate him.

Days passed with no word from the priest. Arthur was becoming agitated, pacing around the house, unable to sit still. Amelia had been screaming for hours, pounding on the walls and hurling objects at the door. She refused to eat anything and had not used the makeshift toilet he had set up in her room for her.

While Arthur was waiting for Father Abraham, Steve and Graham had decided to stay at the house to keep him company. The three of them, all anxiously waiting for the priest's call.

Trish had stayed in Steve's bed with the kids, as someone needed to keep them away from Amelia and the house. Arthur remained by the phone and his laptop, leaving voicemails and emails, hoping that the priest would contact him, but he was unreachable. There was no answer from his phone, and the emails remained unanswered.

"Something's happened. I can feel it," Arthur said as he paced up and down.

Steve and Graham were slouched comfortably on the sofa, watching Arthur twitch in response to any noise that seemed to come from upstairs. Amelia had been banging on the door and screaming for hours, and Arthur was surprised that it hadn't fallen off its hinges yet.

"Should we call him again?" Graham asked quietly.

"Why? He hasn't returned our other hundred calls, so what makes you think he'll return this one?"

"Alright. No need to bite me. I'm only trying to help," Graham snapped back.

"I'm sorry. I'm just really tired and impatient at the moment." Arthur rubbed his eyes, and his shoulders slumped in defeat. "I don't understand why he isn't answering our calls. I'm worried about him."

"We're all worried about him, but there's not much we can do except wait for him to call."

"Well, how come he hasn't bloody called?" Arthur's face flushed as he threw his hands in the air in frustration.

"Calm down, Arthur," Steve said as he stood up, and stretched, trying to ease the tension in his muscles. "You're not thinking straight. It's only been a couple of days."

"Can't you sense it?" asked Arthur, his shoulders clenched as he stared directly at Steve. "Something has happened. He wouldn't have waited this long to call us back."

"Look, I would agree with you on that one, but there is always a chance that he has been distracted by something else—we are right on top of Christmas. And priests don't just perform exorcisms. He might be christening a baby right now. We will just have to wait, and if he doesn't call by the end of the week, we'll make a plan."

Arthur took a deep breath. "But I can't stand hearing Amelia scream. It's driving me insane."

"Perhaps you should take a walk or something." Steve placed a calming hand on Arthur's back and gestured toward the door. "I'll stay here with Graham in case Father Abraham calls. You've been cooped up inside for too long, you need to get some fresh air."

"You're right, you're right. I'll go for a walk and clear my head. If he calls, make sure you call me straight away and I'll come back," Arthur said as he put his shoes on.

Steve gave Arthur a reassuring smile. "Will do, now go and clear your head. We can handle this."

Before heading out into the ice cold air, Arthur paused briefly, looking back over his shoulder at Steve.

Graham watched from the window as Arthur walked carefully down the steps and out of the gate. He breathed a sigh of relief when Arthur disappeared up the road.

"Thank goodness for that. He was driving me insane."

"He's just worried. And he's right, the priest should have called us by now. Something is not adding up here."

"Give him another call and see if he answers." Graham handed Steve the house phone.

Steve dialled the number and waited for the phone to ring. He paced up and down the room, becoming angrier with each passing second.

"He's not answering."

"Then, we'll just have to wait. There's nothing else we can do." Graham headed into the hallway and stood at the bottom of the stairs listening to Amelia's wailing.

"What are you doing?" Steve asked, following him out of the room.

"I was checking on Amelia and now I'm going to watch TV. I can't keep sitting around, waiting for the priest to call."

Steve heard Graham turn on the TV and flick through the channels until he found something to watch. He sighed, equally frustrated with having to wait around. After a few more minutes of listening to Amelia's wailing he went to join Graham in the lounge.

"Is anything interesting on?" he asked, settling down on the sofa and wrapping the blanket around him. The Christmas lights were twinkling on the Christmas tree. It would've been idyllic under normal circumstances.

When Graham didn't respond, he turned toward him, and followed his startled gaze to the TV, yelping as Father Abraham's face filled the screen. He grabbed the remote and cranked up the volume.

"The death of a well-known local pastor has shocked churchgoers. The body of Father Abraham, from St Ben's Roman Catholic church, was found in his car, which had crashed not far from the church grounds. The vehicle was found by a couple on a dog walk on the outskirts of Whitely Bay. Police have not provided any further details at this time. So far, no witnesses have come forward."

The news theme tune blared out from the speakers. Steve turned off the television, stunned.

They sat in silence for a while, trying to process what they'd just heard, until eventually Steve spoke up.

"At least we know why he hasn't called us."

Graham stared at the blank screen, his eyes wide and unblinking. "I can't believe he's dead."

"Do you think the Taranock murdered him?" Steve asked quietly, unsure if he wanted to hear the answer.

Graham looked at him with tears in his eyes. "I don't know."

A heavy silence hung between them as they sat there, neither of them able to speak. Graham sobbed quietly, his head in his hands, the pressure of crying causing his throat to close up. He began muttering incoherent words through his hands and sniffled loudly. Steve sat there watching his friend sob, unable to console him because he, too, wanted to cry. He was fed up with the situation, and it seemed as though their last hope of any peace had been snatched away. Instead, they were left with a screaming banshee upstairs. He knew they couldn't abandon Arthur. He needed them and they had to be there for him.

They needed to form a plan, but how, when they had exhausted all the options for helping Arthur with Amelia? Their lives had been turned upside down since Arthur and his wife had moved across the road from them, and had he known this was going to happen, he would never have let Graham open the front door to them.

Thoughts and questions raced through Steve's mind, drowning any hope he may have had. He couldn't let Graham see him in distress. He desperately needed to create a plan. He looked over at Graham and noticed that his sobs had subsided, and he was now quietly whispering to himself while rocking back and forth.

The deathly silence between them was suddenly broken by a threatening cackle from upstairs, and they both looked up at the ceiling, listening to Amelia's hysterical laughter. Her deep, throaty chortling went right through them, causing the hairs on the back of their necks to bristle. Dust fell from above, onto their heads as she pounded on the floorboards.

Amelia's menacing laughter sent shivers down Steve's spine. He exchanged a quick glance with Graham, confirming that they both shared a sense of unease. The dust falling from above emphasised the gravity of the situation, indicating that whatever was happening upstairs was not merely psychological—it was the Taranock taunting them.

"That answers my question," Steve stammered as he stared at the dust trickling to the floor.

"I want to leave and never come back to this hell hole," Graham pleaded.

"We can't leave. We have to stay here and look after her."

Tears streamed down Graham's cheeks as panic set in. "But I can't stand this anymore! We need to go!"

"Look, Graham, just relax for a second," Steve said gripping his friend's shoulders. "We need to think clearly, and panicking will not help the situation."

"What are we supposed to do? I don't want to die here."

Steve wrapped his arm around Graham's shoulder and drew him in for a hug.

"It'll be fine, mate. Nobody will die. We just need to make a plan."

What about Arthur? What will he say when he finds out that our only hope of helping Amelia has just been murdered?" Graham sniffed.

"We'll deal with that when the time comes, but for now, I need you to stay calm."

"Stay calm about what?" Arthur asked, entering the room, kicking off his shoes and sliding onto the empty sofa next to the Christmas tree. "Thanks for that, Steve. That walk was much needed." Arthur turned to face them, becoming aware of Graham's reddened eyes and sniffling. "What's going on?"

"Well, we may have a problem," Steve said as calmly as he could.

"What problem?" Arthur queried.

"Father Abraham is dead!" Graham blurted out before Steve had even opened his mouth. "He's dead, Arthur!"

Arthur's mouth dropped open as he tried to process Graham's words. He muttered a few words to himself before asking, "how do you know he's dead?"

"It's all over the news! The Taranock got him. I'm sure of it," Graham sobbed.

"Graham, could you please calm down? You're just making matters worse," Steve growled, growing annoyed with Graham's constant wailing.

"He's dead?" Arthur asked, unable to hide either the shock or panic from his face.

Steve nodded. "Yes, he is, and I'm not really sure what to do now. Maybe we should contact another priest."

"If that demon killed Father Abraham, it won't be long before it starts killing us." Arthur reasoned. He looked up at the ceiling, realising that Amelia was silent.

"How come it's so quiet up there?"

Everyone stopped talking, hoping to hear something coming from upstairs, but there was nothing—just silence. Steve put his finger to his lips, shushing them before walking into the hallway. They followed him as quietly as they could until Steve came to a stop at the bottom of the stairs. They all looked up at the landing.

"Maybe she's asleep," Graham said nervously.

"She hasn't slept for days. What makes you think she'll sleep now?" Steve hissed over his shoulder. "Now keep quiet." He shuffled up the creaky old stairs, motioning for them to follow.

Light flooded the shadowy hallway, from the crack beneath the bedroom door, and cast shadows across the wall. Steve took another cautious step toward the door, keeping an eye out for any movement coming from the room. There was none. No movement and no sound. As Arthur watched Steve press his ear against the door, a horrible sinking feeling formed in the pit of his stomach.

"Steve, I have a bad feeling about this. I suggest you take a step back, away from the door," Arthur warned pulling at Steve's arm.

Steve pushed Arthur's hand away.

"Let go. I'm just checking to see if she's asleep."

"Arthur is right. Something doesn't feel right. Get away from the door," Graham pleaded.

"Shush ... I think I can hear something," Steve whispered. He could just make out a soft thudding. Steve pressed his ear closer to the door, hoping to hear the cause.

The noise grew louder and closer until something struck the door with such force that it shattered, bursting out from the frame with a deafening crash, striking Steve in the head and sending him to the floor.

Arthur stood frozen to the spot staring at what was left of his wife. Her once-pretty hair was now black and wiry, and her skin had become scaled, beyond translucent, with obsidian veins mapping her face. Her once delicate, feminine hands appeared old and wrinkled, and her fingers elongated beyond recognition, with sharp claws instead of perfectly polished nails.

As Arthur gazed upon his wife, a mixture of horror and sorrow washed over him. He reached out tentatively, his hand trembling, as if hoping against hope that this was all some twisted nightmare from which he would awaken.

But the cold, hard reality of Amelia's transformation remained. Her once-beautiful features now twisted and distorted, a grotesque mockery of the woman he was married to. He recoiled at the sight of her, his mind struggling to reconcile the image before him with the memories of their life together.

Graham watched in stunned silence, his own shock mirrored Arthur's expression. This was beyond anything they had ever imagined, beyond the realm of rational explanation.

"What ... what happened to her?" Graham whispered, his voice barely audible above the sound of their collective breaths.

Neither of them had an answer. The house felt heavy with the weight of uncertainty and fear. They were trapped in a nightmare, confronted with a reality that defied comprehension.

Nothing remained of her that Arthur could recognise. She had refused to eat since they returned, which had caused her bones to protrude out from her clothing and had also made her face gaunt and sunken. She glared at Arthur. Somehow, the Taranock had completely changed her into something no longer human, something horrific.

As the dust settled and the echoes of the crash faded, Arthur's heart pounded in his chest. Shock and horror gripped him as he stared at the scene before him. Steve lay motionless on the floor, a pool of blood spreading from his head.

Arthur's mind reeled, unable to comprehend the devastation in front of him. Tears welled in his eyes as he stumbled forward, his hands shaking as he stared at Amelia's ghastly frame.

He took a hesitant step back as Graham dragged Steve away from what was left of the fallen door. He gave Steve a quick glance to make sure he was OK before returning his gaze to Amelia, who was now inching closer towards him.

CHAPTER 24
Broken

"What should we do, Arthur? Arthur! What the hell should we do?" Graham yelled, helping Steve to his feet.

Steve was concussed, blood was pouring from his head, his nose was broken, and bruising was already forming on his cheeks.

"We need to get out of here," Arthur said, desperately looking around for something to use as a weapon.

Amelia's frail body took a step toward Arthur, taunting him with that hideous cackle. She then began to chant under her breath, her voice growing deeper and more menacing. Steve struggled to get up, clinging to Graham for support. Amelia slammed her foot down on Steve's left ankle with such force that the crack was audible. He howled in pain and tried pulling his foot away, but he was too slow, and she jumped on it again, breaking several more bones in his foot.

"Get Steve out of here, Graham. Now!" Arthur hollered.

With a swift and forceful motion, Arthur seized Amelia by the neck, his grip like a vice closing around her slender frame, his eyes ablaze with a primal intensity.

Amelia's breath caught in her throat, a strangled gasp escaping her lips as she struggled, her eyes wide with fear and disbelief. But Arthur showed no mercy, his movements swift and purposeful as he dragged her stumbling and flailing into Dotty's old room.

Arthur propelled Amelia forward, his grip unyielding as he threw her violently into the room.

The impact sent shockwaves reverberating through the silence, the sound of her body colliding with the floor a grim echo of the violence that had just unfolded. He pulled the door shut and held onto the handle as tightly as he could while Amelia scrambled to her feet, slamming her body against the hard wood. Fortunately, he was strong enough to hold the handle in place and managed to prevent her from escaping.

He turned his attention to Graham helping Steve as he held onto the door handle, his muscles straining from the effort.

"Just go, Graham. I think I can hold her until you're out safely."

Graham agreed reluctantly, shifting Steve's weight over his shoulder and supporting him as he hobbled down the stairs. Amelia wailed from behind the door, yanking on the handle as hard as she could.

"Please, Arthur. Let me out. The Taranock is going to get me if you don't. Please, just let me out," she cried.

Arthur paused for a moment, listening to Amelia's pleas. It was her voice that he could hear, not the Taranock's. He gathered enough strength to peer through the keyhole, just to see if she was telling the truth. His heart was thumping in his chest and adrenaline rushed through his veins. Her black, penetrating eyes pierced through the keyhole as she punched the door.

"Please let me out!"

"I won't, Amelia," he spoke softly. "You're no longer my wife. Before you start claiming you are, you should take a long, hard look in the mirror."

"I am your wife! Just let me out, Arthur. This is ridiculous. You've kept me in here for days," she wept.

Arthur ignored her and turned to look down the stairs at Graham, who was trying to open the front door.

"What's taking you so long?"

"Every time I try and unlock the door, it locks itself again!" Graham shouted. He dropped Steve and tried again. This time, he pulled on the handle with his entire body strength, but it wouldn't budge.

Arthur was aware that time was running out. He couldn't hold on for much longer. His muscles were beginning to ache as a result of the strain of holding the door closed.

"Try opening a window!"

Graham dashed into the study, leaving Steve sobbing on the floor. Arthur could hear Graham trying to open the windows from the stairs, and he could tell by the rattling, that Graham couldn't open any of them either. It appeared they were trapped inside by the Taranock.

"Shit." Arthur hissed under his breath, looking around for something to barricade the doorway. He spotted the cabinet opposite him in the twins' room, which was too big to move by himself.

"Graham, there's a key in the kitchen drawer, opposite the sink. It's a small brass key, Bring it here and then help me move this!" he yelled.

Graham ran into the kitchen and whipped open the drawer. He then rushed back up the stairs in a panic.

"Here." He inserted the key and locked the door, allowing Arthur to let go of the handle.

"Help me with this." Arthur shouted over the banging of Amelia smashing her fists against the door. He quickly led Graham into the twins' room and pointed to the large cabinet. "This should hold her for a while. Help me drag it."

The two of them dragged the cabinet across the hallway and placed it in front of the doorway in an attempt to prevent Amelia from breaking through. Arthur then ran back into the twins' room and began dragging out other pieces of furniture to build a wall against the door.

"Please let me out, Arthur!" Amelia sobbed from inside the locked room. With bloody, grazed knuckles, she pounded as hard as she could, splattering stains on the wood with each thump. Arthur moved as fast as he could, piling as much furniture as he could in place.

"Come on, Arthur," Graham begged.

"I am." He knew it wouldn't hold her for long. "I need more furniture."

"Will she ever shut the hell up?" Graham yelled above Amelia's screams.

Arthur stepped back; he could see the door vibrating behind the pile of furniture as Amelia repeatedly pounded on it.

"I'm not sure, but one thing I do know is that I'm not going to stay here any longer. I'll call the police—they can deal with her. Hopefully they'll put her away before she causes any more harm."

"I'll get Steve and we'll figure something out," Graham said as he raced down the stairs, leaving Arthur to guard the door.

The banging suddenly stopped, followed by an eerie silence.

"Are you alright, Amelia?"

She did not respond. Arthur took a step back and watched in horror as the furniture, once piled haphazardly in a mmakeshift barricade, now seemed to come alive with a malevolent fury, each piece trembling and convulsing as if possessed by some unseen entity. With a sickening crack, the wooden structures buckled and splintered, succumbing to the relentless assault of an unknown force.

Arthur could only watch helplessly as the hallway descended into chaos, the sound of splintering wood and shattering glass filling the air like a symphony of destruction. Shards of debris flew in all directions, pelting the walls with a hail of sharp edges and jagged fragments.

Arthur's heart pounded as he sprinted down the stairs, each step echoing in the dimly lit foyer. The image of Amelia haunted his mind, urging him to move faster. He reached the ground and scanned the area for Graham.

Graham was pounding on the kitchen door, trying desperately to get out.

"It's no use. The Taranock won't let us leave."

Arthur pushed Graham to the side, hoping he might have better luck, but nothing was going to open it. It was jammed shut.

"Let's go check out the lounge. Help me carry Steve." Arthur took hold of Steve's arms, while Graham took his legs. Steve's face was black and blue, and his eyes had been reduced to slits, due to the pressure from his broken nose. He was unable to see anything. At one point, Graham gripped his broken ankle too tightly, and he yelped.

"Sorry mate," Graham offered as they gently placed him on the floor, before rushing to the windows. It was futile, despite their best efforts.

A loud bang from upstairs stopped them in their tracks. Arthur looked despairingly at the door.

"Graham, we need to barricade this door. Help me."

With a sense of urgency, Arthur and Graham worked together, their movements fuelled by fear and desperation. They dragged the heavy sofa across the floor, its legs scraping against the wooden surface. The loud banging from upstairs spurred them on, each thud echoing like a grim reminder of the danger they were in.

"Push harder!" Arthur urged, his voice strained with exertion.

Graham nodded, his muscles straining as they positioned the sofa against the door. They worked quickly, knowing they had to secure the room before Amelia could break through. Once the first sofa was in place, they wasted no time in piling the second one on top. It wasn't perfect, but it would buy them some time.

Breathless and trembling, Arthur stepped back, surveying their handiwork.

"That should hold for now," he said, though uncertainty lingered in his voice.

Graham nodded grimly, his eyes fixed on the door. "Let's hope so."

"We need to call the police." Arthur managed breathlessly.

Graham nodded and took out his phone, punched in 9–9–9 and waited for it to ring.

When he heard the automated message, he looked at Arthur in fear.

"It's out of service."

"It can't possibly be!" Arthur growled, yanking Graham's phone from his hand, whimpering as he listened to the message.

"This is simply not possible. The police are always available!"

"You might as well give up. It's not going to let us leave. We may as well give up now," Steve moaned.

"I'm not giving up. There must be some way out of here." Arthur looked around the room before catching site of one of the pokers near the fireplace.

"We have to smash the window."

He stepped over Steve, grabbed the poker and marched up to the window, and slammed the poker hard against the glass. It should have shattered instantly, but there wasn't so much as a scratch on it. He tried again and again, until eventually he was angrily slamming his fists on the window, the sound of frustrated pounding echoing through the room.

Graham pulled Arthur away from the window. "Stop. It's not going to work," Graham said firmly, his voice etched with fear.

Arthur's chest heaved with exertion and frustration as he struggled against Graham's hold.

"We have to get out there! Amelia's going to kill us," he protested, his voice trembling with emotion.

"It won't work. We need to try something else." A small smile appeared on his lips as he looked at the fireplace.

"How about we try climbing up the chimney?"

"What about Steve?" Arthur questioned.

"We could try and pull him up?"

Arthur shook his head. "That won't work. I can't pull myself up and hold on to Steve at the same time."

The sudden bang of the lounge door against their barricade sent shockwaves through the room, freezing Arthur, Graham, and Steve in their tracks. Their hearts pounded in their chests as they stared at the door, dread tightening its grip around them.

Without hesitation, Arthur leapt onto the sofa, his instincts kicking in. He slammed the door shut with all his strength, the sound of the heavy wood meeting the frame reverberating through the room. In his haste, he hadn't realised that Amelia's hand was holding the doorframe.

A sharp cry of pain pierced the air as Amelia's hand became trapped. She writhed in agony. Her desperate attempts to free herself only seemed to worsen the situation, eliciting more cries of pain.

"Graham, help me!" Arthur yelled.

Graham leapt into action, prying Amelia's fingers away from the door frame so Arthur could properly close it.

"Bloody hell, she's a fighter." Graham said pushing her hand away.

"Let me in!" a deep voice yelled from behind the closed door.

"Obviously, we're not going to let you in, so you should probably give up, Amelia," Steve yelled back sarcastically.

A piercing scream reverberated through the room, causing the men to wince in pain. They clutched their ears, desperately trying to block out the agonising sound. But even as they covered their ears, they could feel the vibrations of the door as it shook violently.

With a sickening realisation, they watched as the hinges began to loosen, the screws falling to the floor like raindrops. Amelia's rage seemed to give her an unnatural strength as she tore the door from its frame with a primal fury.

The door crashed into the lounge, landing on the makeshift barricade. Amelia stood in the empty doorway, her eyes wild, her hair dishevelled and her clothes torn. She looked like a spectre of her former self.

Fear gripped Arthur's heart as he stared at her, his mind racing with terror.

"We have to do something," he whispered hoarsely, his voice barely audible over the chaos.

"There you are," she said.

They stood frozen in fear, watching helplessly as she shoved the sofa and broken door aside to get in. She was covered in blood, which she smeared on the door frame as she edged her way inside.

"Graham, grab Steve and get into the corner," Arthur hissed. "I'll deal with her. After all, she is my wife."

He slowly picked up the poker and aimed it at her. "Come any closer, and I'll stab this through your heart."

As she took another step toward him, a cruel smile spread across her face. Arthur could hear Graham dragging Steve away. Fortunately, Amelia focused her attention on Arthur, ignoring everything else as she stalked toward her husband, with her arms outstretched, ready to plunge her nails into him. She grabbed him by the neck, lifted him off the ground, and squeezed, smiling as he spluttered and choked, gasping for air.

Graham sprang into action, leaving Steve cowering in the corner. He grabbed Amelia's wiry hair and tried to drag her away from Arthur. She paid no attention to him, as she tightened her grip on Arthur's throat. All of a sudden, she lashed out at Graham's cheek, knocking him backwards, where he hit his head on the fireplace. There was a sickening crack, and then silence, as his body lay twitching, blood seeping from the back of his head and forming a small pool on the floor.

"What was that? I can't see anything!" Steve spluttered, collapsing against the wall.

Amelia cackled and launched Arthur with one shove into the Christmas tree. It collapsed, entangling him in its twinkling lights. He watched as Amelia stomped over to Steve. Arthur panicked, and struggled to free himself, but he was too slow. She scooped Steve up and threw him towards Arthur. Steve screamed, unable to stop himself from falling. The two of them slammed against the grandfather clock, shattering the glass, and spilling its contents all over them, causing Arthur to nearly pass out from the impact. Amelia's face dropped as she stared at the broken clock, instantly realising what she had just done. The clock stopped ticking, but Arthur didn't notice.

The chaos of the moment seemed to freeze as Arthur's head spun from the impact. Entangled in the Christmas lights, he struggled to make sense of what had just happened. Through the haze of pain, he watched as Amelia's expression shifted from one of malevolent glee to one of shock and horror.

Despite the pain throbbing in his head, Arthur couldn't tear his eyes away from Amelia's frozen form. She stood there, as though suspended in time, her face contorted with fear, her body paralysed mid-motion. It was as if the very essence of her being had been halted by some unseen force, leaving her trapped in a moment of realisation and terror.

For a brief, disorienting moment, the room fell silent, the only sound echoing in Arthur's ears the frantic beating of his own heart. He tried to move, to call out, to do anything, but his body felt heavy and sluggish, weighed down by pain and confusion.

"What's going on?" Steve groaned, picking shards of glass out of his hair.

"I ... I'm not sure. She's frozen, I think," Arthur stammered.

Steve shifted his gaze to the direction of Arthur's voice. His eyes had almost completely vanished beneath his puffy cheeks.

"What do you mean she's frozen? I can't see anything!"

"Well, she's not moving, she's not even blinking,"

The sound of rattling chains echoed from inside the clock, and the door burst open, catching Steve on the side of the head. He fell toward Arthur, who quickly caught him before he hit the ground. He wrapped his arms around Steve's body, shielding him from whatever might come next.

As Arthur cradled Steve in his arms, shielding him from further harm, the rattling chains and wailing voices, a cacophony of screams and prayers, seemed to emanate from the very depths of the clock.

The air thickened, suffocating and oppressive. Arthur's heart raced as he looked around, searching for any sign of escape from the nightmarish scene unfolding before them.

"We need to get out of here," Arthur whispered urgently to Steve, his voice trembling with fear.

Steve nodded weakly, his body shaking with terror, but before they could make a move, something silver emerged from within the broken clock, its form shifting and twisting in the dim light, as it slithered towards Amelia.

As Arthur leaned forward to get a better look, his heart pounding in his chest, he realised with a mix of horror and relief that the chains emerging from the shattered clock were the Taranock's. They writhed and snaked through the air, latching onto Amelia's body with an otherworldly force.

Amelia's face contorted once more, but this time, it wasn't with malicious intent. Instead, her features twisted in pain and desperation as the chains tightened around her, ripping the Taranock from her being.

In a flurry of motion, she began to move again, her movements frantic as she scrambled to free herself from the demon's clutches. The black mist that had possessed her seemed to recoil in response, as if repelled by the sheer force of the chains.

Arthur watched in disbelief as Amelia fought against the darkness that threatened to consume her. The chains snatched at the dark figure attempting to re-enter her, each tug accompanied by a cacophony of wails and shrieks.

With a final surge of determination, the Taranock's chains succeeded in dragging the demon back to the depths from whence it came. As the last vestiges of darkness dissipated into thin air, Amelia collapsed to the ground, exhausted but free from the torment that had plagued her.

"What's going on?" Steve asked, struggling to open his swollen eyes.

"I'm not sure, but I think the Taranock has been taken away," Arthur managed to utter, horrified as he watched the chains disappear back into the clock.

Amelia stumbled backwards and scrambled into the corner, whimpering at the screaming demon from inside the clock. Gnarled fingers, like the twisted branches of some accursed tree, clutched at the sides of the clock with an iron grip, their jagged nails digging deep into the ancient wood. And then, emerging from the shadows like a nightmare given form, came the Taranock.

Its long, pointed chin was the first to appear, jutting out from the darkness of the clock like the prow of some infernal vessel. Its hollowed-out eyes gleamed with a malevolent light, fixed upon Amelia with an intensity that sent a chill racing down her spine.

The Taranock's presence filled the room like a suffocating fog, its twisted form towering over them, a dark spectre of doom. Its breath came in ragged wheezes, the sound echoing off the walls with a haunting cadence that sent shivers coursing through the air.

It retaliated angrily as it writhed and twisted, attempting to break free from its chains. The chains, however, held firm as they inevitably pulled the Taranock back into the clock. It screamed and growled, clawing at the doorframe to in an attempt to get out, but the clock's door slammed shut, trapping it inside. The screams and groans instantly ceased, leaving the room in sudden silence as everyone tried to process what had just happened.

"I think … I think it's gone," Arthur muttered, staring at the silent clock.

"I'm not sure what just happened; why would it just leave Amelia?" Steve asked, trying in vain to open his eyes to get a look. He cried out in pain.

"My face is too bloody swollen to see, so thank you very much, Amelia."

Amelia huddled in the corner with her back to the wall, mumbling to herself. Physically, she had reverted back to her old self but had acquired a small streak of pure white hair. She looked exhausted, but Arthur was relieved that she seemed to have returned to normal. The dense atmosphere that had shrouded them seemed to have been lifted, restoring the house to a cosy state.

Arthur dragged himself over to Graham and nudged him. He squealed and groaned loudly, punching at the air and nearly knocking Arthur over.

"Graham, Graham, it's me, Arthur. Calm down, it's over," Arthur said softly, grabbing Graham's flailing arms.

Graham's head spun as he tried to process the chaos that had unfolded before him. His hand came away sticky with blood, a stark reminder of the violence that had just occurred. With a wince, he surveyed the room, his gaze drifting from the shattered remnants of the clock to the sobbing figure of Amelia huddled in the corner.

His heart ached as he took in the sight of Steve's battered face, the bruises and cuts marring his features a testament to the horror they had all endured. Graham's mind raced with a jumble of emotions—relief that they had survived, sorrow for the pain they had endured, and a deep-seated fear of what might come next.

"Are you alright?" Arthur's voice broke through the haze of Graham's thoughts, filled with concern and compassion.

Graham nodded, though the gesture felt feeble in the face of the turmoil raging inside him.

"I'll be fine," he muttered, his voice hoarse with emotion.

Together, they approached Amelia, their footsteps tentative as they crossed the room. She looked up at them, her eyes swollen with tears, her expression one of confusion and distress.

"It's over now," Graham said softly, reaching out a hand to gently touch her shoulder. "You're safe."

Amelia's sobs subsided slightly at his words, though the weight of what had transpired still hung heavily in the air.

As they helped her to her feet, Graham couldn't shake the feeling of unease that lingered in the pit of his stomach. He turned his attention back to Steve. "Damn, Steve looks worse than I do."

Arthur looked over at Steve and nodded. "Well, the good news is that we all survived; the bad news is that the house is in shambles and will take days to clean up."

"I think we should take Steve to the hospital," Graham said, looking at Steve's puffy face.

"I think you both need to go to the hospital. You've got a nasty gash on the back of your head that could use a couple of stitches."

Graham scowled at Amelia. "Yeah, thanks for that, Amelia."

She looked at him through teary eyes. "It wasn't me; it was the Taranock," she said as she began to rock back and forth, crying and mumbling.

Graham leaned in close to Arthur and whispered, "perhaps we should also take her to the hospital."

"How am I going to explain this to the hospital, Graham? Look at her; she looks like she's murdered someone."

"Perhaps if we take her like that and say she attacked us, they might evaluate her and give her the help she needs," Graham explained. "I mean look at her, she needs psychiatric help, mate."

"I agree," Steve said, perking up. "You said you wanted to get rid of her the other day; now is your chance."

"I can't believe it; after everything we've been through, you want me to just drop her off at the hospital and hope they lock her up."

"It's all for the best, Arthur."

Graham nodded. "You need to remember what she did to you, how she made you feel, and why you wanted to divorce her."

Arthur sighed, unsure of what to do. When he saw Amelia crying in the corner, he couldn't help but think that despite everything that had happened, she may well have changed for the better.

"I'm not sure I can do it."

Graham smiled placing a hand on Arthur's shoulder. "We'll help you, besides, I'm bleeding to death here, and we can't leave her here, so she has to come with us."

"All right, I'll call Trish and tell her what happened," Arthur said, his face full of concern and guilt.

CHAPTER 25
The Hospital

Trish smiled at Steve as he awoke in an uncomfortable, lumpy hospital bed.

"So, you've managed to open your eyes."

"Was the operation successful?" he asked. Her face was blurry, but he could tell it was her.

"Yes, they've fixed your ankle and your nose. You should heal just fine. Your face will be puffy for a week or two though, and you'll be wearing that cast for a while." Trish explained.

The stark white room with its plain furniture made his eyes water. The sun poured in through the window, glaring off the white surfaces and blinding him. Trish quietly went over to the windows and closed the blinds.

"Thank you," Steve murmured as he shifted position, in an attempt to relax. "Where are the others?"

"Arthur is visiting Graham at the moment. He's next door, and Amelia wouldn't stop wailing and muttering crap. So, they have taken her for psychiatric evaluation, which I'm guessing was your plan all along."

Steve nodded and grinned. "Maybe."

"She has just been through a very traumatic experience. She's bound to be a little mad after having a demon inside of her," Trish whispered, ensuring that no one else could hear her.

Steve looked away, avoiding Trish's accusing stare. "Don't make me feel guilty. She was a bad person even before this started. At least now she can get the help that she needs."

Trish sulked in her chair. "I suppose you're right, but I still think it's bloody awful."

"She will improve, and who knows, perhaps one day she will become a better person," Steve said cheerfully, hoping to win Trish over.

She relaxed a little, taking in Steve's point of view. "But what will happen to her?"

"They'll probably take some blood and ask her about her physical and mental health. Depending on the outcome of that, they'll hopefully admit her to a psychiatric hospital for further evaluation. Just in case she's a danger to herself or others."

"And how do you think Arthur will feel about this?"

"He's all for it. He wants rid of her, you know that. And he thinks that at least this way, Amelia will get the help she needs. I know it's not nice, but this is the only chance she'll return to her normal self."

"I'll come back later to check on you. I have to talk to Arthur about what the plan is."

"It's already done, Trish!" Steve called after her.

She deliberately left the door ajar, allowing a cold draught in. He slid under the thin hospital blanket and leaned back against the firm pillow. He was still dazed from the anaesthetic, so he closed his eyes and tried falling asleep. After a few moments he drifted off, into a hazy dream.

Trish, however, was stalking the corridor, waiting for Arthur to emerge from Graham's room. She was deep in thought when Arthur quietly closed the door behind him, nearly colliding with her.

“Are you okay?” He could see she was worried.

She sat down and gestured to him to join her. “I need to speak with you.”

He reluctantly agreed and sat next to her, aware of what was coming.

“What's up?”

“Do *you* think it's best that Amelia is evaluated? What if she tells them the whole story? We might also end up being evaluated?”

“They won't listen to the ramblings of a lunatic, and trust me, that's exactly what she appears to be. A lunatic. The Taranock has destroyed her mind, and the doctors will take one look at her and whisk her off to a padded cell. It'll be fine if we stick to our story about how she went insane and tried to attack us.”

“Yeah, but your house and the Taranock story have been all over the news channels. Don't you think the doctors will suspect something?”

“Look, I can't tell you what's going to happen, but I can tell you this: when I brought Amelia in, the doctors took her away immediately. She attacked one of them and tried to rip his eyes out, and she kept rambling on about evil and darkness. In all honesty, I doubt they'll let her out until her sanity returns, and I'm not sure that will ever happen. Try not to worry about it.”

“I'm worried that she'll drag us down with her. Aren't you worried about her?”

“Of course, I'm worried about her. I still bloody care about her. I just can't have her around my children while she's like this. She won't drag us down with her. She's gone mad.”

“You'll need someone to look after the kids while you're at work. I know your childminder is busy studying at college at the moment. Of course I can do it, I'll alternate between school and your house," she announced, changing the subject.

"That'll be great, thanks. I have a lot to sort out when we leave here. I don't even know where to start."

Trish smiled, a mischievous glint in her eye. "Don't worry about the house. I've already sent out my contractors to come out and fix it for you. It will be safe and warm by the time we return."

"What would I do if I didn't have you?"

Her smile widened. "You'd be screwed."

A doctor came towards them, holding a clipboard. "Exciting news, Graham is all ready to leave. He's just getting his things together."

"Thanks Doc, and what about Steve?" Arthur questioned.

"He'll be here for a little while longer. Do you think I could have a private word?" The doctor directed Arthur's attention to a door at the far end of the corridor. "Shall we go to the office?"

Arthur followed the doctor into the room, glancing at Trish over his shoulder, concern written all over his face. Like all offices, it appeared cold and devoid of personality, with plastic plants strewn about in a vague attempt to brighten things up. There was the usual clinical smell of the hospital mixed with the doctor's aftershave, and Arthur shifted in his seat, unable to get comfortable.

"What is this all about?" he asked, nervously.

The doctor motioned for Arthur to take a seat opposite him. Arthur's nerves heightened as he sank into the chair, his eyes flickering briefly on the framed certificates behind the desk before returning to the doctor.

"We need to discuss your wife's behaviour," the doctor began, his tone professional and tinged with a hint of gravity. He cleared his throat before continuing. "As you are aware, your wife has been taken for a psychiatric evaluation. It may take time to get a complete diagnosis but as far as I'm aware, your wife may have to spend some time away from the family."

"How long?" Arthur asked.

The doctor sighed, his gaze sympathetic but firm. "Given the severity of her behaviour and the potential risks involved, it's necessary for her to undergo evaluation and treatment in a controlled and secure environment," he explained gently. "This will help ensure her safety as well as the safety of those around her."

Arthur nodded. "I understand. Where will she be taken?"

The doctor looked slightly taken aback by Arthur's abrupt acceptance of the situation.

"Err, well, she will be transferred to a specialist psychiatric facility across the moors. They have a great mental health team to assess her. I have the necessary documents for you to take a look at." He handed Arthur a small pile of paperwork. "This will explain the process and should answer any questions you have."

Arthur took the documents from the doctor's outstretched hand, his fingers trembling slightly as he flipped through the pages. The weight of the situation bore down on him.

"Thank you," Arthur murmured. "I'll review these carefully and make sure I understand what needs to be done."

The doctor nodded, his expression sympathetic.

"I know this isn't easy. But it's important to prioritise your wife's well-being above all else. She will be transferred tomorrow. You'll receive a call from the facility once she's settled in."

With a final nod of gratitude to the doctor, Arthur stood up to leave, the weight of the documents heavy in his hands.

Trish spotted him coming out of the office looking dishevelled. She hurried over to him, concern etched on her face as she reached out to gently touch his arm.

"What did the doctor say? Is everything alright?" she asked, her voice filled with worry.

He took a deep breath, trying to steady his racing thoughts. He handed the documents to Trish, his expression solemn. "It's Amelia," he said quietly. "The doctor said that she will be taken to a psychiatric facility for further evaluation. The facility will ring me tomorrow with more information."

Trish squeezed his shoulder reassuringly, her eyes filled with determination.

"We'll get through this together," she vowed. "Amelia will be in the best place to get help."

Arthur nodded. "You're right. Let's get Graham home and await the facility's call."

CHAPTER 26
The Burning

Arthur and Trish stood in the lounge later the following morning, staring at the broken clock. Its hands were frozen in time, the glass cracked like a spider web with shards missing, and its once-ticking heart silenced.

Arthur sighed heavily, running his hand through his hair in thought. "Well, should we get rid of it?" he asked, his voice tinged with fear.

Trish nodded, her brow furrowed in concern. "We should get this thing as far away from the house as possible."

She stepped closer to examine the damaged clock face and reached out, feeling the surface of the wood beneath her fingertips. Despite the chill in the room, there was a strange warmth emanating from the broken timepiece, as if she could feel the demon's lair radiating heat from inside.

She pulled her hand away in disgust. "Let's get rid of it. I don't want any more surprises."

"We can build a fire in the garden and burn it." Arthur offered, trying to think of ways to rid themselves of the Taranock. "That way, it can't come back if there's no opening from its realm to this one. The garden is more than big enough to burn this thing."

Arthur's suggestion hung in the air, the weight of its implications settling over them like a heavy shroud. Trish glanced at the clock's door, feeling a shiver run down her spine as she thought about what lay beyond it.

"Are you sure that will work?" Trish asked, her voice laced with uncertainty. "What if burning it only angers whatever's on the other side?"

Arthur hesitated, his brow furrowed in thought. "I don't know," he admitted, his gaze fixed on the broken clock. "But we have to do something. We can't let this thing continue to haunt us."

Trish nodded in agreement, her resolve hardening. "We'll do it," she said firmly. "We'll build the fire, burn the clock, and seal whatever portal it opened. And then we'll bring the kids back home, where they belong. I'm still concerned about their behaviour. They keep talking about this 'Theo', and I'm worried sick that the Taranock still has a grip on them, but hopefully after we burn the clock, the boys will return to normal. We need to get rid of this demon for good, not only for our sakes, but for the boys as well."

There was a sense of grim determination in her words; a refusal to let fear dictate their actions any longer.

She grabbed the side of the clock and gestured for Arthur to grab the other side. "Let's just get this over and done with," she glanced at the logs piled by the fireplace, a silent reminder of the warmth and comfort they had once provided. "We'll take it outside, prepare a space, and use the logs from the fireplace to burn it."

Her hands trembled slightly as she grasped the side of the clock, feeling the weight of their decision pressing down on her. Arthur nodded in agreement, his expression grim but resolute. Together, they lifted the broken timepiece, its once-familiar shape now feeling foreign in their hands.

With slow, deliberate movements, they carried the clock outside, the winter air sending chill through them. The garden lay silent and still, the gloomy-looking clouds casting only a bleak grey light, making it feel much later than midday.

Reaching the centre of the garden, they set the clock down on the ground, the wood creaking softly beneath its weight. Trish swore she heard a low growl coming from inside it, but pushed the thought to the back of her mind as she watched Arthur run back into the house to collect the logs and kindling from beside the fireplace.

Arthur appeared moments later, struggling to carry the bundle of logs in his arms and clutching the small bag of kindling. His breath came out in puffs of mist, his face set in a determined expression despite the strain of his burden.

Trish hurried to his side, offering her assistance as he carefully lowered everything to the ground.

"You shouldn't have carried all of this yourself," she said, concern evident in her voice.

Together, they cleared a large space, placed the clock into it, and began to arrange the logs around it, creating a pyre which seemed to pulse with an otherworldly energy.

"I hope Graham is doing alright at home," Arthur said, breaking the silence between them.

Trish picked up the small bag of kindling and began arranging it in between the logs.

"I'm sure he's fine. He was asleep when I left earlier after visiting Steve's mum to make sure they were all alright. He was resting in his room and Steve's mum was playing with the twins downstairs. Heard anything from Steve?"

Arthur nodded. "I had a call from him earlier this morning. He's doing alright, but he can't wait to sleep in his own bed. He said the hospital ones are too lumpy for his back."

Arthur made his way into the shed and grabbed a small cannister of fuel. He carefully poured some on the logs and the clock for good measure, his eyes squinting from the fumes. He took a step back and smiled.

"Ready?"

Trish nodded. "Yes," she replied, her voice steady despite the uncertainty that still lingered in her heart. "Let's put an end to this once and for all."

With a shared nod, Arthur pulled out a box of matches from his pocket and lit one. Throwing it into the logs, they stepped back from the pyre, leaving the broken clock at its centre. In the flickering light of the flames, it seemed to take on a life of its own, its shattered form a stark reminder of the darkness that had threatened to consume them.

As the fire roared to life, Trish felt a sense of hope stir within her. She watched as the flames engulfed the clock, igniting the wood within seconds. They stood and watched as the fire consumed it and there was little left but the metal fixtures.

As the roar of the fire gradually became the crackling of embers, Arthur frowned, deep in thought. He was concerned that there had been no retaliation from the Taranock. There had been no screaming or wailing as the fire decimated its portal into this world. He fixed his gaze on the smouldering remains. The absence of any reaction from the Taranock was deeply unsettling, a stark departure from their previous encounters with the malevolent entity.

"It's too quiet," he murmured. "I don't like it."

Trish grabbed Arthur's hand and squeezed it lightly.

"The clock is destroyed. The Taranock cannot come back."

Arthur's grip tightened on Trish's hand, a silent reassurance amidst the growing unease.

"We need to stay vigilant," he said, his voice firm. "We can't let our guard down, not for a moment."

She pulled Arthur to face her. "Arthur, look at me," she began, lifting his chin up for him to look at her. "We've destroyed the only way it can come through. There is no other way for it to come back."

Arthur stared into his sister's eyes, a wave of relief washing over him. "I know. I'm just worried that it'll find some other way to haunt us."

Trish met Arthur's gaze with a reassuring smile, her eyes reflecting the same concern that weighed heavily on his mind.

"It can't," she said, her voice firm. "The Taranock is gone."

Trish wanted desperately to believe her own words, but a nagging feeling inside her was telling her otherwise.

As they stood in the flickering light of the dying fire, tension hung heavy in the air, each of them acutely aware of the danger that could potentially still lurk in the shadows.

And then a dreadful thought entered Arthur's mind. He looked at Trish with fear etched across his features.

“What if the clock wasn’t a portal? What if it was a lock? What if it was the only thing tying the Taranock to his realm or the house? What have we done? Amelia ...”

“The boys ...” Trish whispered, horrified.

CHAPTER 27
A Beginning

As Amelia gazed out of the window of the van, the world outside seemed to blur into one big blob of scenery rushing past. Trees whizzed by in a dizzying blur, their branches looming over the narrow country roads.

She couldn't remember how she had ended up in the van, her memories shrouded in a fog of confusion, but she did remember what the doctor had said to her in the hospital.

All she knew now was the rhythmic hum of the engine and the steady drone of the road beneath them. She squinted against the harsh brightness that filled the interior of the van, the stark white hurting her eyes as she struggled to make sense of her surroundings. Everything looked bleak and plain, devoid of any warmth or comfort.

The interior of the van felt like a sterile, empty cell. The walls, the floor, even the ceiling seemed to blend together in a sea of sterile uniformity. The only splash of colour in the interior were the blue seats. Their faded upholstery stood out against the white backdrop.

As she took in her surroundings, a sense of claustrophobia washed over her, the confines of the van closing in around her like a suffocating blanket.

As the van travelled further into the countryside, the landscape seemed to stretch out endlessly before her, a vast expanse of nature unfurling on each side of the road. Amelia felt a strange sense of disconnection from it all, as if she were merely a spectator in her own journey. Anxiety gnawed at her insides, but beneath it all was a glimmer of hope—hope for understanding, for clarity, for a chance to make sense of what had happened to her.

A man in a crisp, white uniform sat opposite her, quietly writing things on a clipboard. He glanced up every few minutes, observing Amelia's actions.

She shifted in her seat, acutely aware of the man's scrutiny. His steady gaze and the sound of his pen scratching against the clipboard only added to her discomfort.

She wondered what he was writing, what observations he was making about her. Did he see her as just another case to be analysed and evaluated?

With a deep breath, she forced herself to meet the man's gaze, her eyes searching for any hint of understanding or compassion in his expression. But all she found was an inscrutable mask, his features betraying nothing of his thoughts.

Feeling a knot tighten in her stomach, she looked away, her gaze returning to the ever-changing landscape outside the window. She tried to push aside the unease that gnawed at her, focusing instead on a flock of birds in the sky which seemed to be following the van.

As they continued on their journey, the man's presence remained a constant reminder of the uncertainty that awaited her at the psychiatric facility. She had been told what was going to happen to her before she left the hospital by a snooty doctor who looked down on her as if she were a bug needing to be squashed, and as she braced herself for what lay ahead, she couldn't shake the feeling that her every move was being scrutinised, her every action weighed and measured by those who held her fate in their hands.

She turned away from him again, casually staring up at the birds in the sky. They swooped and glided, moving effortlessly with one another. As they followed the direction of the van, they seemed to dance in the air, their wings outstretched as they rode the currents. Amelia couldn't help but marvel at their freedom, their effortless grace a stark contrast to the confines of the van.

As she focused her gaze on the birds soaring overhead, she realised with a pang of frustration that she couldn't quite make out their distinctive features. Their silhouettes appeared blurred against the cloudy sky, their movements swift and elusive.

She stared at them, trying to discern any tell-tale signs that might identify their breed. She had never seen birds like these before. Even though they were high in the sky, they still looked huge.

As she strained her eyes to get a better look, she couldn't shake the anxiety that washed over her. These were not ordinary birds. Their size alone was enough to set them apart, towering high above the landscape as they pursued the van with an almost majestic grace.

She furrowed her brow in confusion, trying to recall any birds she had ever seen that matched their description. Yet, despite her efforts, she couldn't place them. They were unlike any species she had encountered before, their presence in the sky both captivating and unsettling.

Amelia pointed out of the window at the birds. "Have you seen this type of bird before?"

The man looked up from his clipboard, studying her, before glancing out of the window.

Amelia shivered as the man's gaze shifted from his clipboard to her, then towards the window. She watched with bated breath as the man studied the birds, his features betraying no emotion.

There was silence in the van, broken only by the hum of the engine and the rush of wind outside. The air seemed to crackle with tension as the man's eyes lingered on the birds, his expression unreadable.

Then, without a word, he returned his attention to his clipboard, his movements deliberate and measured. But Amelia couldn't shake the feeling that he had seen something that had sparked his interest.

With a sense of unease settling over her, she turned back to the birds, her mind swirling with questions. Squawks and shrieks echoed across the fields, sending a flurry of smaller birds into the trees nearby for safety.

Amelia's heart quickened its pace as the screeching grew louder, piercing the air with an unsettling intensity. She watched in growing apprehension as the birds dipped closer to the van, their massive forms casting shadows over the country road.

The air inside the van grew heavy as her eyes darted between the birds outside and the man opposite her. His expression remained stoic, but Amelia couldn't shake the feeling that something was amiss; these birds were more than just a random occurrence.

As the van continued its journey, the squawking seemed to intensify, their cries echoing off the surrounding trees and fields. It was as if they were trying to communicate something, their voices pulling something inside her towards them.

Her hands clenched into fists as she struggled to contain her rising panic. What did they want? And why were they following the van with such determination?

The man looked up from his clipboard at the window, watching as the birds drew nearer. Amelia's heart raced as she watched his expression shift, his eyes widening with a newfound sense of interest as the birds swooped down to fly alongside the van. She felt a surge of apprehension at the sight, the proximity of the massive birds was disturbing.

The man's gaze flicked from the birds to Amelia, a glimmer of curiosity shining in his eyes. For a moment, there was a silent exchange between them, the intensity of the situation hanging heavy in the air.

As the birds continued to fly alongside the van, their wings beating in unison with the steady rhythm of the engine, the man leaned forward slightly, his focus unwavering. It was as if he were trying to decipher some hidden meaning in their behaviour, some clue to the mystery that surrounded them.

Amelia's heart leaped into her throat as the van lurched forward, its sudden movement causing her to grasp onto the seat in front of her for support. The sound of screeching tires filled the air as they skidded across the road, swerving dangerously from side to side. Panic surged through her, the world outside spinning into a blur of motion. She cast a frantic glance towards the man opposite her, his expression mirroring her own shock and fear.

The screeching grew louder, mingling with the chaos of the moment as they continued to surround the van. With each passing second, Amelia braced herself for impact, her mind racing with a jumble of thoughts and fears.

Shattering glass pierced the chaos, sending a shockwave of fear coursing through them both. Their hearts pounded in their chests as they exchanged a wide-eyed glance, a silent acknowledgment of the danger that surrounded them.

Amelia's hands trembled as she reached out, her fingers gripping the edge of her seat with white-knuckled intensity. The sense of helplessness was suffocating as they were unable to see beyond the panel which separated them from the driver.

The van swerved wildly, the sound of metal scraping against asphalt adding to the cacophony. Amelia's mind raced with a million possibilities, each one more terrifying than the last.

A loud scream burst from the driver's cab. It was the sound of raw terror, unmistakable in its desperation. As it echoed through the van, Amelia's heart clenched with fear, her mind racing.

Beside her, the man's expression grew even more grim, his eyes widening in alarm at the sudden elevation of noise. The shrieking birds coupled with the human screams added to the sense of impending doom in a discordant symphony of terror.

Amelia's breath caught in her throat as she strained to work out what was happening, her senses heightened to breaking point. Her world spun in a dizzying blur as the van slammed into something nearby with bone-jarring force. The impact was so sudden and powerful that it threw her and the man from their seats, sending them crashing to the floor in a tangle of limbs.

Pain shot through Amelia's body as she landed hard, her head spinning from the force of the collision. She struggled to catch her breath, her heart racing in her chest as she tried to make sense of what had just happened.

Beside her, the man groaned in pain, his voice barely audible over the chaos of the moment. Amelia reached out a trembling hand, her fingers brushing against his arm in a silent gesture of solidarity.

The van was filled with the sound of creaking metal and the groaning of strained machinery as it came to a shuddering halt. Outside, the world seemed to hold its breath, the air heavy with the scent of blood.

As the dust began to settle, Amelia and the man slowly picked themselves up from the floor, their bodies aching from the impact. With a shared glance, they braced themselves for whatever awaited them on the other side of the doors. The screeching of the birds had abruptly stopped after the van crashed.

The man stared at the window, his eyes full of fear as two beady black eyes stared back, their gaze fixed directly on Amelia. She returned the stare, transfixed. The bird was intense, unnerving, as if it could see straight into her soul. Beside her, the man trembled in terror, his eyes wide with disbelief. He opened his mouth to speak, but no words came out, his voice lost in the overwhelming dread of the moment.

A cold panic swept through Amelia as she felt a stirring within her—a presence that seemed to emanate from the depths of her own being. It was a sensation both familiar and foreign; a creeping darkness that sent her mind into a frenzy.

She clutched at her chest, her breath coming in short, ragged gasps as the darkness threatened to consume her from within. It was as though a malevolent force had taken root inside her, twisting and writhing with a hunger that could not be sated.

Alarm and horror gripped her heart as she struggled to resist the dark tide that was fast beginning to overwhelm her. She felt as though she were teetering on the edge of the abyss where the Taranock lurked, waiting to devour her whole.

She could feel the Taranock stirring angrily within her once more. Beside her, the man stared at her face, his eyes wide with shock. He reached out a trembling hand, his fingers brushing against her arm in a desperate attempt to anchor her back in reality.

A low, guttural growl escaped her lips, a sound so primal and raw that it vibrated through her body. It was a sound unlike anything she had ever heard herself make, a manifestation of the Taranock that lurked within her. It echoed through the van, filling the air with tension that seemed to suffocate everything around her.

Beside her, the man recoiled in horror, cowering in the corner of the van, as far away from Amelia as he could.

The thing which had once been Amelia turned to look at him, its obsidian eyes like the void. Its pale face broke into a slow, too-wide grin.

It was free, and it was ravenous.

Willow Hewett is a 28-year-old mother of two, who lives in the smallest city in the UK. She began writing short stories for herself at the age of seven and has been writing ever since, publishing her first works in 2021.

Willow writes in a variety of styles and across several genres: As well as novels, she writes short stories and even scripts. She loves to write horror and suspense, but she also writes YA for teens, as well as short stories for young children. Her work has been shortlisted in multiple writing competitions.

www.ingramcontent.com/pod-product-compliance
Lightning Source LLC
Chambersburg PA
CBHW070436170726
48291CB00002B/534